"I'm sorry I'm not
expected, my lord,
or alter."

Rhun found himself held against his will by the gaze that boldly met his. Her simple statement, yet one of pride, drove a blade into his bowels, and once again, he cursed the duty that lay like a yoke about both their necks. For the truth was, this woman he was bound to wed was as fettered and as wronged as he and innocent in spite of her bloodline. She was given to him, through no wish of her own, as belated compensation for a crime against his family.

"How could you know what I expected or what I did not, my lady?" he asked.

Eleanor's chin tilted higher, and he saw much more than challenge in the deep green depths of her eyes. There was courage and honesty and a vitality of spirit that seemed to come from the very essence of her. "By your reception of me tonight, my lord, that is how. I hope you don't welcome *all* your guests in such an indifferent manner!"

Author Note

In the autumn of 1294, eleven years after the conquest of Wales by King Edward I, rebellion broke out, led by men who fought to restore freedom and dignity to their people and their country. When I began this book, I knew at once that my hero would be one such man. But he would also be a patriot who was torn, as so many were, by the social and political tensions, strategic intermarriages and divided loyalties that shaped the borderlands of Wales and England known as the March.

Born and bred in Wales, I am constantly inspired by my country's rich and turbulent history and dramatic landscape. When I look up at the mountains of Snowdonia—Eryri in Welsh, which means "place of eagles"—or walk Wales's stunning coastline, I feel truly blessed to live in a land so steeped in beauty, language and heritage. I hope you enjoy reading this, my debut novel.

LISSA MORGAN

The Welsh Lord's Convenient Bride

If you purchased this book without a cover you should be aware
that this book is stolen property. It was reported as "unsold and
destroyed" to the publisher, and neither the author nor the
publisher has received any payment for this "stripped book."

HARLEQUIN®
HISTORICAL™

Recycling programs
for this product may
not exist in your area.

ISBN-13: 978-1-335-40790-0

The Welsh Lord's Convenient Bride

Copyright © 2022 by Lissa Morgan

All rights reserved. No part of this book may be used or reproduced in
any manner whatsoever without written permission except in the case of
brief quotations embodied in critical articles and reviews.

This is a work of fiction. Names, characters, places and incidents
are either the product of the author's imagination or are used fictitiously.
Any resemblance to actual persons, living or dead, businesses,
companies, events or locales is entirely coincidental.

For questions and comments about the quality of this book,
please contact us at CustomerService@Harlequin.com.

Harlequin Enterprises ULC
22 Adelaide St. West, 41st Floor
Toronto, Ontario M5H 4E3, Canada
www.Harlequin.com

Printed in U.S.A.

Lissa Morgan hails from Wales but has traveled far and wide over the years, usually in pursuit of the next new job. She has always pursued her love of history too, taking in as many castles, abbeys, hill forts and museums as possible along the way. She once worked as a costume tour guide at Hampton Court Palace, where she donned her sumptuous Tudor gowns in Catherine of Aragon's dressing rooms!

Now happily back home, Lissa lives between the mountains and the sea in rugged North West Wales, where she works in academia and web design. She has also recently returned to her first great literary love, historical romantic fiction, not just reading it now but, amazingly, writing it too! Visit her at lissamorgan.com, Facebook.com/lissamorganhistoricalromance/ or Twitter.com/LissaMorganAuth.

The Welsh Lord's Convenient Bride
is Lissa Morgan's debut title for Harlequin Historical.

Look out for more books from Lissa Morgan coming soon.

For my sister

With thanks to Lynne Blanchfield
for the Englyn

Prologue

Castile, Easter 1294

My beloved son,
By the time you read this, I will be dead and you
will be lord of Castell y Lleuad and all that goes
with it. I deeply regret our long estrangement,
but I ask you now to come home and honour the
pledge of marriage that I made on your behalf
ten years ago. You were a boy then and you didn't
understand my motives. Now you are a man and
you must realise that we need an alliance in the
March if our line is to prosper.

Banish the hate from your heart, Rhun, and
heal the enmity of the past by joining our house
in friendship and in peace with that of Richard
de Vraille.

Even if you cannot forgive me, I pray you will
grant this last wish of your dying father,
Owain ap Iorwerth

Rhun ab Owain stared long at the letter, the script beautifully etched yet its matter abominable, and then crushed the parchment into a ball in his fist. 'My father died seven months ago?'

The messenger, who stood behind him in the empty hall, weary and ill at ease, took a moment to respond. 'At Michaelmas last year, my lord.'

'Then why, in God's name, do I only hear about it *now*?'

Rhun whirled around to see the man's face flush. 'Castile is a long way from Wales, my lord, and it has taken many months to reach you.' His voice was thick with the accent of their homeland. 'Harsh weather and misdirection halted my journey several times.'

It was a miracle that the man had found him at all, Rhun acknowledged. In the six years he had been abroad, in France and now here in Castile and León, he could hardly remember spending more than a few months, sometimes only a few weeks, in one place. However, despite the rootless existence of an adventurer, the endless, restless wandering, he had never once considered returning to Wales. But now duty demanded that he return to his homeland and claim his birthright. A birthright he had renounced when he'd quarrelled bitterly and irrevocably with his father over the matter of his marriage to the daughter of his enemy.

'What was the manner of his death?' he asked, his voice barren of feeling as it echoed back at him. 'There are no wars in Wales that I have heard of.'

'A pestilence fell heavily on the castle and the village. Many died, my lord.'

Rhun tried to picture his father, his once strong body wasted by disease, but no image came. Was it possible to forget so completely what the man who had sired him looked like? Or was it rather that the image of his mother's bloodied face and broken body was so painfully etched in his memory that it shut out all else?

He looked down at the letter, still scrunched tightly in his hand. Live in peace? Banish hate from his heart? How, in God's name, could that sound so simple yet be so hard to do? He hadn't known peace since he'd witnessed his mother's murder, but hate was something he knew only too well. Hate had become an indelible part of him that day and it had not faded over the passing years, only grown strong, until it had finally driven him from Wales to foreign lands, to support causes that, however just, were not his own.

Now he discovered that it wasn't as easy to stop hating as it was to start. He doubted that he even *wanted* to stop. And neither did he want to marry Eleanor de Vraille, a girl he'd seen once, ten years ago, all wide green eyes and unruly hair the colour of wheat. A child who'd retreated behind her mother's skirts at first sight of him, tripping over the hem of her gown in her haste to hide away. Had she smelt the lingering stench of his prison cell on him, despite his fresh clothing and scrubbed skin? Or had the thought of marriage, even then, been as abhorrent to her as it had been, and still was, to him?

'Is there any answer to the letter, my lord?'

The question of the messenger, a man from Castell y Lleuad but unknown to him, crossed the abyss of Rhun's thoughts, pulling him back to himself.

'Or do you intend to return home at once?'

Home. The word seemed to pierce his soul—a soul that had somehow got lost here, far from the misty black mountains and thick green forests of Wales. A soul that was suddenly tired of wandering and longed for rest. But to return to his homeland he must carry out his father's wish, become friends with his enemy and marry a woman he neither knew nor wanted to know. And in so doing condone the wrong that had been done to his family that day twelve years ago.

But there was no alternative. He had to take up his duty as lord of Castell y Lleuad, the place where he had been born, his home for more than half his lifetime. On the fringe of the border between England and Wales, it would need defending, for all the so-called peace that existed now in the March. And he was the only one who could do so. But he would never forget nor forgive in the doing of it.

He nodded, his head aching but his mind made up. 'I will journey with you back to Wales.'

Opening his fingers, he let the letter drop into the fire. The flames flared high as the vellum and his father's last wish withered to ashes, and justice along with it. And Rhun felt his heart do the same.

'We leave tomorrow.'

Chapter One

Wales, September 1294

'We have arrived at last, cousin.' Guy de Barfleur turned stiffly in his saddle and looked back at Eleanor, the rain dripping off the tip of his long aquiline nose. 'Although the devil himself must have thought it a fine jest to make our last effort all uphill.'

Eleanor reined in her mare alongside her kinsman and pushed back the hood of her cloak. The mist that hung low in the valley caressed her face with cold fingers and settled in droplets on her hair. High above them, on a rocky crag, stood the castle that was their destination, set square and grey against an even greyer sky. At sight of it a shudder ran through her that had nothing to do with the cold or the steady drizzle that soaked through her clothes to her very bones.

From behind came the voice of her maid, Alice, her teeth chattering. 'Then p-pray to God there's a fire waiting for us. For it is impossible that the Welshmen can b-be as inhospitable as their land.'

Eleanor managed a smile, though her teeth were chattering too. When they'd set off two days earlier from her father's estate in Herefordshire the September morning had been glorious, the sun warm on their backs and the way lined with late blooms as if to cheer them on their journey. However, the moment they had forded the River Severn at Pool, where the swollen waters had reached almost to the horses' bellies, the change had been startling. The rain had started to fall like pebbles out of a sky that had turned swiftly from blue to black, while the terrain had become too harsh for even the hardiest flower to show its colours. Mountains had loomed up on all sides and the dense oak trees that choked the landscape had been almost leafless, even though the trees at home were alive with autumn colours. And as they'd ridden through the fading daylight the country around them had seemed more unwelcoming than any Eleanor had ever known in all her nineteen years.

Now, as she looked up at the forbidding fortress that was to be her new home, the clouds that hung over its gloomy battlements descended over her heart too. Castell y Lleuad. She'd been told that, in English, it meant Castle of the Moon. It seemed to her far too beautiful a name to give to such a bleak place.

'Fire or not, this place will seem very different from home, Alice,' she replied, her voice equally bleak.

The daylight was fading as they rode through the gatehouse and into the bailey, where a chorus of foreign voices greeted their arrival. Out of the twilight men appeared like ghosts, their feet squelching in the mud underfoot as they took the packhorses, unloaded their baggage, and helped her and Alice down from their mounts. As her feet sank, Eleanor's heart sank too, but she picked up her skirts and followed a beckoning torch to where the lights of the hall shone. Guy walked a step or two ahead of her, his hand hovering where his sword hilt should be, even though he and the other men had relinquished their arms at the gatehouse, as was customary.

Over the threshold, Eleanor blinked and tried to take in her surroundings. Supper had obviously just finished, for the boards were being stacked against the walls and in obscure corners pallets were already being laid out for the night. Everyone stopped what they were doing and regarded their little party in stony silence.

The Welsh were all dressed simply, in dark rustic colours, and their eyes without exception held a mix of curiosity and suspicion. In the stillness, the only sound was from the hearth, where a peat fire hissed, its flames casting dancing shadows on the grimy white-washed walls and its smoke rising to hang like a grey-blue cloud in the rafters. Eleanor coughed as it caught at her throat, the noise loud in the silence, making the tension crackle even louder.

One of the Welshmen said something in his own tongue and everyone turned back to their business, some of the men hurriedly laying a table again. The man who'd spoken approached and, bowing awkwardly, addressed her in English.

'Lady Eleanor, I bid you welcome to Castell y Lleuad. We expected you earlier.' He rubbed a hand over the thick reddish beard that covered his chin. It was threaded with grey, as was the once red curly hair on his head.

'I will see about some food and drink for you and your party. Come, sit before the fire.'

He was so tall that Eleanor had to tip her head back to meet his eyes. She found them to be bright blue, and his face, although weathered and lined, was not old. 'Thank you... Sir...?'

'My name is Huw ap Gruffudd. I am *distain*...er... steward here, and instructed to welcome you.'

'Lord Rhun is not at home?'

'Ay, my lady, Lord Rhun is above. I have sent someone to advise him of your arrival.'

Eleanor coloured at the tactful yet pointed correction of her pronunciation of the name—*Rheen*. Why wasn't it written that way, then, on the missive that had summoned her, if that was how the letters were to be sounded? Everything was so strange here—the quiet murmuring of the people around her in a language she didn't understand, the lack of colour everywhere compared to the splendour of her father's great hall... Even the scent of the rushes on the floor was different, as if the herbs and heather grew wilder here than anywhere else.

They settled themselves at the table that had been set up next to the hearth and their damp cloaks at once began to send clouds of steam spiralling up to the rafters. Wrapping numbed fingers around her cup, Eleanor drank deeply, feeling the warm ale burn her throat and set a torch to her insides. Bread, cheese and cold meats were brought, and she sensed some life seeping back into her body.

Her companions looked ready to fall asleep where they sat, apart from Sir Guy, her father's cousin and marshal of his household, who was erect and watchful as always. An old warrior, he had fought countless battles in the Welsh wars, and even though there had been peace between England and Wales for many years now unrest always bubbled beneath the surface on either side of the March.

The steward returned. 'I have made sleeping arrangements for your men, my lady. Your bedchamber is above and is ready for you and your maid.' He paused. 'Before you retire, however, the Lord Rhun would speak with you.'

A sense of dread settled on Eleanor's cold shoulders. But she would have to greet the lord of the castle sooner or later, so it might as well be now.

Bidding goodnight to Guy and his men-at-arms, she rose and followed the Welshman up the stone staircase that led from the hall to the level above, Alice close behind her. As they reached the top and proceeded along the narrow, dimly lit passageway, her heart began to beat frantically, the blood rushing in her ears and leaving her light-headed.

For she was about to come face to face with the man she had been sent here to marry.

She had met Rhun ab Owain just once before, and her scant memory—a child's memory, since she had passed only nine summers at that time—was of a sullen black-haired youth who had scowled at her and at everybody else present at the Christmas feast in her father's castle. Eleanor had been aware that the Welsh faction had been invited for reasons other than festive ones. Part of the peacemaking done between her father and Owain ap Iorwerth that winter following the last Welsh war was the marriage between her and the Welshman's only son, Rhun.

Her protests, appeals, tantrums and finally tears on hearing that the betrothal had been agreed had done her no good. However, as the years had passed and no more had been said Eleanor had begun to believe the agreement rescinded and the matter forgotten. But then a few months ago—ten years after that Christmas feast—the letter had come.

They stopped outside an oaken door at the end of the passageway. Huw ap Gruffudd turned to her and indicated the doorway a few paces back. 'Your bed-chamber is that one, my lady, if your maid would care to wait within. This is the Lord Rhun's room. He will see you alone.'

'Mistress?' Alice glanced at her uncertainly.

'It will be all right, Alice. Please unpack our things and make ready for bed. I shall not be long.' Eleanor drew herself a little taller, stiffening her spine and lifting her chin. 'Sir Huw, please lead on.'

Rhun had been on the battlements when the English party had arrived, and at first there had been just the sound of harness and hooves through the gloom. Then the barely visible shapes of horses and riders in the bailey below and the glint of helmets in the torchlight. But instead of going down to meet them he'd gone back to his chamber and sat staring into the fire, refilling the cup of wine in his hand until the knock had come.

'Dewch.'

The door opened in response to his invitation and his

steward informed him of what he already knew. 'Lady Eleanor de Vraille is here, my lord.'

'*Diolch*, Huw.' For the lady's benefit, Rhun changed to English. 'You may retire. I shan't need you again tonight.'

The door closed behind his steward and still he did not rise and turn to greet the woman who stood waiting. His bones seemed to have become part of the chair in which he sat, while his bad leg, broken that day twelve years ago, had gone to sleep on the stool upon which it rested.

'You wished to speak with me, my lord?'

Her voice was soft and low, although a little muffled, as if she'd caught a chill. Mayhap she had, given the inclement weather she must have ridden through, for the rain had been falling steadily for days now. Rhun shifted his leg and let it drop to the ground, his heel landing on the tail of the hound that lay sleeping at his feet. Cai, the closest creature to a friend he had, got up with a growl and moved away, to flop down again a little further from the fire.

The wind outside growled too, and the heavy linens that hung over the windows stirred ominously. Eleanor de Vraille said nothing more, just waited, and not even the sound of her breathing reached his ears. If it weren't for the prickling at the back of his neck and the sense of dread churning in his belly, Rhun might have imagined himself still alone. But he wasn't alone, and there was no putting the moment off any longer.

Placing his cup on the low table beside him, he stood and turned to face her, unprepared for what he might meet despite the last few months of knowing this moment would come.

He found his future wife to be tall and slender, fair of hair and green-eyed. Her face didn't conform to any sort of beauty—her nose was too small, her mouth too wide, and there was a petulant tilt to her chin that hinted at temper. She seemed younger than the nineteen years he knew her to be, and in spite of her obvious fatigue her skin was as fresh as a spring morning and her eyes were like a sunlit forest. He, on the other hand, felt aeons older than his four and twenty years, and spring mornings and sunlit glades were things he had long since ceased to notice.

He stepped towards her, inhaling as he did so the scent of rain and earth, for the bottom of her travelling cloak was sodden and rimmed with mud. The thought occurred to him that her feet must be frozen, and beneath her damp clothing he saw that she shivered. He gestured towards the hearth, and after a slight hesitation she approached the fire, stretching out her hands to its warmth. The flames bathed the folds of her clothes, making them glow, and as he went to stand beside her Rhun felt the same heat bathe him too, yet leave him chilled to the bone.

'I trust you had a good journey, Lady Eleanor, in spite of the inhospitable weather that welcomes you?'

A flush of pink swept over the high cheekbones and a spark lit in the eyes that turned to meet his. 'We did *not* have a good journey, my lord. It is a wonder we got here at all, given that we had to wade through water practically all the way!'

* * *

Eleanor hadn't been able to keep herself from blurting out the complaint. She was cold, she was wet, she was tired and she was unhappy, and now she had the distinct impression of not even being welcome at the end of it all. She saw Rhun ab Owain's gaze narrow, and then his mouth twitched, but there was no telling if it was meant to be a smile, or a smirk, or even a scowl, so fleeting was the motion.

'Then you are fortunate not to have suffered anything more than a pair of wet feet and a dirty gown, my lady.'

Eleanor's unhappiness slid into puzzled despair. She looked down at her hands again, feeling her fingertips beginning to tingle in the heat of the flames and the peaty smoke stinging her eyes. She hadn't known what to expect from the Welshman, although she had hoped for courtesy at least, as befitted a nobleman of his standing. Yet he hadn't even invited her to sit down! Perhaps the ideals and etiquette of nobility were very different here from how they were in England.

Living in the March, she'd grown up hearing tales of the Welsh—a strong-willed race that clung to their ancient language and laws and fought bitterly for their freedom. Of wild men who ravaged the borderlands in the summer, stealing cattle and burning crops, retreating into their mountains to wait out the winter until the raiding began all over again in spring. Was Rhun ab Owain such a barbarian, despite his noble blood?

'Was that meant to be a jest, my lord?' she asked.

'It was not meant to be anything other than what it

was, my lady. Journeys into Wales are often fraught with dangers far worse than the weather or the terrain.'

With growing dismay, Eleanor searched his face. It was fine-boned, and would not have been unpleasant to look at if it hadn't been marred by such an ill-humoured mouth. His eyes were nearly as black as his hair, and beneath the frowning brows they glittered with something that sent a shiver down her spine, making the cold that racked her body feel as nothing.

For Rhun ab Owain was looking at her as if he hated her.

'I would have dried my feet and changed my gown, but your steward informed me that you would speak to me at once. So I came at once.' Her voice quivered, but she kept her eyes steady on his. She was the daughter of a baron, and as such was the equal of Rhun ab Owain in that respect. 'However, if there is nothing of particular importance you wish to discuss with me tonight, perhaps you won't detain me any further.'

'No, I won't detain you for long, my lady. I merely wanted to greet you.'

Greet her? Was this what passed for greeting in this inhospitable land? And why had he summoned her now, when surely the morrow would have served just as well? He hadn't even bothered to attire himself suitably for his reception of her, but was dressed as simply as his steward, in a long tunic of russet-brown with a grey surcoat over, both garments faded and well worn.

'Then now that you have done so, may I retire to my room?' she asked, eager to be gone from this cheerless chamber, filled with the aroma of stale rushes and the smell of the hound that snored by the fireside.

Rhun ab Owain's eyes narrowed and he looked at her as if he was assessing her worth, studying her face and then her hair, hanging limp and sodden over her shoulder. He stared for so long that Eleanor moved her hand self-consciously to the thick twist of her plait, to find that it wasn't the neat braid she'd set out with that morning. Tendrils of hair had escaped in the wind and clung damply to her neck and cheek, doubtless making her look even more bedraggled to his sight.

'I regret my dishevelled appearance, my lord,' she went on, lifting her chin. She knew nothing of men, and even less of this particular man. Was he disappointed in her? Was she not what he'd expected or hoped for? Well, neither was he what *she'd* expected, still less what she'd hoped for in a future husband. 'As I said, I had no time to change and prepare myself.'

'I can see that, my lady.' His eyes clouded and for a moment he looked like the boy of ten years ago, gaunt and pale, and seething with injured pride that his two years as her father's hostage had not dimmed but only fuelled. She'd been told that Rhun's captivity was to ensure his father turned coat and fought for the English, but she hadn't understood then, for she'd only been a child herself. Now she saw, with a knowledge that went beyond sight, that the man burned as fervently as the boy had done.

And as their eyes held Eleanor felt her own grow wide as something that she understood in the same instinctive yet intangible way made her face heat and her breath catch. His lashes flickered and scarlet stained his cheeks too, and then he turned abruptly and stood with his back to her. Against the leaping flames his tall, rigid figure looked even taller, his body lean and hard, and the gleam of the fire caught his black hair, overlong and unkempt, making it shine like pitch.

Eleanor's heart began to beat faster, although she didn't know why it should, or why her stomach was spiralling like a leaf that floated from the top of a tree down to the forest floor. 'If there is nothing else, my lord,' she said for a second time, 'I will bid you goodnight.'

Yet her feet seemed reluctant to move, and as his shoulders heaved and he dragged in a deep breath it was too late.

'There *is* something else, Lady Eleanor—something that we must have clear now…tonight. I would have you understand that were I given a choice I would not marry in this manner.' He paused, and with his foot pushed back a lump of turf that had tumbled from the fireplace, making the dog wake and bound to its feet with a growl.

'Taw!' He silenced the animal with a word she didn't understand and then turned back towards her, the firelight brightening the shadows on his face. 'This match is to seal the pledge of peace made between our families— to end the long animosity between our two houses. I did not seek it and neither did you.' His eyes bored into hers, burning hotter than the peat in the hearth, and the intensity in them was just as scorching. 'I trust you understand what I'm trying to say?'

Eleanor felt as if all the blood in her body had flooded into her cheeks, washing her in a tide of humiliation and rejection. She knew full well the terms of the agreement, and why she was here, so what else had she expected? Affection? Companionship? Love, even? No, she was not such a fool as that surely!

'I understand perfectly, Lord Rhun. This marriage is a necessary obligation and nothing more.'

Nothing more? Despite her reasoning, despite her resignation, Eleanor's heart rebelled. Her parents' marriage had been a strategic match too, but her father and mother loved each other deeply, often to the exclusion of everything else—including their three daughters, something that she had been aware of even as a child. Perhaps they had grown to love each other over the years they'd spent together, but even if she and the Lord Rhun spent a hundred lifetimes together could she *ever* come to love such a man? Or could *he* ever come to love her—a man who clearly disliked her without even knowing her!

'Then I'm glad we are agreed.' The dark head inclined stiffly, as if even that courtesy was too much of an effort for him. 'When you have rested we'll discuss the wedding feast. I would rather not tarry over the arrangements.'

The announcement couldn't have been less practical and impersonal, but if she had to marry this man, if she had to lie with him on her wedding night, if she had to bear his children, Eleanor would not let him see her disappointment or her fear. And nor would she lose her dignity in front of him—not now, not ever.

'Neither would I wish to delay, my lord. Best to get what needs to happen over and done with as soon as possible.'

His brows arched and she saw the ripple of surprise on his face. And then his features set into granite once more. 'Then, since we are agreed, I bid you goodnight, Lady Eleanor.'

He crossed to open the door for her, and as Eleanor went to pass through it she stopped and turned to look once more into that black and daunting gaze. There was something more still to be said, and if there was to be any chance of concord between them, if nothing deeper, now was the time to say it.

'I am sorry I'm not what you wished for or expected, my lord, but that I cannot help or alter.'

Rhun found himself held against his will by the gaze that boldly met his. Her simple statement, one of pride, had driven a blade into his bowels, and once again he cursed the duty that lay like a yoke about their necks. For the truth was this woman he was bound to wed was as fettered and as wronged as he, and innocent in spite of her bloodline. She was given to him through no wish of her own, like an offering at an altar, in belated compensation for a crime against his family that had no retribution.

'How can you know what I expected or what I did not, my lady?' he asked.

Her chin tilted higher and he saw much more than challenge in the deep green depths of her eyes. There was courage and honesty and a vitality of spirit that seemed to come from the very essence of her.

'By your reception of me tonight, my lord, that is how. I hope you don't welcome *all* your guests in such an indifferent manner!'

The fire hissed in the taut atmosphere and the room

seemed to smoulder with tension until Rhun's ears began to ring.

'I rarely welcome guests here at all, my lady,' he said, his voice rougher than he'd intended.

Something in her seemed to reach out and pass through his clothes, through his skin too, and grip at his vitals. An unexpected and unwelcome reminder that he was flesh and blood after all, and as vulnerable as any man to the allure of a woman—even this woman!

'And you are hardly a guest. But, while we may not relish this match, we must endure each other's company all the same.'

Her mouth dropped open and then snapped shut again. Stepping over the threshold, she marched away down the passageway to her own room, her backbone rigid and her hands clenched at her sides. She didn't look back at him once, but the slam of the door behind her echoed around the walls. And then there was silence once more.

Closing his own door rather more softly, Rhun crossed slowly back to the fireplace. A heavy sigh rose up out of his chest, and as if in agreement the hound at his feet gave a deep whine. Dropping to his haunches, he fondled its ears and stared into the flames.

'Well, Cai, *ychan*, what would *you* have me do?'

Cai couldn't answer him, of course. Nobody could. He only had himself to berate and to blame for this state he found himself in. *Why* had he let himself be bound to such a crushing, impossible to bear burden? Granted it was a burden another man might welcome. Another man might embrace and enjoy such a woman as his soon-to-be wife. Any other man but he! There had been too much harm done, too much wrong, for any hope of reconciliation or forgiveness. That was something his father hadn't understood when he'd sealed this marriage and made peace with Richard de Vraille—a man who turned a blind eye to injustice and excused murder in the name of politics and war.

And the fact that his daughter, that timid and elusive little child of ten years ago, had grown up into an arresting and intriguing woman, as proud as she was noble, only made his cross all the heavier to bear.

Rhun's mouth twisted into a mirthless smile. It was cruelly ironic that if his father had wanted to condemn his only son to a lifetime of purgatory, he couldn't have chosen a better way to do it.

Chapter Two

'Endure each other!' Tearing off her mantle and flinging it to the floor, Eleanor paced her chamber, her feet
squelching in her sodden shoes. 'That is actually what
he said to me, Alice!'

'Not a very promising welcome, mistress.'

She turned to face her maidservant, fisting her
hands on her hips. *'Welcome?* The man doesn't know
the *meaning* of the word!'

'I knew we should never have come.' Alice picked
up the discarded cloak, shaking it out and hanging it on
a peg in the wall to dry. 'But now we *are* here, there's
nothing else but to make the best of it.'

Her maid's gloomy practicality didn't help. The
chamber was cold and the faded tapestries on the walls
barely covered the stone beneath. The wind pummelled
like battering rams against the walls, making the rushlights flicker in their holdings.

Eleanor took up her pacing again, unbraiding her
hair with furious fingers. 'Just because we're here, that
doesn't mean we have to stay!'

Although what choice did she have? This was her home now and, like it or not, she did indeed have to stay. She paced faster and the toe of her shoe caught in a hole in the floor covering where it had started to fray. Viciously, Eleanor stamped the rushes back into place, the tears she'd wanted to shed since the moment she'd arrived rising up inside her to burn against her lashes.

Sinking down on the edge of the bed, she bit her lip and balled her hands in her lap. She wouldn't cry, because if she did she might never stop. This was her fate and her future and she had to—what had *his* word been?—*endure* it!

'Is he handsome, though, mistress?' Alice sat down beside her and began to dry her hair with a cloth. 'That would be some consolation, at least.'

Eleanor leaned her head into the brisk, yet comforting rubbing and tried to picture Rhun ab Owain's sullen face. It came all too clearly, and so did the strange and unsettling feelings she'd had when she'd stood staring at his straight back and rigid shoulders at the fireplace.

'I suppose he *might* be handsome if he knew how to smile!' she conceded.

'A clever wife can learn how to make her husband smile.'

Wise words—but could she ever be that clever? Did she even want to try? Not when she was bound to fail and be humiliated in the process. After all, she'd grown up knowing she wasn't clever or accomplished or beautiful like her two older sisters. Joan and Margaret could do no wrong in their parents' eyes, whereas she could do no right. Why should her future husband find her any different?

Even in the matter of marriage her sisters had been blessed—Joan wedded to a handsome and flamboyant young English lord and Margaret to a kind if older and less handsome baron of the Scottish March. While she... She'd got the Welshman!

'I fear the effort would be too much for him, Alice,' she retorted, 'and for me as well. He's as unapproachable as the rock his castle stands on!'

Her maid put aside the cloth and took up a comb. 'Perhaps we've arrived at a bad moment, mistress. Perhaps he is preoccupied today and will appear a different man altogether tomorrow.'

'I doubt it! That frown he wears is too deep to be fleeting. I've never met a man so uncouth and so... Oh, I don't know! He...*confuses* me.'

Eleanor stood up abruptly, the comb tugging at her hair, and moved to the fire. Alice's words had made her think. Why should Rhun ab Owain frown so? Was she really so abhorrent to him? Or was it solely their marriage he resented? But they were one and the same thing at the end of the day.

'That's enough. I'll wash now.'

Alice undressed her and began to bathe the stains of travel from her limbs, though the water in the pitcher was tepid. In the firelight that cast a rosy glow over her naked body her disfigurement didn't look so bad. But even so Eleanor pulled her hair over her right shoulder, so that it covered her breast. Only to have her maid, in the next instant, sweep her hair back again and wash that part as if it were no different to any other.

'You've nothing to be ashamed of, mistress, and

nothing to hide. Your body is as God willed it and a
kind husband will see deeper than the skin.'

Eleanor said nothing. Nobody, not even Alice, knew
how her sisters had teased her as a child, cruel without
meaning to be. The thoughtless fun of children had cut
deeply and permanently, leaving inner scars to mirror
the outer one. Joan and Margaret had long forgotten
their tormenting, of course, and Eleanor never reminded
or rebuked them. But she was a woman now, soon to
be wedded and bedded, and if Rhun disliked her fully
clothed, he would surely find her repulsive unclothed.

Alice, oblivious to her thoughts, rubbed her dry and
then slipped a night shift over her head. She slipped
some sound advice into her ear as well. 'A woman must
hope for kindness if not love in her marriage, mistress.
And if it doesn't come from her husband, then her children must be her consolation.'

There was that word again. *Consolation*. As the soft
linen fell to her feet Eleanor wondered if the man on
the other side of the wall was also looking in vain for
the consolation in this marriage. Was he as puzzled by
her as she was by him and even now wondering at that?
Or was he, more likely, ruing that he'd ever sent for her
at all? If he wasn't ruing the fact now, then he surely
would on their wedding night!

Turning from the fire, she helped her maid gather
up the discarded clothes and hang them alongside the
cloak to dry. 'You talk like a married woman, Alice,
and not a maid!'

Alice shrugged. 'Mayhap I do, mistress, but imper-
fections of the body matter little to a man in the moment of coupling.'

Eleanor gasped, her eyes flying in shock to the other woman's face. 'How would you know anything about it?' Her maidservant was always outspoken, but this was forward even for her. 'Have you ever...lain with a man?'

'Not as far as that, no.' A secretive smile flittered over her lips as she said the words. 'But there are plenty of other pleasurable things a man and a woman can do together.'

Alice was barely older than she, but Eleanor knew that her maid, pretty and bold, had had dalliances with several of the young knights of her father's house, making her leagues ahead in experience if not in years. It was on the tip of her tongue to ask what those allegedly pleasurable things were when she was pushed gently but firmly in the direction of the bed.

'Sleep now, mistress. You're tired and everything seems ill, but you're bound to feel better in the morning.'

The low, square bed didn't look any more comfortable than those of the abbey and the inn they'd stayed in on their way here, but Eleanor crossed gratefully towards it, her bones aching after two days in the saddle. Alice was right. She was tired—they both were—and sleep would at least bring forgetfulness, if only for a while.

But her foot, bare now, caught again in the same piece of frayed matting and she nearly tripped headlong.

'God's bones!' she swore and, hopping the rest of way, sank down and inspected her big toe to find a puncture where a splinter had caught the skin.

It wasn't deep and, rushing to her aid, Alice pulled it out easily, with a smile to make light of the trifle. And it *was* a trifling thing, but the sting it left behind and the small drop of blood that oozed seemed only to mock Eleanor's misery. She'd always been clumsy, ever since her childhood, but to be reminded of that flaw right now was almost too much to bear.

'Curse this place,' she muttered between gritted teeth as she climbed under the coverlets, 'and curse its lord too.'

'Goodnight, mistress. Everything will look better by daylight, you'll see.'

The next morning, after a cheerless breakfast—at which her future husband had been conspicuous by his absence—Eleanor left Alice making arrangements with the laundress for the cleaning of their soiled travelling clothes and ventured out into the courtyard. Unlike the bustling and expansive courtyard of home, Castell y Lleuad's bailey was small and cramped, the ground rocky and uneven. Opposite the keep was the gatehouse, with the two narrow flanking towers she'd ridden in through last night. Was it really only so short a time ago? Already it felt much longer, for the castle was no more welcoming in daylight than it had been in darkness.

And as that realisation dragged at her heart Eleanor saw Rhun ab Owain coming through the gatehouse from outside the walls, his hound at his heels and his eyes cast down to the ground. His hair was wet, as if a rain shower had drenched it and left it glistening with droplets in the sunlight. He limped slightly on his left leg, but despite that moved with the same alert grace of a warrior, just as Guy de Barfleur did. But whereas

Guy's face bore a deep scar that ran from brow to jaw, Rhun's face was unmarked by any weapon.

He hadn't seen her yet, and Eleanor half turned to disappear back inside before he did. For in the wake of her observations came the same confusing and exposing awareness of him that she'd felt last night before the fire. But it was too late to hide as he glanced up and their eyes met across the courtyard. For a moment he looked as if he was going to walk right past her, but instead he stopped to greet her, his voice courteous but without any warmth.

'Good morning, Lady Eleanor. I hope you slept well?'

The dog, which was grey and hairy and the size of a stag, wagged its tail and sniffed at the hand she stretched out hesitantly, towards it. He at least was friendlier than his master!

'Yes, thank you,' she replied, although nothing was further from the truth, for she'd slept fitfully, woken at intervals by the wind and her worries.

The Welshman fell silent, averting his gaze and looking away over her shoulder. Eleanor stood in silence too, as lost for conversation as he appeared to be, and lowered her gaze to the ground. She noticed the calfskin boots that reached to his knees were old and worn, and more suited to the feet of a lowly squire than a lord.

'Did you find your chamber comfortable?' he asked.

She lifted her head to find him still looking into the distance. 'Yes, quite comfortable,' she replied. 'But…'

He met her eyes swiftly, his brows drawing together. 'But…?'

'The rushes need replacing or mending. They are old and starting to wear.'

'I will see it's done.'

Despite the assurance, Eleanor saw nothing in his face that she hadn't seen the previous night—unwelcome, resentment and dislike. In the daylight his eyes weren't black, as she'd assumed, but the darkest brown, with glints of gold around the irises. That didn't make his hostile glare any warmer, however, although it did make it startlingly compelling.

'And have you breakfasted, my lady?'

'Yes...thank you.'

Their stilted politeness was even worse than the discomfort of the previous evening. Alice had been wrong. Things *weren't* better by daylight. If anything, they were worse.

Eleanor shifted her gaze and looked around the bailey, taking in the little wooden chapel that was attached to one side of the keep, a primitive clay oven on the other side, at which a cook was busy baking bread, and the stables and pens for livestock that ran along the wall.

'Is this the extent of your castle, my lord?' she asked, for the false courtesy between them had surely been done to death now.

Too late she bit her lip, having not intended either the complaint or the criticism he evidently took her words to be. She saw lashes as black as his hair flicker and his lips draw into a tight line. He wore no beard, but instead of making him appear clerk-like the fact only served to emphasis the sullen curve of his mouth and the sharp angularity of his jaw.

'Did you expect something grander, Lady Eleanor?'

'I... No, of course not.' She didn't crave luxury, but the stark neglect of this place compared to the comfort of her childhood home made her feel even less welcome. 'It's just that I didn't see it properly when we arrived last night.'

His shoulders squared. 'This is the extent of the castle, yes. It is a small household, as you've discovered. My lands stretch for a considerable distance beyond the walls and, inhospitable as they are, they contain a village, a river, pasture and forest.' His eyes burned a challenge into hers. 'Is there anything *else* you'd like to know?'

The defensive pride in his words rang out as clear as a bell, silencing any further comparisons she might make between her new home and her old. Pride was one thing, but what she saw in that black gaze seemed to go far beyond. The enmity that had raged between their two houses might be ended with this marriage, but to look at Rhun ab Owain's face it seemed only to have taken on a new form, with words instead of swords.

Eleanor shook her head. 'No, there's nothing else I would like to know.'

'Then this morning, if it pleases you, we will meet with Father Robert, the abbot of the Cistercian monastery nearby. The priest here died of the sickness last year, and has yet to be replaced, so Father Robert will be marrying us instead.'

'This morning?' A lump of dread thudded into her stomach, but he'd said the previous night—and she had agreed—that it would be best to get the matter over with quickly. She hadn't expected it to be *this* quickly, however. 'I would have liked some time to settle in first…to get used to this place.'

'This *place* is your home now.'

Under different circumstances Eleanor might have laughed at the term. Castell y Lleuad wasn't and never would be home to her, even if she passed her whole lifetime within its sombre grey walls. 'But if there is no priest, how is Mass observed?'

'A monk comes on Sundays.'

So they weren't completely heathen here. But all the same her heart shrivelled in her breast. 'Then by all means let us speak to the abbot as soon as you wish.'

If only wishes were so easily fulfilled, thought Rhun, life might be far less complicated. He'd spent the night tossing and turning in a useless effort to rid himself of his dreams, which had been worse than usual. He'd woken drenched with sweat long before daybreak and so, despite the chill in the autumn air, he'd gone down to the river and bathed, scrubbing away the remnants of his nightmare until his skin stung. Then he'd walked until his legs had ached and his stomach had growled with hunger.

Only when the dawn had crested the mountains had he turned for home. But seeing Eleanor standing in the courtyard, looking like a lost lamb, had driven away the rare state of peace that had been the reward for his exertions.

'We won't have to travel to the monastery—which in any case is not so far away,' he informed her. 'Father Robert will come to us. It would be beneficial for you to meet him before the ceremony. And, if it reassures you, he speaks French and English as well as Welsh.'

'If he didn't, the proceedings would be rather one-sided, would they not, since I don't speak your language!'

A tinge of irritation ran along Rhun's nerves at the testy reply. It was becoming very clear to him that he did not know how to talk to a woman in *any* language. During his self-imposed exile he'd known women occasionally, driven by the needs of his body to seek out camp followers and harlots who gave their favours easily or for money. He hadn't spared any of them much thought when the coupling was over—but then none of them had been his prospective wife.

'Then it would be good to learn it,' he said. 'Most of the people here have no other language than their own.'

'Will it be very difficult to master?'

Although he knew she was referring to his native tongue, she might equally have asked the same question of their future life together. 'That depends on you, my lady, and on your will and your ability.'

Rhun studied her profile. Her skin was as pale and as smooth as buttermilk and her lips were the colour of soft, ripe berries. Even if she did master his native tongue, and spoke it as fluently as he, she would always be a stranger here—like a dove that had landed in the midst of the hens that scratched and clucked in the mud around them.

'Then I will do my best, Lord Rhun.'

The words might be conciliatory but he saw the knuckles of her clasped hands were white, as if she was holding her temper with a great effort. Even Cai, who'd stretched out on the ground to ease his old bones, had sprung up, ears pricked, as he sensed the tension in the air.

'Until later, then, my lady.'

Rhun clicked his fingers to his hound, turned and walked away. If he hadn't, he might have listened to the little voice in his head that was arguing with him, and had been doing so since the moment Eleanor had passed under his gateway. For even though she herself might be innocent of her father's crime, nevertheless she embodied everything he'd grown up to hate.

For that alone this marriage was doomed, and she surely knew that as well as he did.

To Eleanor's surprise, it was Rhun himself, and not she, who seemed ill at ease as they entered the small chapel. A mason was chiselling at a stone tomb against the wall to the right of the altar and the Welsh lord dismissed him with a nod. The abbot was there already, and the discussion was brief and perfunctory. The date of the wedding was set for three days hence, to allow for the banns to be read. If Father Robert sensed the awkward atmosphere that had accompanied them through the door, he made no sign of it.

'Will your family be attending, my lady?' he asked, in faultless English.

'Sadly, no,' Eleanor replied. 'My mother is unwell, and my father will not leave her, so my cousin Guy de Barfleur will be giving me away.'

'Are none of your other kin attending?'

She shook her head, shame mingling with sorrow. The thought that not one of her family would be at her wedding made her feel lonelier than ever. 'One of my sisters is in childbed and the other is too far away in Scotland.'

The Cistercian smiled, his grey eyes old, yet clear-sighted. 'Then I imagine you are pleased, in that case, to be living rather closer to your parents?'

Rhun, who had been standing with his back to them, staring at the unfinished tomb, suddenly turned and spoke, his features as hard as the stone behind him. 'The distance is immaterial, Father, as it is unlikely we will be visiting our neighbours in England very often—if at all.'

For a moment or two the cool air inside the church seemed to become even colder and Eleanor suppressed a shiver. Rhun hadn't said the words as such, but his meaning was clear. He might be making peace with her family through this marriage, but that was to be the extent of the relationship.

She glanced at the abbot to find his expression pensive as he nodded in Rhun's direction and then bowed to her.

'It was a pleasure to meet you, my lady, and I look forward to seeing you again soon and joining you in marriage to the Lord Rhun.'

Then he left them.

At a loss to know whether she was expected to go too, or stay, Eleanor looked around the chapel. It was modest, to say the least, the painted walls muted compared to the devotional splendour of her father's chapel. Would her wedding day be equally devoid of colour, let alone joy? Her heart sank at the thought and her gaze returned, as if drawn, to the unfinished tomb.

There was a second carving beyond the one the mason had been working on—an image of a woman. It was splendidly coloured, beautifully etched, with a face that was serene and poignantly young. Eleanor couldn't see the lettering on the tomb clearly, and wouldn't have been able to read the Welsh anyway, but the wide brow and the curve of the mouth, the fine lines of jaw and cheekbone were unmistakable, for they were the same as those of the man who stood behind her. The woman could be no other than Rhun's mother, long dead and part of the reason that this marriage was taking place at all.

'Is that your parents' tomb, my lord?' Eleanor asked without cause, for the answer was right there before her.

'Yes.'

The response didn't invite any further discourse on the matter, nor the asking of the questions she longed to know the answers to. But she probed anyway. She was part of his family now, after all, and his kin were her kin, dead or alive. 'I know your father died last year, and I'm sorry for your loss. Your mother died long before, I believe?'

There was no answer at all this time, so Eleanor moved from the tomb towards the stone altar. Daylight slanted in from the small square window above it, turning the specks of dust in the air to dancing silver motes. The solitary cross and two flanking candlesticks were made of pewter and the linen altar cloth was faded and worn. She traced a finger along its nap, feeling the roughness of the texture. The poor quality sparked a prick of remorse. This wasn't her father's house and she shouldn't be so naive as to expect it to be like it.

But was it so naive to hope for contentment in her union with the glowering, puzzling figure behind her? Naive to hope, if not for love, at least for a marriage built on friendship as well as strategy? And perhaps, with time, even on trust—not this conflict that already seemed to mark their future life together?

As if her thoughts had called him forward, she heard Rhun step nearer, until he was standing close behind her. Her skin began to prickle, and had she been able to she would have inched away. But she was caught between the altar and his tall imposing form. There was nowhere to go. Eleanor cleared her throat and turned around, snatching in a breath as she saw just how close he was.

'Why do you not wish to visit my family after we are married, my lord?' she challenged, hoping he wouldn't notice how her breathing quickened, making her breasts rise and fall unevenly.

His expression gave little away, but the tone of his reply was clear enough. 'Because it is a two-day journey and I have enough to do here—as will you when you are mistress of this house.'

'And what if I wish to visit alone?' she persisted, urged on by the need to wrestle some control over her situation which, for all her noble birth, was still that of a chattel at the end of the day. 'Will you *forbid* it, my lord?'

Rhun stared into the bold green eyes. Had he thought her lacking beauty last night? He'd been wrong. The aroma of rose petals invaded his nostrils, as though he stood in a summer meadow and not in the musty interior of his chapel. Unlike the straggling plait of the previous evening, her hair shone and coiled neatly over her ears. A fine wool tunic and surcoat the colour of holly leaves made the emerald eyes seem brighter still, and a soft grey cloak was fastened at her collarbone with a clasp of rubies set in gold.

Eleanor de Vraille was indeed beautiful, but that didn't change what she was—the proud and pampered daughter of an English baron and totally unfitted for a life here. Equally unfitted for him as a husband.

'That would require an escort,' he answered. 'And I cannot spare the men. I'm sorry.'

The sky brightened suddenly at the window behind the altar, and in the beam of sunlight that came through he saw her face fall. For the second time in as many days Rhun realised just how difficult a burden his father had laid on his shoulders.

'So I'm to be cooped up here like a bird in a cage?'

'You have the freedom to go wherever you wish, Lady Eleanor, both within the castle and, as long as it is safe to do so, outside its walls too.' He fixed his gaze on the wall behind the altar, with its painted depiction of the Virgin and Child, and spoke to the cold stone and not to the warm, vital being beside him. 'But if you do venture out, take an escort with you and stay this side of the river. Do not cross the bridge to the village.'

'Why not?'

But Rhun didn't have a chance to answer. An image, swift and unbidden, had flashed across his vision, blotting out the faces of the living and the dead, and darkness eclipsed the daylight. A cold sweat broke out on his skin as the horror took him, sucking him down as it always did into a swamp of memory that choked him with fear and split through his skull like an axe. The thunder of a destrier's hooves, the flash of a sword, a blaze of bright red and that single, awful, gurgling scream before the silence of death. Despair beyond any he'd ever known and then the empty chasm of guilt that had followed and left his heart a hollow shell.

Too late, and unprepared for what was coming, Rhun fisted his hands and tried to fight it. But still the trembling began—first in his hands, then his arms, then his legs, until it finally possessed his whole body. The confines of the chapel grew smaller, pressing in on him, and there was nothing he could do to prevent it.

Eleanor was looking at him in astonishment, her features swimming in and out of focus as his vision faded to black and then exploded into scarlet. He lurched past her like a drunken man, groping for the support of the altar, falling heavily against it as his knees buckled beneath him.

'M-my lord?'

Through the roaring of noise that filled his ears her voice came, hesitant and tinged with alarm. Rhun tasted blood in his mouth and realised, dimly, that his teeth were clenched so hard he must have bitten his tongue. He was shaking violently now, as if an earthquake was taking place inside him, but all he could do was wait for it to subside. At least he was still standing, still breathing, although the rasping in his throat was terrible, even to himself, he who'd heard it so many times.

'Are you not well, Lord Rhun?'

Long moments later—or it might have been hours— the sound of his name pierced through the fog. Gradually Rhun's vision cleared and his mind regained its senses, however piecemeal. And then the inevitable shame fell upon him. Why in God's name had the weak-

ness had to happen *now*? And why had *she*, of all people, had to witness it?

'Leave me…please, Lady Eleanor.'

His hand jerked to wave her away, accidentally
knocking over one of the candlesticks. It fell to the floor
with a loud clatter, making his nerves tighten all over
again. But the fit was passing now; he'd been through
them enough to know the signs. He also knew that despite his instruction Eleanor hadn't left him, but was
standing just behind his left shoulder.

'I asked you to go,' he said, louder this time, forcing his head up to glare at her. Her face was white, her
expression a mix of curiosity and confusion, and her
eyes were filled with a pity that made his shame all the
more unbearable. 'Now!'

Eleanor wavered, unsure what to do, almost afraid
to stay, but unable to leave him like this. It was a miracle he was still on his feet, and if he hadn't gripped
the altar the way he had she suspected he would have
collapsed to the floor. Even now his face was bathed
with perspiration and blanched of colour, his lips greyer
than the altar cloth that was still bunched in his hands.

Forcing herself to calmness, she picked up the fallen
candlestick and placed it carefully opposite its mate
beside the cross. 'I thought I was supposed to be the
clumsy one,' she said lightly, yet with care.

The over-bright eyes found hers and his brow
creased, as if he'd heard but not understood. 'What?'

Eleanor stepped a little closer. 'I've always been awkward since childhood. I don't know why. My sisters are

the epitome of grace and I've never understood why I shouldn't be graceful too.'

It was nonsense—at least in part. Idle talk to fill a chasm that needed to be filled. And the distraction seemed to be working. After a moment or two longer, during which he stared at her as if drunk or delirious, the colour began to seep back into his cheeks. His breathing became easier and finally, relinquishing the altar cloth, he straightened up and stood tall again— taller, in fact, as if to make up for the weakness that had taken possession of him.

'You look graceful enough to me, Lady Eleanor.'

'Appearances can be deceptive, my lord,' Eleanor replied.

His certainly were. Standing upright and strong before her now, it would have been impossible to imagine him any other way if she hadn't seen it with her own eyes.

'Do you suffer from a malady of some sort?' she asked, reluctant to pry but wanting to help. For the incident, as terrible as it had been, had opened up a doorway between them—invited her into his presence properly, for the first time since she'd arrived. 'Is there anything I can do to help?'

The dark head shook. 'It's nothing.'

It was far from nothing. It had been frightening to watch and be unable to help or understand. She might not know Rhun ab Owain, nor ever hope to like him, but neither did she wish to see him suffer.

'Then shall I accompany you back to your chamber?' she offered. 'Or bring you some wine?'

That door slammed shut again, closing her out with

only one foot over the threshold. 'I said I'm well, so please leave me be!'

Eleanor turned away, stung by the rebuff, and reached to smooth out the altar cloth, still crumpled from his grip. Before she could do so, Rhun's hand came down and covered hers. The contact was startling, and she bit back a gasp and stared down at the long fingers and clean, square nails, keenly aware of his warm breath on her cheek, as soft as a caress.

'I'm sorry. That was ungrateful of me.'

Meeting his gaze again, she could have counted the gold and amber flecks in the dark brown eyes. They were like the sparks that flew up from a bonfire into the night sky on All Hallows' Eve. As if a tempest raged inside him…as if his very soul was engulfed in a hell-fire of its own.

'There is no need to apologise, my lord. I'm the one who's sorry that you are ill.'

Eleanor bit back on the rest of what she'd intended to say. That she was sorry he didn't want her sympathy or her help. That she was sorry, too, that he didn't want *her*. Sorry that, while she was prepared to bend and make the best of things—for what other course was there?—he stood remote and resentful.

'Then I trust you will keep what happened here today to yourself.'

It was a command, not a plea, but even had it been Eleanor knew she wouldn't speak of it to anyone. Whatever it was that afflicted him, it was a matter he clearly wished kept hidden.

'I will, of course. But…' She wavered, torn between pity and pride. 'Have you not consulted a physician?

There may be some remedy…a medicine. I have some small skill in herbs. Perhaps I could—'

'Er mwyn Duw!' He released her hand and dragged his fingers through his hair. 'There is no remedy and I have no need of physicians or herbs or potions. I'll thank you not to suggest it again!'

So much for sympathy!

Eleanor's patience snapped. 'If that is your wish, then I won't!'

Rhun looked at her, his eyes as cold and as empty as they'd been feverish and full of anguish a moment earlier, further away from her now than ever. 'Wish? No, Lady Eleanor, I don't *wish* it. I insist upon it.' He hesitated, and then inclined his head stiffly. 'But I'm grateful to you for your concern nevertheless.'

And with that he spun on his heel and strode down the aisle and out through the door. A blast of wind swept in, and then silence fell as the door creaked shut.

Eleanor was left at the altar where she would soon be joined in wedlock with a man who, although still a stranger to her, and more puzzling than ever, now had her pity. Not just because he suffered, but because he chose to suffer alone and in silence.

But from what?

Chapter Three

Eleanor's wedding day dawned wet and windy, and she awoke to a sense of dread. The dullness of a sleepless night throbbed at her temples and, rubbing her eyes, she threw off the heavy bed coverings that smothered her. Beyond the curtains she heard Alice moving around, getting dressed, requesting a fire and hot water from the man who knocked at the door. Later came the hissing sound of peat burning—so different from the logs they burned at home—and the smell of smoke, sweet like rotting apples. And then the curtains were drawn back with a flourish and a little shower of dust.

'Good morning, mistress. Did you rest well?'

'No.' Eleanor sat up and stretched her arms above her head, feeling the cool air of the chamber bathe her skin as the fire struggled for life. 'Is it late?' she asked, hoping that it wasn't, and that she had hours yet before she had to face her wedding.

'A little after dawn,' replied Alice, handing her a cup of warm spiced wine. 'Though it is so dark outside you wouldn't think it was daytime at all. I've put your wedding gown out to air, mistress. Isn't it lovely?'

Eleanor sipped her wine and looked at the pale blue silk dress trimmed with silver thread that hung from a peg in the wall. It *was* lovely, but that didn't change the fact that she would soon be fastened into it as if it were a dungeon, not a dress.

'And the silver slippers match perfectly!' Alice took them up and turned them over reverentially in her hands. 'Such soft material and fine stitching.'

Soft and fine and totally inadequate for a wedding in the rain! Although even if the sun had been blazing in the sky it wouldn't have made any difference.

Eleanor got out of bed and went over to the window, her bare feet unscathed this time, for Rhun ab Owain hadn't had the hole in the rushes repaired, as he'd promised, but replaced them for new ones. The aroma of fresh herbs rose to her nostrils as, drawing back the linen, she peered out. Yesterday, the view had stretched as far as the eye could see, to rolling hills beyond and the sun rising over the eastern horizon. Today, thick grey clouds lay low over the landscape, shrouding the castle walls, blotting out any sign of sky, let alone sun.

'They say rain at dawn, sun at noon, so perhaps the weather will bless your nuptials after all, mistress.'

Eleanor dropped the curtain back. On any other day the cheery chatter of her maid would be welcome. Today it wasn't just unwelcome but annoying, because Alice seemed as excited by the wedding as she herself was dreading it.

'Stop dawdling, Alice,' she replied sharply, 'and fill my bath.'

The ceremony was set to follow the hour of Sext, the midday prayer, and the hour came all too soon.

Eleanor was sewn into her wedding gown, a belt studded with amethysts was wound twice around her waist to loop low on her abdomen, and her feet were eased into the silver slippers. Alice finished combing her hair, threading tiny white autumn flowers into the locks that fell to her hips, and finally placed a silver circlet on her brow, around which she wound a delicate coronet of evergreen. Then she stood back to survey her handiwork.

'You do make for a beautiful bride, mistress, and no doubt about it.'

'I don't feel like a bride at all.' Eleanor lifted a hand and scratched at her temple, where the evergreen was already starting to irritate. 'Do I have to wear this ridiculous weed around my head?'

Her maid reached up and adjusted the circlet. 'You *will* feel like a bride at the ceremony and your wedding night *will* make you a wife.' Her maid's eyes twinkled. 'They do say the consummation of marriage can go either of two ways—a due given in obligation, or a bond forged between a man and his wife never to be broken.'

Inspecting her appearance in the little enamelled mirror that had been a gift from her mother, Eleanor wondered which it would be for her—a begrudging due or a lifelong bond. She couldn't imagine *any* bond was possible between her and the man she was about to wed, if their relationship thus far was anything to judge by.

'You and your sayings, Alice!' she said. 'You talk like a troubadour!'

Though she'd talked and dreamed like that too, once,

when she'd been young and carefree, believing in the songs of fools. And if she didn't know any better she could almost believe now, in the image that stared back at her from the glass. Her face—if not her body—was pale and unblemished, and with the meagre adornments available, Alice had arranged her hair with a skill that couldn't be denied. She looked like a spring bride, even if it was winter in her heart, and for the first time in her life Eleanor beheld a sort of beauty that she didn't really possess.

But perhaps all brides blossomed from a girl into a woman on their wedding morn. Outwardly at least.

'Better to hope for joy than to look for sorrow, anyway,' said her maid with maddening practicality, having the last word as she usually did.

Despite everything, Eleanor smiled. Whatever her mood or her tone, it was all water off a duck's back to Alice. At times it felt as if they were sisters, not mistress and minion, and today she was thankful for the company and the comfort of their relationship.

'We'll see if you think so on *your* wedding day!'

At that moment a knock came at the door and it opened to reveal Guy de Barfleur, big and reliable, on the threshold. His eyes roamed approvingly over her attire, but when they lifted to hers it was with a shadowed concern. Was he also overwhelmed by the pervading gloom of this unwelcoming place? Or did he, like she did, wonder why the lord of the castle ignored his guests as if they weren't under his roof at all? For since that day in the chapel Rhun ab Owain had neither looked at her nor spoken to her—or only when it had been impossible to do otherwise.

'Are you ready, cousin?'

No, she wasn't ready—she'd never be ready. But Eleanor nodded all the same, for she could do little else. 'Yes, I'm ready, Guy.'

Downstairs in the hall, people were laying out tables and benches for the feast later, strewing fresh herbs on the floor, placing new candles in sconces. Their open-mouthed stares were lost on her as she passed between them. Because, at the far end of the hall, his tall, dark figure filling the doorway, Rhun ab Owain was waiting, looking as if he was going to his execution instead of his wedding.

In contrast to his grim features, his dress was more resplendent than she'd previously seen it—a rich blue tunic, the cuffs and neckline threaded with silver—and his thick black hair was shining and brushed neatly to his collar. He appeared so different, and so striking, that her feet faltered as he stepped forward to greet her.

'Lady Eleanor.'

His voice was steady, his face impassive as always, but she hadn't missed the quick flare of his eyes or the flush that had swept up into his cheekbones. And as she inclined her head and returned his greeting she saw the pulse that beat rapidly at his throat.

'Lord Rhun.'

His gaze fixed on hers in silence for a moment, and she would have given anything to read the thoughts behind it. But she didn't need to; he'd told her plainly how he felt about this match on the night she'd arrived.

'Are you ready, my lady?'

It was the second time she'd been asked that—once upstairs by the man who would be giving her away, and now by the one who would receive her. She was a possession simply passed from one sort of ownership to another. And her new owner was staring down at her as if he didn't want her now any more than he had three days ago.

But Eleanor could give no other answer than the one she'd given to Guy earlier. 'Yes, I'm ready,' she said, stepping before him and descending the stone steps that led down into the bailey.

With one hand on her kinsman's arm and her head held high, she walked, steadily enough, across the courtyard to the chapel.

As Alice had prophesied, the rain had stopped some hours since, although the wind threatened to blow all the flowers from her hair. Rhun, his steward at his side, followed in her train, and behind them came the wedding guests.

There weren't many, although all the people of age from the nearby village were present, as were the inhabitants of the castle. There was even a minstrel, his instrument nestling silently in the crook of his arm, its strings presumably to be played at the feast that would follow.

Father Robert was waiting outside the chapel and it was there, before the narrow shuttered doors, that Eleanor's courage threatened finally to desert her. As Guy stepped back and Rhun came forward to take his place her mind emptied, leaving her body adrift and her feet longing to flee. But she fixed her gaze on the lips of the abbot like an anchor, as he began to speak the words that would join her irrevocably to the man at her side.

The man who, a moment later, astonished her by tak-

ing her hand, quietly and without hurry, and enclosing
it in the warmth and strength of his.

'And should anyone know any reason why these two
ought not to be joined in wedlock, let him speak now.'

The solemn question hung loud and ominous in the
still air. Even the wind dropped for a moment, as if
awaiting an answer. But no objection came from anyone, although Rhun's fingers tightened around hers.
Glancing sideways, Eleanor saw him swallow once,
and then a second time, and half expected him to announce a reason of his own. But he said nothing and
the moment of uncertainty passed.

The dowry was read, the vows spoken, and then
came the exchange of rings—slender silver bands en-
graved with their names. Eleanor went through it all
as if dazed, looking down at herself from somewhere
seemingly far away. Then the chapel doors were opened
and, hand in hand still, they went inside and up to the
altar. Under the white cloth that was hoisted over their
heads the nuptial Mass was read.

Finally, the sacrament of marriage complete, Father
Robert blessed them and gave Rhun the kiss of peace.
Her new husband bent his head and passed the kiss
to her, his lips so light that she hardly felt them. And
when his hand finally relinquished hers Eleanor felt her
old life fall away with it, leaving her new one looming
lonely and bereft before her.

The feast held afterwards in the hall was sumptuous.
In place of the usual beef and mutton, pottage and oat-
cakes, and the hare stew they called *cawl*, the boards
were laden with platters of boars' heads and suckling
pig, swimming in rich sauces, and roast fowl glazed

with mustard. There were sweets too, honey cakes and nutmeg custards and autumn apple paste spiced with ginger.

Sitting at the top table, Eleanor had no appetite for any of it. Guy, to her left, did his best to engage her in conversation, but her responses were only half-hearted. Rhun ate and spoke little too, and even then it was to Huw ap Gruffudd, not to her. The minstrel's music was obviously much to the liking of their guests and Eleanor concentrated on that, even though she didn't understand the Welsh songs.

It was as one tune ended and another began that Rhun turned to her, breaking the long silence between them. 'I have a gift for you, Eleanor.'

Eleanor turned to him, startled by the informal use of her name as much as by the fact he was speaking to her at all. But now they were man and wife it was his right to address her and use her as he pleased.

'You have already given me a gift,' she replied, not able to bring herself to say his name yet. It was too intimate a way to address a man she hardly knew, even though he was now her husband.

'I don't mean the purse of coins.'

The money was symbolic, she knew—to show everyone that she was mistress of his house now, and that its economic management would fall in a large share to her. The thought sent a sudden shaft of panic through her. What did she know about the running of this place that was so different from anything she'd learned at home?

'There is another gift I wish to give you, as is customary.' From the pouch at his belt he drew out a little brooch, holding it out to her in the palm of his hand.

'The silver is from the mines on Ynys Môn,' he said, his tone gruff, almost begrudging. 'The stones come from the East.'

'Oh.' Eleanor half lifted her hand to take the lovely and unexpected gift and then stopped, a sudden shyness confusing her, causing her tongue to trip. 'It's… it's very pretty.'

A tinge of disappointment ran through Rhun as his new wife looked blankly down at the brooch. Did she consider such a plain and simple ornament a poor offering, when to him it was the most valuable thing he could give her? It was small—trifling, almost—but it had been his father's wedding gift to his mother, and because of that it weighed like a boulder in his hand. The hand that, almost without his realising it, had sought Eleanor's during the marriage ceremony and held on fast.

'You don't have to wear it, now, of course,' he said, his tone incongruous with the act of giving a gift, as his thoughts dwelt on how cold and still her fingers had been in his. 'Or at all if it doesn't please you.'

But she took up the brooch and pinned it to the neckline of her gown, just at the point of her collarbone. Amid the rich splendour of her clothes the green semi-precious topaz lacked lustre, and yet it caught the brilliance of her eyes all the same. But the jewels could never match her beauty, no matter how much they were polished…a compelling beauty that drew his eyes even now, away from the brooch and to hers.

'Thank you. I'm honoured to wear it. I have a gift for you too, but I was so…preoccupied this morning I left it in my chamber.'

He saw her brow crease, and as she bit her lip he realised she was even less equipped for this marriage than he.

'Should I send for it now, or shall I give it to you later?'

Bile began to churn in Rhun's stomach. *Later* meant their wedding night—the time when he would come to her bed and they would be alone for the first time as man and wife.

'Later will suffice.'

She gave a little nod and then reached for her eating knife. But it slipped from between her fingers and onto the floor with a clatter, though nobody else noticed above the noise.

Rhun stooped to retrieve it, only to find that Eleanor had beaten him to it. Their heads bumped, not painfully but shockingly, and she shot upright in her chair again. He straightened too, the knife in his hand and the tantalising scent of roses in his nostrils. Her hand was over her mouth, but her eyes were torn between shock and laughter.

'I see you weren't exaggerating the other day in the chapel!' he said into the embarrassment that followed. He failed to return her smile and hers faded. He wasn't good at conversation, less still at humour, and up until now he'd seldom troubled himself over either. But this was his wedding feast, and his new wife looked as uncomfortable as he must, and no doubt that was exactly how she felt—as did he.

'What do you mean?' she asked, her eyes wary now.

Rhun wiped the knife on his napkin and placed it by

the side of her trencher. 'Did you not complain to me of your clumsiness?'

'Oh! I didn't think you'd remember that.'

'Why not?'

'Because you were clearly...not yourself then.'

'No, I wasn't.'

He lifted his goblet to his lips, drinking deeply as silence fell between them once more. Neither of them had referred to what had occurred in the chapel until now, and he'd had no intention of ever doing so. And yet by trying to make light of a triviality, to break the brittle tension that sat between them, he'd unwittingly brought the occasion up himself.

'I am myself now, however,' he added. 'And I remember everything.'

But *was* he himself?

As the evening wore on her warm, slender figure next to his became hard to ignore, no matter how much he tried. The tumble of golden hair about her shoulders, entwined with the hardy flowers that bloomed late on the hillsides, drew his gaze more than once. She was a beautiful woman and she was now his wife, and he was expected to do his duty by her that night like any good husband.

Leaning forward, Rhun cradled his cup between his palms and stared down the hall. The mood was festive, especially among the villagers, who were more used to home-brewed ale than the heady mead from the castle kitchen and the rich wine from Gascony. Eleanor leaned forward too, seemingly reading his mind, and perhaps also sensing the tension in his body that surely must be evident to all.

'I haven't had the opportunity to thank you for replacing the rushes in my chamber.'

He gave a curt nod, berating himself for that neglect. 'There is no need, since they should have been seen to *before* your arrival and not afterwards.'

'Well…thank you all the same.'

Silence dropped once more like a stone between them. Out of the corner of his eye Rhun watched as she turned her cup slowly round and round in her palms.

'Everyone seems to be enjoying themselves anyway,' she said, moving her goblet to one side before resting her elbows on the table as he did. 'Just in case I knock it over, you understand,' she added, as if she were teasing him and challenging him at the same time.

'Eleanor, you could upset every cup on this table and it wouldn't matter,' he replied, forcing his tone to lightness even while his senses sparked at the feel of her arm next to his. 'The revelry tonight will no doubt lead to all sorts of mishap.'

'Still, I wouldn't like to give your guests the impression that your wife can't hold her wine.'

She wouldn't be the only one, judging by the relaxed and carnal behaviour that was being indulged in in shadowed corners the more the wine flowed.

'They couldn't accuse you of that when you've hardly touched either food or drink,' he said.

He hadn't eaten much either, although he'd lost count of how many times his own cup had been refilled. But the wine wasn't having the numbing and incapacitating effect he craved. And in a little while he and Eleanor would be far more intimate that even the most amorous among his guests.

But how could he ever lie with this woman and expose her to the terrors that assailed him while he slept? Let her hear the cries that woke him sometimes from his nightmares and left him wondering if he'd been thrown headlong into hell at last?

Rhun's skull began to ache as the noise in the hall grew louder and the guests became merrier. Even Dafydd Genau'r Glyn, his *bardd*, had left off entertaining the room and was becoming acquainted with Eleanor's maid—Alice, was it? Or rather he was struggling piteously to engage her in conversation while the woman herself clearly only had eyes for Huw ap Gruffudd.

'Your kinsman and his men leave tomorrow, I understand?' he asked of Eleanor, even though he knew the answer. He was struggling just as feebly as his hapless poet for something to say.

'Yes,' she answered, her gaze meeting his briefly. 'There is no longer any reason for them to stay.'

There was a forlorn note in her voice that tugged at his conscience and Rhun stared deeper into his cup. Would Eleanor find it lonely here with only her maid for company? Huw's wife, Non, would have been a good companion, and a wise advisor as to the business of running the household, but she'd died of the pestilence last year, like so many others.

A sudden stirring in the hall brought his gaze upwards again. The two long tables fell silent as Dafydd gave up trying to charm Eleanor's maid and returned to his *crwth* once more. Every eye watched as he seated himself on a low stool in the centre of the room and, facing the top table, lifted his instrument and began to play.

In the hush, the first haunting strains of music rose to the roof and the hairs at the back of Rhun's neck lifted too. And then, as the poet began to recite, his heart stopped.

Yn y nos daeth y Lleuad—un hudol.
Ysbrydol, blodeuad
ein gobaith heb amheuad.
Dechreuad heb ddagreuad.

It was the *englyn* to Castell y Lleuad—the very same song another *bardd*, this one's father, had declaimed at his parents' wedding. He should have expected it, of course, and been ready for it, but he was neither. Nor was he ready for the way Eleanor leaned in towards him, her fingers touching his forearm and her gaze eagerly seeking his.

'What does it mean?' she asked.

Rhun's pulse began to pound in his ears. Not loud enough to block out the words of the poem, and even if it had he knew it line for line anyway. Almost without realising it he translated it for her, his lips moving of their own accord.

'"*In the night came the Moon—a magical one. Spiritual, a flowering of our hope without doubt. A beginning without tears.*"'

As the last notes of the *crwth* died away, the strings echoing to a silence heavy with sentiment, applause rang out from every corner of the hall. Rhun turned his head and looked into Eleanor's eyes to find them full of feeling. And he knew an ache in his soul so intense that his whole body seemed to shrivel to dust inside his clothes.

'I've never heard anything so lovely,' she breathed. 'The melody was sad even though the words were ones of hope.'

Her voice was like a caress that seemed to reach out and touch him. His new wife was lovely too—something he hadn't really seen that first night, when she'd arrived unwelcome, travel-stained and soaked to the skin, yet with a vitality that had shone then as it shone even more brightly tonight.

'The poets of Wales have a knack for melancholy.'

His tongue felt loose and thick, as if the sentiments of the poem were contagious, spreading through his hall like a fever. Or had the song opened up a well of feeling he'd long sealed shut and in doing so released a desire for this woman that he didn't want to feel?

'The *englyn* has been declaimed at wedding feasts here for many years, long before I was born, to welcome the bride and bless the marriage.'

From the shadow that darkened her eyes Rhun saw that the irony wasn't lost on her. But she had the grace—or the wisdom—not to voice it.

'Is that why this house is called Castle of the Moon?' she asked.

He nodded, his head suddenly too heavy for his shoulders, his ears still ringing with the words of the *englyn*. 'It's really called Castell Caledfryn, but, at some point a poet sang of the way the walls are turned silver by the full moon in wintertime and it's been called Castell y Lleuad ever since.'

She smiled at him, and her gaze sparkled like moon

and stars put together. Or perhaps it was the wine and the song that dazzled him. 'And do the walls *really* turn silver?'

'No, it's just a trick of the heavens…nothing more.' He sat back, away from the bewitching gaze of her eyes, and took a deep drink from his goblet. 'I've never seen it, but poets waste no time in turning such nonsense into legend to entertain their lord. And, if they are good poets, to earn a reputation that keeps them well for the rest of their lives.'

'Oh, don't cheapen it, please!' She moved back too, and the space between them, so full of awareness a moment earlier, became a void again. 'The song has a meaning that I can appreciate. And even if I'm not welcome in your house, Lord Rhun, unlike all those other brides who have come, it doesn't matter. The words are lovely all the same.'

Rhun blinked as her accusation hit him like a broadsword. For he *hadn't* made her welcome—not from the moment she'd stepped over the threshold. In fact, he'd told her bluntly that she *wasn't* welcome at all! His fingers tightened around his cup but he couldn't drag his gaze away from the eyes that glowed like green fire. How could the poem touch her so deeply, its lyric kindle such passion in her heart, but leave him cold with rage and yet burning with pain?

Silently, he cursed Dafydd for his *englyn*—but not as bitterly as he cursed himself for providing the occasion for it.

'Perhaps you should have asked somebody other than me to translate it for you!' he said, his bitterness clutching him by the throat and making his words ungracious.

Getting to his feet, he banged his cup on the table to silence the hall and called Dafydd forward. Thanking him for his praise, for he could do nothing else, he threw a trinket at the *bardd*'s feet.

Picking it up, the man responded in turn with the traditional blessing. *'Gad i'r noson hon ddod â phleser a phlentyn i chi'ch dau!'*

Pleasure and a son!

The wish of every man and woman on their nuptial night.

Rhun turned back to Eleanor, forcing his body and his voice to obey him. Because the moment had come for him to take the last step in the bargain he'd fulfilled. To consummate the marriage and make it real and binding. Or at least show that intent to all present.

'The feast will continue, Eleanor.' His words were hoarse, his mouth so dry he might well have drunk nothing at all. 'But we should retire now—if it pleases you?'

'Of course.' Eleanor nodded, rising to her feet too. She might be glad to finally escape this ordeal, but it evidently didn't please her new husband to leave the hall and go upstairs. That fact was clear from every line of his face, where the skin was drawn so tightly that the bones stood out sharp as blades.

His face had turned crimson at his poet's words a moment ago, and a frown of displeasure had fallen so heavily on his brow that she hadn't dared ask what they meant. Now, as his eyes gleamed brightly down at her, she wondered if he were drunk—for what else could explain such brusque manners?

Bidding goodnight to Guy, she rose and, her eyes

fixed blindly in front of her, walked down the length of the hall behind Huw and Alice. Rhun strode unsmiling at her side, his bad leg dragging more than usual.

Everyone stood to see them out, and the thumping of cups on boards and lewd cheers shook the very roof. None of the guests followed them to the doorway, however, or tried to get a piece of her clothing for luck, as she knew tradition demanded. The garter she wore on her stocking stayed where it was, firmly tied below her knee, and even though she'd dreaded the embarrassing ordeal it was even more shameful that it seemed no one wanted to share in her fortune on this occasion.

They climbed the stairs, Huw lighting their way, just as he'd done the night they'd arrived. At the top, Rhun went ahead of them without a word and disappeared through the door of his chamber, slamming it shut behind him. Outside Eleanor's own door Huw, his face flushed, but not with drink, bowed low and bade them goodnight.

Standing at the hearth in her chamber, Eleanor felt none of the fire's warmth as her maid replaced her wedding gown with the new shift of pale gold that had been made especially for this night. The flowers were removed from her hair and it was combed until it shone like spun flax. In the mirror that Alice held before her she saw she looked as a bride ought to look—virginal, yet resigned—but that was as far as it went.

On her sisters' nuptial nights Eleanor had brushed their hair in the same way, and helped them prepare for their husbands' persons. Amid excitement and anticipation, giggles and nerves, the three of them had discovered a closeness that they'd never had as children.

Would she feel more like a bride if Joan and Margaret were here now, reassuring her that marriage was a blessing not a curse? That it was the lot of a woman and should be welcomed as such, and that it was better to be wed than go into a convent?

She tried but failed to count those blessings as she climbed into bed. The curtains were left open in invitation and the rushlights burned brightly to illuminate her husband's way. Too brightly!

'Douse these candles near me, Alice,' she ordered, her voice thin through the nerves that had closed her throat. 'Just leave the one at the door alight, and one for yourself.'

Her maid did as she was bade and then settled herself on a stool near the hearth, until such time when she would be dismissed. In the dimness, the noise of merriment from the hall below made the quiet of the chamber ominous. Even Alice was silent for once, her chatter exhausted, and she bent her head low over the piece of needlework in her lap.

Long moments passed while Eleanor—her fingers worrying at the hair that lay over her breast, hiding the ugliness that would soon be discovered and reviled—awaited Rhun's knock at the door.

It never came.

Chapter Four

'You wish to ride, my lady?'

Huw ap Gruffudd squinted down at her in the afternoon sun and Eleanor nodded. For the first time since she'd arrived the sky was blue and cloudless, the hills were bright with red bracken and the breeze blew warm and gentle.

'That is precisely what I wish, Sir Huw,' she said, her heart starting to sing at the thought of a few hours of freedom outside the confines of the castle walls.

'Then I will arrange for an escort.' The squint became a frown. 'Lord Rhun is absent today, or he would mayhap have ridden with you.'

'Oh…?'

Eleanor doubted that very much. She'd grown used to seeing little or nothing of her husband by now. Apart from sitting at her side at mealtimes, where his occasional attempts at strained conversation were worse than his long periods of sullen silence, Rhun had not come near her since their wedding day, three weeks ago. It was as if it had never happened at all.

'Where has he gone?' she asked, her curiosity aroused all the same.

'To the farmland beyond the village, my lady. To discuss the harvest and winter stores with the hayward.'

Eleanor had seen the village from the battlements. It lay not too far distant to the southeast of the castle, beyond the bridge that he'd warned her not to cross that day in the chapel. Now, for the first time, she wondered why.

'As my maid will be riding with me, Sir Huw, I won't require an escort. We'll not go far. I simply want to see something of the land hereabouts, and my mare requires some exercise.'

'I would urge you to take some men all the same. Or I will accompany you, if you prefer?'

'Why? Is there likely to be any danger?'

He shook his head. 'Close to the castle it is improbable, but—'

'Then we'll keep the castle in sight at all times.'

'But, my lady—'

'Sir Huw, no more discussion, please!' Eleanor lifted a hand and the steward fell silent. She sent him a reassuring smile. 'I promise we'll be careful, so please see that our horses are made ready.'

'Yes, Lady Eleanor.' The man bowed and, looking far from happy, turned in the direction of the stables.

'Shouldn't we allow Sir Huw to come with us, mistress?' Alice's eyes glowed as they always did whenever she was near the handsome yet taciturn steward, and it was clear she'd set her cap at the man. 'After all, we might get lost. Or robbed... Or worse.'

Eleanor shook her head. Shunned by her new husband, she wasn't going to be piggy in the middle in a dalliance between Huw and Alice by any means! Smoothing her palms down over her kilted riding skirts, she stifled a sting of jealousy that her maid could flirt, desire a man—contemplate love, even—while she, though wed, could not.

'No, we'll go alone. Nothing will befall us—why should it?'

As he turned his horse's head towards home Rhun felt his knee complain, the ache pulling at the sinews of his entire leg from ankle to hip. Cai trotted alongside, keeping pace as he always did, though his old legs must be aching too. How long had he been out? Four, five hours? More, even? He'd lost track of time, although the sun hadn't yet reached its zenith when he'd ridden out through the gatehouse that morning, and now the shadows were starting to encroach on the landscape, like black brooms sweeping the daylight away.

As he rode he brooded on the poor harvest this year. The crops had been spoiled by heavy rainfall, and although there were enough animals to be slaughtered for winter he would have to obtain more salt to preserve them as long as possible.

But the prospect of a cruel winter was something he could deal with head-on—tackle with the means at his disposal. Why, then, couldn't he face the far simpler ordeal of sitting next to his wife in the hall? Why did his feet halt and turn swiftly in another direction whenever he spied her across the courtyard? Why did he spend his days abroad on horseback, absenting himself from mealtimes in an effort to avoid her as much as he could?

'Uffarn dân!' Rhun cursed aloud, causing the stallion to toss its head and take a startled leap forward.

He gathered the reins and patted its neck contritely. He'd had Eryr since a colt, and his horse was as sensitive to his human moods as he was to its animal moods. And just at that moment his mood was blacker even than the shining coat beneath him. Because he found himself confronted with something that he wasn't prepared for and could neither fight against nor retreat from.

His marriage.

He'd never been afraid to take risks, seek adventures, launch himself headlong into the fiercest of tournaments. Now he'd sooner face enemy hordes in their thousands than spend a moment in the company of his new wife—a wife in name only—and find himself blushing and stuttering as he tried to string two intelligent words together.

The shame of that was still burning in Rhun's brain as he skirted the village and rode along the riverbank. Two riders on the slope of the hill below the castle caught his attention, and in the still afternoon air snatches of laughter came to his ears, interspersed with an occasional word of French. It could only be Eleanor and her maid, out riding alone and defenceless.

The blood chilling in his veins, he dug his heels into Eryr's flanks and set off at a gallop towards them.

As he clattered over the wooden bridge that spanned the river the women reined in their mounts. The laughter ceased abruptly and their mouths dropped open in astonishment, their faces like pale moons against the green hillside behind them. And, as those faces got rapidly nearer Rhun realised he was going too fast. Far too fast!

Hauling on his reins, he managed to slow and pull his horse to a skidding halt—but not before Eryr had collided violently with Eleanor's grey palfrey. The mare squealed and shied backwards, knocking into the maid's mount, and chaos ensued. The maid's animal reared and the woman slid slowly over its rump, landing with a yelp on the ground. In the stunned quiet that followed the only sound was the riderless horse galloping high-tailed for home, with Cai in eager pursuit.

'Iesu mawr!' With a whistle to call the dog back, Rhun leapt from the saddle and picked the maid up, setting her down gently upon her feet. Anxiously, he examined her face, which had gone as white as snow. 'Are you hurt?'

'N-no, I don't think so.'

The woman's eyes brimmed as she brushed the dust off her skirts, but she seemed unharmed apart from her fright. So Rhun took no further notice of her tears and whirled around to face her mistress, who sat tall and rigid in her saddle, her face as ashen as her maid's. When he spoke his voice—though even he hardly recognised it—roared like thunder around the hills.

'Er mwyn Duw! What are you about, madam?'

Eleanor stared speechless at the man before her, his face contorted with fury and his eyes blazing up at her like hot coals. His steed sidled and snorted beside him and the hound began to bay, making her mare dance nervously on the spot, nearly unseating her.

Grabbing a handful of Mistletoe's mane to steady

herself, she found her voice at last. 'What am *I* about? I think I could ask *you* the same question, my lord!'

'I saw you riding towards the bridge from the other side of the river.' He put out a hand to silence his hound, the other hand taking hold of her reins. The mare settled at once and stood quietly under his command. 'What on earth possessed my steward to allow you to leave the castle unescorted?'

Eleanor felt her cheeks flame and her temper rise. But it wasn't just temper that was making her blood gush through her veins. The short riding tunic and hose Rhun wore hugged his lean, strong body, moulding the muscles of his arms and thighs, the expanse of his chest and broad shoulders. And with his eyes so intensely alive, and his black hair windswept, her new husband appeared both formidable and attractive. And even though she didn't understand how the two went together, somehow they did.

'Sir Huw is blameless,' she said. 'You said I could venture wherever I chose, did you not? Except for over the bridge to the village—though I can't see for the life of me what harm there could be in that.'

'That may be.' He ignored her deliberate mention of the village completely. 'But did you not think to take an escort with you?'

'I *have* an escort. As you see, Alice is with me.'

'Your maid would hardly be able to defend you any more than you could her.' He cast a contemptuous glance over his shoulder to where her maid stood, quiet and clearly in shock. 'She can't even sit a horse properly!'

'She rides as well as I do,' Eleanor bit back, sharpening her tone now to match his.

Having said hardly two words to her for the last three weeks, the Lord Rhun was eloquent enough, it seemed, when his anger was aroused! But berating his unfortunate steward was one thing—blaming her poor maid was unacceptable.

'It's not her fault she fell off. What do you *expect* to happen when you come galloping up, yelling like the devil himself, and frightening us out of our wits?'

He had the grace to look discomposed at that, for a fleeting instant at least, before his mouth set into a scowl again. 'She isn't hurt. And, believe me, a lot worse can happen to women who are foolish enough to venture out alone.'

'Such as what?' Eleanor gestured towards the tranquil countryside around them, the quiet landscape so at odds with the turbulent and inexplicable conflict that was taking place. 'Abduction? Or murder, perhaps?'

If she'd thought she'd seen Rhun angry before, she'd misjudged him. For now, as she looked back at him, his eyes were glittering with fury. His hand began to shake where it held her mare's reins, and it suddenly felt as if an explosion was about to happen right beneath their feet. Her stomach tightened with apprehension and all at once she was ten years old again, cowering before the wrath of her father, awaiting the inevitable punishment for something she knew not what.

'You are ignorant of life this side of the border,' he answered, after a taut moment that in the end came to nothing. 'And ignorance can be dangerous as well as foolhardy, my lady.'

.Since their wedding feast, the fledgling connection she'd felt when he'd given her the brooch and explained the lovely poem to her had long withered. And gone too was the intimate use of her name. Even in private, on a rare occasion, they were now *my lord* and *my lady* again, as if he'd never married her at all!

Eleanor held her husband's eyes. She was a grown woman now, not the child who had lived in fear of her sire, and she would not allow herself to live in fear of her husband. 'I may be ignorant, but I was also born and raised in the March, and I hardly think there is any more danger on one side than on the other.'

'Even so, you are my wife, and in future I forbid you to leave the castle without suitable escort—is that understood?'

'Forbid?' She drew herself up straighter in her saddle and snatched her reins out of his grasp. 'I will go where I please, escorted or otherwise. And I am *not* your wife yet in the full and proper sense—as we both well know!'

Rhun's face turned crimson, and behind him Alice's eyes grew wide with shock. It was no secret from her maid that the marriage was as yet unconsummated, even if no one else suspected. But to voice the fact bluntly and before a servant shamed him far more than it did her.

And shame him she had. That much was obvious as, with another grating and unintelligible curse in his own tongue, Rhun spun on his heel. Picking up her maid as if she were a feather, he flung her up onto his horse's back, making Alice shriek and grab at the stallion's long mane for dear life.

The magnificent courser was so big that she looked

like a sparrow perched on top of a barrel, and despite
the tension—or perhaps because of it—Eleanor giggled.
Rhun whirled back towards her and hastily she swallowed her amusement. God prevent that she should find
anything funny in a situation that he obviously viewed
with dire gravity!

'Come, I'll escort you back to the castle myself.'

And without another word he strode stiffly away, his
hound and his horse at his heels. Eleanor sat glaring at
his retreating figure for a moment, sorely tempted to
continue with her ride alone, if only to show him that
she was not some dumb and obedient creature, content
to follow at his heels too. But finally she nudged Mistletoe into a walk and trailed along behind him.

The whole thing, for all its startling violence, had
been a brief but passing storm, and now, in the lull, there
seemed nothing to do but wonder at it.

Not once did Rhun look back as they climbed the
hill towards Castell y Lleuad. His limp grew more and
more pronounced the further they went, and Eleanor
felt the sting of tears rise up behind her eyes. For now
that the storm was over it had left her drenched with an
uneasy foreboding. Was this to set the pattern for her
married life? A union that would veer for ever between
mute tolerance and stormy clashes of will? And was
she destined to live her whole life under his roof as his
wife and yet remain despised and childless all her days?

What sort of man had she married, for heaven's sake?
And what if the terrible ailment that she'd witnessed in
the chapel three weeks ago wasn't of the body at all—
but of the mind? After all, what else could explain his
strange and unpredictable behaviour?

* * *

Rhun's leg was on fire and he gritted his teeth so hard his jaw ached. *Myn diawl*, what else was he supposed to have done? Left them wandering blithely about the countryside, prey to any lurking knave, robber or murderer?

The maid had started to sniffle quietly, getting on his nerves, but from his wife there was no sound whatsoever. Although he could feel Eleanor's displeasure like a sword thrust deep between his shoulder blades. And her accusation of his neglect of her—as just as it was accurate—twisted it with venom deep into his heart.

But even that was nothing to the sense of fear that had gripped him when he'd seen them riding unaccompanied by men-at-arms. Their close proximity to the castle—a fact he'd been aware of with some small part of his mind—hadn't mattered. All he'd seen was danger, and the fact that there had been none apparent was irrelevant. There hadn't been any apparent danger that autumn day he and his mother had set out for the village twelve years ago, and still…

Rhun shook his head and stepped up the pace, pushing the terrible memory away before it took hold. He fixed his eyes on the castle gatehouse, no more than half a league away, and as he looked two men on horseback emerged in haste. As they trotted nearer he recognised Huw ap Gruffudd, and saw that the second man rode the chestnut rouncy that had unseated the maid.

'My mare is lame.'

He turned around at the quiet statement behind him and stifled a groan. For Eleanor was on her knees in the dirt, her head bent and her fingers gently probing her horse's fetlock. Giving Eryr's reins to the maid, he issued a command that he hoped she'd have the sense to obey—otherwise his stallion would be away like the wind for home. 'Hold these tight and sit still until my steward gets here.'

Striding back towards Eleanor, Rhun dropped down next to her and inspected the animal's leg. Just above the hoof there was a deep gash from which blood oozed— not fast, but thick enough for concern. He realised at once what had happened. When he'd come to a sliding stop in front of the mare earlier, one of Eryr's hooves must have struck her.

Looking up at Eleanor, his eyes met hers, and in the sinking sun the colour of them was deep and dazzling. Quickly, he dragged his gaze away, but his eyes went instead to her mouth, just as her lips parted.

'Is it bad?'

Rhun cleared his throat, clogged suddenly with both remorse and something far more carnal. 'It's deep, yes.'

She nodded her head, the sun catching at the gold strands of the single thick plait that hung over her shoulder. Her head was covered with a coif, as befitted a married woman—although, as she'd accused him, and rightly, he'd not made her a married woman in the full sense…a failing that insulted her and shamed them both.

'Then I'd best not ride her back to the castle. I'll walk instead.'

Her voice cut through his thoughts. 'It's not so very far now,' he said. 'But it's not fitting that you should walk all the same.'

They were kneeling so close that he'd only need to

dip his head a little to kiss her. But that would undo all the effort he'd made over the last weeks to keep that temptation at bay. And if he gave in to it now would he be able to stop there? Would he want to touch her too? Feel the body that lay beneath the folds of her riding gown?

He never got the chance to find out—which was perhaps all to the good. A blast of warm air hit the back of his neck, followed by the tickle of the mare's muzzle lipping at his hair.

Eleanor burst out laughing, the sound tinkling like silver bells into his ears and rippling over his senses. 'I think Mistletoe is trying to say thank you!'

Rhun felt his mouth lift into a smile and almost succumbed to the impulse to laugh too. 'There is no need for thanks, since it is Eryr and I who are at fault. I fear that his hooves caused this damage.'

But she hadn't accused him at all, and that only made his remorse bite harder.

'Then it was by accident, and there is no fault involved.'

His heart began to thud so loudly that its echo filled his whole chest, thundering against his ribs and knocking the breath from his lungs. His blood began to roar through his veins, setting his body alight, and he might well have kissed her, right there and then, on his knees in the mud, if the sudden activity of Huw ap Gruffudd's arrival not pulled him to his senses.

Leaping to his feet, Rhun spun away from temptation and glared up at his steward as the man drew rein before him.

'My lord, is anything amiss?'

'As you see full well there is much amiss!' he ground out through lips that were still thinking of Eleanor's. 'What were you about, man, allowing my wife to venture out unescorted?'

Behind him, he heard Eleanor get to her feet and come up behind them. And then her hand found his forearm, light and imploring.

'Please don't berate your steward, my lord. Sir Huw advised me to take an escort and I disagreed.'

The slender fingers seemed somehow to reach through the material of his tunic to his skin. Rhun tensed, every nerve in his body aware of her. 'From now on, Huw, whenever Lady Eleanor wishes to ride out you will accompany her yourself, with men-at-arms, whether she disagrees or not. Is that understood?'

'Yes, my lord.'

The man flushed, and Rhun steeled himself not to relent. Huw had been a member of his household for a score and more years, since he was a boy of fourteen, but service and loyalty would matter little if the worst happened.

'Now, if you please, take the ladies back to the castle. The mare is lame, so my wife will ride with her maid upon Eryr.'

'No, that won't be necessary.'

As Eleanor spoke her hand dropped from his arm and she walked back to her palfrey, taking its reins and turning to look at him serenely. Her tone and the stubborn set of her chin were becoming annoyingly familiar, and Rhun could almost have predicted his wife's next words even before she said them.

'I will lead Mistletoe back myself. It's not very far in any case. So pray go ahead and I'll follow.'

Eleanor saw Rhun's jaw clench and tightened her fingers on Mistletoe's reins. All four faces, even that of the man-at-arms, were turned to her in astonishment. Was that because she'd chosen to walk back to the castle when she could ride in comfort? Or because she'd dared to gainsay her husband's command in public?

Her answer came soon enough as he approached and, dipping his head, spoke in a voice quiet enough so that only she could hear it. 'Eleanor, you are being foolish, and you are making me look foolish too.'

So they were back to the intimacy of names now! But the familiarity didn't stop there, since his forehead was almost touching hers and she couldn't help but breathe him in. His skin and his hair bore no perfume, unlike some of the English and French lords. Rather Rhun's essence was of open countryside, of wild weather and heather-covered hills, of health and strength and vigour.

Her gaze dropped from his eyes to the harsh line of his mouth. A mouth that only a few moments ago, when they'd been kneeling together, had almost relented into a laugh—or had she imagined that? Had she imagined, too, as his eyes had lingered so long on *her* mouth, that he'd thought about kissing her? But then Huw had arrived and she'd never know for sure, or know what she would have done if he *had* taken her lips.

'That isn't my intention.' She lifted her eyes to his again. 'Mistletoe is mine, and I'd rather not trust her to anyone else.'

It was partly true. The mare *was* dear to her—both for her sweet nature and also because she had been a wedding gift from her sisters. But she couldn't capitulate now...not after she'd defied her lord husband in front of everyone. If she did, the precedent would be set and any hope of asserting her own will in this marriage would be a forlorn one.

The sun dipped behind a cloud, and in its shadow she saw Rhun's frown darken. 'Then will you trust her to me?'

'To you?' Eleanor felt herself waver before this new tactic, voiced with a new and beguiling softness. Or *was* it a tactic? 'What do you mean?' she asked cautiously.

'I mean I'll lead the mare home while you ride with your maid on Eryr, as I suggested.'

He hadn't suggested, he'd *ordered*, and it was on the tip of her tongue to point that out when his next word took the wind completely out of her sails.

'Please.'

It wasn't a plea, but neither was it a command. Whatever it was, it worked.

Inclining her head as meekly as she knew how, Eleanor handed Rhun the reins, for it seemed now both foolish and purposeless to dig her heels in any longer. 'Very well. As that seems the most sensible thing to do, I will ride with Alice.'

She wasn't prepared for his next move, however, although perhaps she should have been. Looping Mistletoe's reins over his elbow, he picked her up, and before she could draw breath she was sitting astride the great black courser behind her maid.

And as they set off, she clutching on to Alice for

dear life and feeling indeed like a sparrow on top of a barrel, Eleanor would have sworn that there really *was* a smile on Rhun's mouth now…a barely concealed smile of victory.

Chapter Five

Leaving Huw to see to the women, Rhun led the mare into her stable and called for his constable of the horse to come and clean the wound. He secured her to the wall, after which she tried to nip his arm, and, stepping back, studied her for the first time. A light dapple grey with fine lines and a dark and spirited eye, she was a pretty and valuable animal with a mind of her own. A fitting mount for her mistress!

As if the comparison had called her forward, his wife entered then and came to stand at his side. 'Your palfrey will be well looked after,' he said. 'You have no need to worry or to linger.'

'I will treat Mistletoe myself.' She smoothed her skirts down and a flush mounted her cheek. 'I have a tincture in my chamber that is good for wounds, both in man and beast.'

Rhun felt a flush mount his cheek too. When he'd lifted Eleanor up into the saddle earlier his blood had been boiling with annoyance and the need to have done with the situation. But the intimate brush of her body against his, the arms that had clung to his shoulders, the soft gasp of shock that had feathered his cheek, had made his blood boil in quite another way and brought other, more urgent needs to his body.

'As you wish,' he replied, feeling those needs still barely in check. 'Although my constable is adequately skilled in the ailments of horses.'

'All the same, I will tend to her myself.' Eleanor removed her cloak and riding gloves and passed them to her maid, who stood hovering in the doorway. 'Please take these things to our chamber, Alice, and bring me the pot of green ointment as quickly as you can.'

The woman dropped a curtsy, though her legs were visibly stiff after clinging to Eryr's saddle so tightly, and hurried off. Suddenly he and Eleanor stood alone in the stable, both of them seemingly lost for words. Yet what was there to say after the storm between them that afternoon and the remnants of it still hanging there now, like a last remaining thundercloud? Along with the more recent storm of desire which she knew nothing of but that scorched along his nerves like wildfire!

Turning to him, his wife inclined her head and dismissed him as succinctly as she had her maid. 'Well, don't let me detain you, my lord. I'm sure you have other tasks to see to.'

Rhun shook his head. Like any enemy, meeting lust head-on was the only way to vanquish it. And the only remedy for temptation was in proving that it could be resisted. 'Nothing that cannot wait until the morrow, my lady.'

Rhodri ab Ifor entered and began to clean the wound with salted water. Eleanor went down on her knees beside him, watching intently but saying nothing. Rhodri knew no English. The maid arrived with the ointment and promptly left again, no doubt having had enough of horseflesh for one day.

When the work of cleaning the fetlock was complete, Rhun dismissed his constable with a word of thanks and, going to the mare's head, took hold of her halter.

'I will assist you, since my constable has other things to attend to.'

Eleanor made no answer, but he saw her shoulders set, as if she was bracing herself against his presence. Her bended head was just level with his knee and her neck was pale below the white linen coif. Her hands worked with skill and tenderness as she began to apply the ointment. They were deft and gentle, displaying none of the clumsiness she had claimed for herself.

Would those hands be as skilful on a man as well? Lust flared again in his loins at the thought, and he drew a deep breath as his body hardened.

'Did you speak, my lord?'

Focused on what her hands were doing, Rhun realised too late that his wife had looked up at him, her gaze sharp. 'I was wondering where you learned your skills with herbs,' he lied. 'Not a pastime that many noblewomen practise, I imagine.'

'As to that, I can't say.' She sat back on her heels and wiped her fingers on a piece of cloth. 'I find it to my liking. As for teaching—I taught myself. Herbs challenge my capabilities less than embroidery does.'

Rhun looked down again at the slender fingers, stained with the ointment she'd worked into the wound.

They seemed more than capable, and once again the image of them on his body turned his vitals to fire.

'Why does embroidery challenge you?'

She shrugged. 'It is too delicate…too frivolous. I prefer more meaningful pastimes—and besides, if I see hurt or suffering anywhere I want to offer help.'

Like the help she'd offered him that day in the chapel—a tincture for his wound that he'd refused without any grace or gratitude.

She glanced up at him again and her green eyes gleamed as if she'd seen right into his mind. 'But even the most effective of herbs is of no use when the sufferer is too stubborn to admit he requires any help.'

If she hadn't seen the impact of her comment on his face, Eleanor would have felt it in the spasm that ran through Rhun's body. How could she not when his leg, the lame one, rustically clad in dun-coloured trews, was so close to her shoulder that it was almost touching her? When she could feel the warmth of his flesh, the hard play of muscle, all the way though her tunic and into her skin? But his reaction told her that her reminder had hit its target, despite the dismissal that came all too swiftly.

'Not all wounds heal, no matter how much ointment is applied.'

'Perhaps not.' She held his gaze as their talk played out more like a game of chequers than a conversation, with both care and guile. 'But don't you think, my lord, that where a wound exists treatment should be sought all the same?'

'Not always. Sometimes wounds are best left alone to heal themselves.'

'And if they don't heal themselves?'

'Then they must be endured, like anything else.'

Rhun was staring down at her so intently that she couldn't look away. His eyes were dark, unreadable in the failing daylight beyond the stable. For dusk had come all of a sudden and shadows enfolded them, locking them into a secret world.

'And my name is Rhun, as you well know.'

Eleanor's heart began to race and her fingers grew clumsy. She remembered how Huw ap Gruffudd had corrected her pronunciation of the name the day she'd arrived. She'd said it over and over in her head since then, practising so as to perfect it. But she'd not had cause to use it without his title, and never in the intimate and inviting way in which Rhun said it now.

'And mine is Eleanor—as *you* well know. Although you seem as reluctant to use the name as I am to use yours.'

Carefully she placed the pot down, even though she hadn't finished the treatment, afraid it would slip out of her grasp. Was it her probing into the illness that he refused to acknowledge, or had her remark earlier, about their marriage being as yet unconsummated, sparked this new and sudden intimacy? Now she wished she'd never said it, for the longer Rhun kept away from her bed, the longer her disfigurement would remain undiscovered.

'I think I've done enough for now,' she said, suddenly feeling too exposed for comfort, despite the shadows that loomed around them. 'And it's getting too dark to see properly in any case.'

Eleanor started to rise, but the hem of her gown

caught beneath her and she half fell to her knees again. In a trice, Rhun's hands had closed about her arms and he lifted her gently to her feet, turning her towards him. She felt his breath on her face as they stared at each other, and then his hand lifted and he pushed the coif she wore back from her head.

'Eleanor...'

She stood as still as a statue as he put his finger-tips to her hair, stroking along her temple, over her cheek, along her jaw and down her throat. In the wake of his slow and tender touch an ache began to gnaw in her belly, and a strange longing pulsed between her legs. Her breasts were rising and falling rapidly, and her throat went dry as his hand travelled lightly along her collarbone. Her limbs began to quiver, her flesh responding instinctively to what he was asking of it, her very bones melting and becoming soft and pliable, ready to bend to his touch, to his will.

But then his fingers found the birthmark, where it crested over her shoulder and, even though he couldn't see it beneath her clothes Eleanor jumped backwards so that his hand was left suspended in mid-air. Her heart pounded and her whole body seemed to be poised on the threshold of some excitement or expectation. But fear choked her, stronger even than what she knew to be desire, and whatever spell had been cast over her was shattered in an instant.

'So you shun my bedchamber, my lord, but would tumble me in a stable like a common leman?'

A tide of scarlet swept his face and immediately she wished the insult back again. It had been bitten out in desperate self-defence. For whether Rhun eventually discovered her disfigurement in her bed, or in the straw at this very moment, the result would be the same. Her husband would find her hideous to look at, and she would find it utterly unbearable to be so exposed to his disgust and his contempt.

But she'd already earned his contempt, it seemed, as he shrugged and turned away.

'I beg your pardon, madam.' Stooping, he picked up the coif that had fallen to the floor and held it out to her with a little bow that was more ironic than contrite. 'I forgot myself completely. But be comforted to know that it won't happen again.'

Eleanor clutched the linen to her midriff as misery churned in her belly, dowsing the warm honeyed feeling that had swirled there a moment ago. 'Perhaps you mistook me in what I said before…about not making me your wife in…in the full sense of the word.' She heard her tongue form desperate excuses, and for the life of her didn't know if they were truth or lie. 'It wasn't a complaint—quite the contrary. For I assure you that our…arrangement suits me as well as it suits you.'

He said nothing, and in the darkness she couldn't read any expression at all on his face as she went on, speaking so fast her words tumbled out of her mouth.

'Obviously I understand that you must have an heir one day, but we have years yet before we need to think of that, surely?'

The night encroached further into the stable, and in the quiet that came with it her words echoed loud and damning. What she'd just said was tantamount to refusing him her bed, and Eleanor waited, her breath coming even faster than her words had. For if he disagreed entirely—if he demanded entry to her bed, to her body—what could she do to prevent it, after all? She was his wife, his to use as he pleased. And his answer, when it finally came, proved that fact.

'Yes, we have time yet before we need to think of children. However, you need not think that any other woman but you, Eleanor, will bear me those children when the time comes.'

'When the time comes?' Eleanor's stomach turned over. It was as if he'd lifted a blade above her head and now she would be forever watching and wondering when it would fall. 'So I'm meant to wait for your call, like your horse and your hound, when the moment pleases you?'

'*Arglwydd mawr*, Eleanor! That is not what I meant.'

'Then what *do* you mean?' But she didn't wait to hear his answer. 'And don't shout at me in your own tongue! If you must curse me, at least be so good as to use English, so I can understand *why* I'm being cursed!'

His eyes blazed, even through the gloom. 'If you didn't challenge me at every turn I would have no need for curses in *any* language!'

'*At every turn?* How can that be when we hardly ever meet? And even when we do meet—at table, for instance—don't think I haven't noticed how you sit as far away from me as you possibly can, and will converse with anyone rather than with me.'

Eleanor dug her nails into her palms as the confusion and tension of the last few weeks bubbled up inside her like a boiling cauldron of oil.

'Heavens, even if I ask you to pass me the salt you look as if you'd like to empty the whole pot over my head. And God forbid our elbows should accidentally touch for, if they do, you'd jump clean out of your skin!'

She ran out of breath, her breasts heaving and her throat convulsing. For a long moment neither of them said anything, and then he spoke, his tone low and his words as unsettling as they were accurate.

'Yet just now, when I touched you, it was *you* who flinched and jumped out of your skin, was it not, Eleanor?'

'Th-that's different.'

'Is it?' He moved a step towards her. 'I had no intention of tumbling you in the straw, as you seem to assume, but surely the privacy of a dark stable is a more appropriate place for a man to touch his wife intimately than at table in front of the entire hall?'

Eleanor felt herself blush and shook her head. 'Fine words from a man who, although married nigh on a month, hasn't deigned to touch his wife *at all*!'

'So you would have your cake and eat it too?'

'What does that mean?'

'It means that you complain when I touch you and complain even louder when I don't.'

This time she felt herself blush all over. For it was true, wasn't it? And therein lay the reason why this marriage could never last. For when the night came, when they were neither in the hall nor in a stable, when he came to her room and claimed his husband's due, she wouldn't have the right to complain either way.

Eleanor turned her head and stared out beyond the door. The moon was just peeping over the walls and in the clear darkening sky stars were beginning to twinkle. It promised to be a calm and beautiful night, yet here were the two of them, caught up in a maelstrom that was completely the opposite.

'Perhaps…in that case…' she spoke to the moon, not to Rhun '…why not settle this discord and have our marriage annulled? We're not suited, and that is abundantly clear, so is it not better to undo this union before either of us insults the other beyond repair?'

Rhun felt the air leave his lungs in a rush, though he made no outward sound of breath or words. A fortnight ago he would have agreed with her wholeheartedly, escorted her personally to the border—to her father's very door if she had insisted upon it. So why did the thought of it bring a sour taste to his mouth now?

Eleanor, too, must have been wondering, because she turned back to him and drew a little nearer. 'It's not too late for us to put things right, Rhun, and part amicably instead of in enmity.'

The scent of rose petals came to his nose, mingling in his senses with the aroma of sweet straw and horse-flesh. Beyond the door he heard Cai whine, the hound missing his company and wanting his supper. Somewhere behind him a rat scuttled, the sound scraping over his nerves.

'No.'

There was a gasp and she lifted her arms, spreading them wide in disbelief, the coif in one of her hands showing startlingly white in the dark, like a flag of truce. 'But… I don't understand. Why would you wish to continue this pretence?'

Why, indeed? Hadn't she just offered him—offered them both—the release they craved? Mistakes, even the worst of them, were not totally irreparable, so why wasn't he snatching this chance to put things right like his hawk snatched at a songbird in the hunt?

'We are wed and we will remain wed.'

Her hands dropped slowly to her sides and he could almost hear her mind turning.

'Is it the alliance you are concerned about? Surely there can still be an agreement of peace between our houses, despite our separation?'

She was so near to him that all he had to do was stretch out his arms to their fullest extent and he could pull her to him. Or push her away! 'There will be no separation, Eleanor.'

She hissed something under her breath and moved abruptly to the doorway, the straw rustling at her hem. Outlined in the twilight, she stood and stared at him for a long time, and then she nodded. But if it was an agreement then it was a grudging one, and when she spoke there was more resolve than resignation in her words.

'Then there is nothing more to be said on the matter. We are wed and we will remain wed, as you wish it. But don't forget, my lord, where one can shun and despise, so can another!'

And with that she was gone, like a queen leaving her court. The darkness crept nearer and nearer, until only the light coat of the mare was visible, shimmering like a ghostly marsh mist. All was quiet without the stable, and as Rhun went to move his foot struck something hard on the ground, sending it rolling. Stooping, he found the little clay pot that held Eleanor's ointment. The aroma of marigold came to his nostrils, and something else—something that reminded him of the pungent, sickly remedies that had reeked in the pilgrims' hospice at Santiago de Compostela. He hadn't noticed it before, while she'd been applying the ointment, but now it filled his head like sweet choking nectar.

With a groan, he clenched his fist in the mare's mane, and as the moon rose over the castle wall and began to spill like a trickle of silver blood across the earth he cursed himself. For who but a fool or a madman chose imprisonment instead of freedom? Who but a monster consigned another as well as himself to a lifetime of purgatory?

If only he *could* despise his wife, perhaps this marriage would be easier—or bearable, at least. But he couldn't despise her. The more he shunned her, the closer Eleanor seemed to come, challenging all his vows and beliefs and tempting him to desires he didn't want. For she'd been right, even though he'd denied it. He might well have tumbled her right then and there, so hot had his blood burned to possess her. And for that grossness he despised only himself.

Eleanor's hand paused on the door latch of her chamber. What on earth had she done with the ointment?

She thought back to that moment when Rhun had drawn her to her feet, evoking strange and disturbing responses within her—before their argument had blazed up like a bonfire out of nowhere. And then she thought of her fear. Fear of the desire she'd felt and of the discovery that would have resulted—a fear that had driven her from his presence with bitter words.

The pot had been forgotten as a result, but it could only be where she'd put it—on the stable floor. It couldn't be left there because Mistletoe might crush it beneath her hooves and spill the precious balm. So, taking a deep breath and prising her fingers from the doorknob, Eleanor turned and headed back down the staircase.

The moon was high now, and had turned the court-yard to a burnished lake, so she didn't need a torch to find her way across. All was silence around her. Everyone was already at supper, apart from the watch above the gate. Somewhere an owl screeched, and more distant still the haunting howling of a wolf made her flesh shudder.

Reaching the stable, she searched for the door—but her hand froze even as her fingers curled around the cool hard wood. For the moonlight not only bathed the bailey, but also lit up the scene within the stable brighter than any torch could have done.

Rhun was crouched down beside Mistletoe's side, his head bent to the task of finishing the treatment she'd abandoned, wrapping a clean linen cloth around the fetlock to keep the ointment undisturbed. He must have brought food for her mare too, for Mistletoe's nose was deep in a bucket on the floor, the sound of her munching loud in the stillness.

Eleanor stood as rigid as a stone, her heart fluttering in her breast, hardly daring to breathe and impose on this startling moment.

Something brushed against her legs and she drew a quick gasp, but it was only Rhun's hound, still waiting faithfully for his master. Although she herself had made no sound, or at least she thought not, Mistletoe had heard her, or perhaps sensed her. The mare's head came up and she gave a low whicker. Rhun's head lifted too, swift and alert, and both turned to look towards the entrance just as Cai, as if to make her discovery complete, began to bark.

But Eleanor was already gone, her feet flying back the way they'd come, skirts lifted high so as not to trip her. All the same, she stumbled headlong up the steps to the keep, biting down on a little cry of pain as her knee struck sharply at the stone. She picked herself up and didn't stop until she'd regained the safety of her chamber.

Using the bruised lump on her knee as an excuse, she didn't go down to table that night, but sent Alice to fetch their supper. But the next day, when she stepped over the threshold of her chamber, the little clay pot of ointment was there on the floor outside her door.

It wasn't until supper that evening that Eleanor met Rhun again. He was already seated at the table when she came down, and he rose stiffly to greet her with a bow and a guarded face. She dipped her chin briefly in response and took her chair next to him. Huw ap Gruffudd was seated to her right, and the chair to Rhun's left was taken by Father Robert, the Cistercian abbot, whom she hadn't seen since her wedding day.

The abbot smiled at her and explained that he'd called in on his way home from the cathedral of Bangor, in the north. But the kind old eyes were sober, the lines around them deeply scored, and Rhun too seemed preoccupied. The hall was noisier, busier than usual, and as she received a cup of wine from the servitor Eleanor felt a pulsing excitement in the air.

Huw gallantly served her with meat. 'I trust your maid has recovered from her mishap yesterday, my lady?'

She glanced at him in surprise, for there was a note of diffidence in the question and his usually frank blue gaze wavered a little away from hers. 'Alice is well. Thank you for asking.'

'And your little mare is doing well too?'

She nodded. 'The wound looked worse than it was.'

'My Lord Rhun tells me you are treating her yourself?'

She nodded again, wondering at this idle talk from the usually reticent steward. 'Yes. Although healing herbs don't work for every kind of wound, of course.'

As the balm she'd applied to her grazed knee hadn't worked, leaving it bruised and painful today.

The steward fell silent and turned back to his meal. The two men at her other side were quiet too, conversing almost in whispers, each toying with their trenchers rather than eating the mutton upon them. To her surprise, they were speaking in French, and Eleanor caught an occasional word when a lull fell in the noisy hall. And although the significance of them evaded her, the words sent a thrill of terror to her heart.

'Fled for their lives...burned to the ground...hanged over his own doorway.'

And interspersed between that list of horrors was a name she'd never heard before—Madog ap Llywelyn.

She looked towards the two long tables where the castle folk sat, talking as they ate, their faces more alive than she'd ever seen them. It was as if everyone else knew a secret that she didn't. Alice was seated halfway along the right-hand wall, looking lost and bemused between with the laundress and another woman, who talked busily across her. Dafydd Genau'r Glyn was entertaining the hall, as he did every evening, but tonight there was a different tone to his music. It was lively, rampant, his bow raking the strings of his *crwth* as if he were wielding a weapon, not an instrument.

Eleanor turned to ask Rhun what the strange and disturbing music was, but checked herself and asked Huw instead. After all, she and her husband had hardly parted on good terms the previous night, and her angry final words seemed both childish and cruel to her now. It wasn't in her nature to shun and despise anyone—not even her husband, and not even if he did the same to her. And what she'd witnessed in the stable soon after had left her with a strange sense of remorse for having said them.

'What is this music the poet is playing, Sir Huw?' she asked.

The man put down his knife and looked out over the hall. 'Some of the old tunes, my lady, from times long past.'

Out of the corner of her eye Eleanor saw Rhun's head half turn towards her, his ear clearly catching the conversation, and a feeling of unease began to prickle at the nape of her neck. Something was amiss—something huge, important…threatening, even.

'And what times would those be?' she asked calmly, while her blood quickened and latent expectation filled the hall until it seemed the very walls would burst apart under its force.

It was Rhun who answered.

'The times when Wales was ruled by its own princes, my lady, and its people were free and proud.'

Eleanor turned to look at him at last, but he too was staring down the hall now, the lines of his face taut with determination and a sort of passion she'd never seen in him before. The abbot, however, met her gaze and seemed to be about to speak, but whatever words he was about to utter were cut off as Rhun pushed his trencher from him and got swiftly to his feet.

'We'll continue our talk in private, Father Robert, if you please. It's too noisy in the hall.'

Once they'd departed the chatter grew louder, with people getting up from their seats and moving to join other tables to engage in urgent speech, hands gesturing wildly. Dafydd's bow scraped harder and faster on the strings, until the grating inciting music began to scrape on her nerves too, shredding them until she couldn't stand it any longer.

'For pity's sake, Sir Huw, tell me what has happened!'

The steward answered frankly, his tongue perhaps unchecked by his lord's absence, or his blood perhaps too ardent to contain his words any longer. 'Only rumours, my lady, as yet, and therefore I cannot tell you in absolute fact. But if the news the abbot brought with him today is true, Wales will soon be at war.'

Chapter Six

Later that night Eleanor stood at her window and listened to Alice's excited recounting of the rumours that were running like wildfire through the castle. It seemed that it wasn't only Huw ap Gruffudd who was certain of war, and she shivered as a memory of the steward's words crept over her skin like icy fingers of doom.

'What else did you hear?' she asked, when her maid finally paused for breath.

'They say the whole of the north is aflame, mistress, and the south too! And Welshmen are flocking in their thousands to the banners of the rebel leaders. A nobleman called Madog ap Llywelyn in Gwynedd, Cynan ap Somebody in the March, and another… Oh!' She wrung her hands. 'Oh, it's terrible!'

Eleanor curled her fingers tighter around the curtain edge. If there *were* flames lit throughout Wales they weren't visible yet, and beyond the castle walls everywhere was dark and hushed, the moon obscured by black clouds. There was no wind, and it was so quiet that the bell from the distant monastery could be clearly heard, sounding the hour for evening prayer.

'No Englishman or woman is safe anywhere now,' her maid went on. 'Even children are being cut down by the rebels' swords, as if they were nothing but corn.'

'This is all mere gossip!' Eleanor let the linen drop and turned around. But all the same she knew that Rhun and Father Robert must be discussing the same news at that very moment, in secret, in the chamber next door. 'Who brought these tales, Alice?'

'The layman that accompanied the abbot to the north. On Michaelmas Day he saw Caernarfon town burning with his own eyes—the church on the island too, from across the water. The rebels hanged the sheriff of that district from the lintel of his own door, he said, and now they mean to drive all the English out of Wales if they leave any of us alive at all!'

Alice's tone had changed from excitement to panic, driven headlong by her own words. Eleanor too felt foreboding settle on her shoulders, although giving way to panic would serve for nothing. 'The knave should have curbed his tongue instead of spreading stories that might not be true at all,' she said sharply.

At that, the creak of Rhun's door opening and closing broke the silence. Footsteps sounded in the passageway without, and then they stopped outside the chamber. A tap came quietly at the door.

Alice gave a little gasp. 'Wh-who can that be at this time of night?'

'Go and open it, you little ninny, and we'll find out!' But Eleanor heard the tremor as well as the exasperation in her own voice too.

Her maid shook her head, her hands clutching at her skirts. 'Hadn't we best ignore it, mistress?'

'God's bones, Alice! Do you think the rebels would bother knocking so politely if they'd come for our blood?'

She strode over and opened the door herself, to find Father Robert on the threshold.

'Good evening, Lady Eleanor.' The abbot's calm voice and serene tone made the scurrying alarm of a moment ago seem absurd.

'Good evening, Father.'

'I am about to observe Compline in the chapel, my lady, and wondered if you and your woman would like to attend?'

Since her arrival Eleanor had only attended Matins in the chapel, led by Dafydd Genau'r Glyn, who seemed to hold several offices beside that of *bardd*. There was still no priest in the castle, but a monk came from the monastery to administer Mass on Sundays, though Rhun never attended. She did her other devotions in her chamber, but now—especially now—the chance to attend Compline was more than welcome.

'Thank you, Father, we would indeed. We'll come down with you.'

The abbot's layman was lighting the candles on the altar as they entered the chapel. Huw ap Gruffudd was seated on one of the small benches to the left, and two people whom she knew to be his sister and her husband occupied the bench behind him, but that was all. No doubt everyone was still in the hall, drinking and gossiping, consumed and incensed by the talk of rebellion.

Alice—brazen once more now her fear had abated—

promptly sat down next to the steward and flashed him a coy smile. Eleanor took her place on the foremost bench that was reserved for the lord and lady, although it was devoid of cushions and as narrow and as uncomfortable as all the others. Rhun, however, didn't appear, and as Compline began it became clear he didn't intend to.

The abbot's voice was younger than his face as he sang the devotional end-of-day prayer. The pure notes of the Latin words sent shivers up and down Eleanor's spine and her lips moved instinctively in the responses.

But even so her mind wandered out beyond the walls to where uncertainty lay and turmoil reigned. And inexplicably to the stable, where the previous night Rhun had touched her hair, her cheek, his eyes burning with something that had set her senses alight. And for a moment she'd almost succumbed to his caresses, to the strange yet delicious sensations they'd evoked deep within her, and then his fingers had found her birthmark…

Compline seemed hardly to have begun before it was over, and Father Robert was bending at her side and offering to escort her back to her room.

'Thank you, Father, but I'll stay a while and continue my prayers,' she replied. Although in truth she hadn't yet prayed at all—at least not conventional prayers!

The abbot blessed her, making the sign of the cross over her forehead, and then with a bow of farewell turned and left her.

On the bench behind, Huw rose to his feet and cleared his throat. 'I'll be glad to escort Mistress Alice back, my lady—unless you wish her to remain with you?'

At his side, her maid's lashes were lowered, though

not so low as to hide the cow's eyes she was sending the steward. And, judging by the pink tinge on Huw's cheeks, it seemed Alice's admiration had not gone un-noticed or unwelcomed by the man himself.

'Thank you, Sir Huw.' Eleanor looked pointedly at Alice. 'I'll not be long behind you, so make sure our beds are ready, please, Alice.'

'Yes, mistress,' her maid replied, demurely enough, as the steward held his arm out to her.

And then they were gone, the door closing behind them with a soft thud.

Left alone, Eleanor sat quietly and watched the flick-ering candles die lower and lower. The sound of rain started on the wooden roof and she pulled her cloak more snugly around her, trying to harness her thoughts. But now the chapel was empty they clamoured even louder, until they filled her head and drove her to her feet to light more candles from the few that remained.

As the interior glowed warm and bright again she moved to the stone tomb of Rhun's parents and looked down at the serene faces, chiselled to repose in death.

It was finished now, and not for the first time its unusual design struck her. The Lady Morfudd's face looked upwards to heaven, but her husband's head was turned to one side, his open sightless eyes gazing not at God, but directly at her. His arm was lying across his body, his hand covering hers where they lay across her breast.

Had they been happy together, the Lord Owain and his wife? Had they desired, comforted and even loved each other? For if they'd been put together unwillingly, chafing and resentful as she and Rhun were, surely they would not have been laid to rest in such a striking and poignant way?

Behind her, the door opened. The sound of pattering rain came in and then was cut off as it closed again. Eleanor turned, and her breath caught as she saw her husband walking up the aisle. His gaze was downcast and it was evident he thought the chapel empty. And then, as if he'd sensed rather than seen her, his feet stopped dead in their tracks. His head lifted and he pushed back the hood of his cloak.

'Eleanor.' As he said her name the tranquillity of the chapel was suddenly shattered. 'What are you doing here?'

Eleanor's hand froze where it had been tracing the lettering on the tomb. 'I came to hear Compline with the abbot and then stayed behind to pray.'

Rhun seemed as cold and as still as an effigy himself. Why was he here at this time of night? Was he too come to seek peace and quiet in this neglected church, the resting place of his parents? If so, perhaps *she* should be the one to go and leave him alone with whatever devotions he intended. If any.

But she didn't go. Instead her fingers began to move over the lettering again, spelling out the two names: Owain and Morfudd.

'Why are they carved so?' she asked, after several moments had passed and it had become clear that neither of the two living beings in the chapel were willing to speak. 'Why is the Lord Owain's gaze turned to his wife and not to heaven?'

There was a beat of silence and then the answer came

gruffly, almost reluctantly. 'It was his wish to look upon her for all eternity.'

The delicate frozen features on the tomb seemed suddenly to come to life, as if the stone was warming beneath her touch. 'I don't wonder... She was very beautiful.' If the carving was a faithful representation of how the woman had been in life, the fact was undeniable.

'Yes, she was, but that's not why my father asked to be depicted that way.'

Eleanor turned as Rhun moved forward to sit down on the foremost bench. A strange tension thickened the air, and one of the candles on the altar hissed and then went out. In the rafters, the wind moaned softly.

'Then what was his reason?' she asked.

Perhaps by learning about his family she might begin to know Rhun too. Even if they were never truly to be man and wife, there must be something to salvage—some common ground on which they could walk through life together, as they had vowed to do at this very altar.

'Do you really need to be told, Eleanor?' His head lifted swiftly and then dropped again. 'What is there to tell that you don't know already?'

'I know nothing.' Eleanor stepped forward despite the bitter tone that warned her off. But tonight, bathed in the light of the candles, truth seemed to hover in the air. Unlike the obscurity of the stable the evening before, she felt herself coming within reach of a chance of understanding. 'I know only what I was told when I was a child—that your mother was killed in a skirmish in the last war.'

'A *skirmish*?' Rhun glanced up at her and she saw his

jaw clench. 'Is that what they told you? No, it wasn't a "skirmish", Eleanor, it was slaughter. And my father's eyes are turned towards his wife because that is the only atonement he could make.'

'Atonement? For what?'

The rain on the roof grew heavy, its noise almost obliterating his reply. 'As my father can't explain, and I have no desire to, you'd best ask *your* father!'

'He isn't here to ask.' Eleanor shivered, though it wasn't the chill in the air that clutched at her bones but the ghostly shadows that had seemed suddenly to gather, as if they too wanted to hear the truth. 'So I'm asking you.'

Rhun leaned forward on his elbows and stared down at the floor. He'd come here tonight to think about the present, not the past, but Eleanor made that impossible, challenging him as she always did.

Could it be that she really *didn't* know?

'It was twelve years ago.' The scene loomed bright before his eyes, as clear as if it was yesterday, right down to the smallest detail. 'An English force, led by a knight on horseback, attacked the village.'

'The village? But why?'

'My father was fighting for the Prince of Wales, to the north. They were too few to make an assault on the castle…mayhap they had no intention in any case.'

The sound of rain was so loud now on the roof that she probably couldn't even hear him clearly.

'But they burned every house in the village, slaughtered the cattle and pigs, and killed many of the men, women and children. My mother was among them.'

Eleanor made no sound, but when Rhun lifted his eyes to hers he saw they were filled with horror, her face pale. With the folds of her fine wool cloak wrapped around her, and her head covered by a white linen veil, she looked like an angel, standing there before his parents' tomb.

'But why was your mother at the village instead of in the safety of the castle?'

'She went to help someone who was ailing from a fever. Like you, my mother knew the healing properties of herbs.' Rhun swallowed as the unbearable irony of that rose up and choked him. 'She often helped those who were ill, inside the castle and out. But that day she should have stayed put!'

'Were you with her, Rhun?'

He nodded, her soft, inevitable question driving into his flesh like spikes. 'Although I escaped with only an injured leg!'

A lightning flash filled the chapel with vivid blue for an instant and a faraway rumble of thunder sounded. When it died away he was no longer alone on the bench, for Eleanor had come to sit beside him, bringing with her the warmth and scent of a living body, a woman of flesh and blood, not stone and gilt and paint.

'I'm so sorry, Rhun. I didn't know, truly.'

He turned his head away. 'How could you *not* know, Eleanor, when they were your father's own men?'

Her sleeve brushed his as her hand flew to her mouth. 'That can't be!'

'Can't it?' Rhun brought his eyes back to hers, saw the candlelight reflected in them, the way her skin glowed warm and alive. 'It was so, Eleanor. But when my father identified and accused the knight who'd led the attack, Richard de Vraille turned a deaf ear.'

'No, it's not true! My father can be capable of many things, I admit, but nothing like that!'

'It *is* true, Eleanor.'

Rhun got to his feet and walked towards the altar. Why was she arguing? Denying what she'd asked to know in the first place? There was another flash of lightning, another rumble of thunder. The storm was closer now than before. As it died away her voice came, still doubtful, but filled with less denial now.

'If it *is* true, then who was the knight? What happened to him?'

He shook his head. The hated name was buried so deep in his heart that it wouldn't come to his lips. 'He fled the realm and your father let him go. It was *we* who were punished. My father was captured and forced to fight on the side of the English. And to ensure he continued a traitor I was sent as hostage to Hereford.'

'That I know.'

He sensed Eleanor get to her feet, knew the moment when she moved forward for the familiar scent of rose petals came to his nostrils.

'It was on your release that I first saw you, at the Christmas feast,' she said.

'So you remember that?' he said bitterly, the humiliation of those two years rising as bile into his mouth. 'My release was part of the peace pact, and in return for our submission we got the right to keep our castle and our lands as long as we pledged fealty to the King.'

'And you got me too.'

He nodded. 'That was the *galanas*.'

'Galanas?'

'The bloodwit. My father lost his wife so his son gained a wife. An honourable exchange that had no honour in it at all!' Rhun turned to face her and his voice echoed off the bare chapel walls. 'And that's why he looks at her in death, Eleanor, and not towards God. To make atonement for a crime that can *never* be atoned for. He should have been here to protect her, but instead he made a deal with the man who condoned her death.'

'Perhaps he did it for you? To ensure you at least were safe...that you would survive the war?'

'Then he paid too high a price!'

The next flash of lightning through the window behind him lit her face with stark illumination and he saw the sheen of sorrow in her eyes.

'I'm sorry. Nobody ever told me that our marriage was so...so callously arranged.' She turned away and lifted her hand, as if to dash away tears before they fell. 'If only I'd known that right from the start I'd have understood things better.'

Rhun passed a hand over his eyes too—not to dash away tears, for he'd done all his weeping long since, but because he suddenly felt empty, weary, as if all that talk had wiped his mind clean of the ability to think any more.

'Understood what, Eleanor?'

'Why you forbid me to ride over the bridge to the village...why you resent this marriage so bitterly and... and why you hate me so much.'

There was a sharp intake of breath behind her, like the tearing of silk. The storm raged louder overhead, as if now the truth had come out the very wrath of heaven had come down to herald it. And then she felt Rhun's hand touch her arm.

'Eleanor...' Her name floated on his breath, caressing the nape of her neck, and where his fingers rested lightly on her sleeve a feeling of utter desolation seemed to emanate from him into her flesh.

She didn't turn to look at him. She couldn't. 'Yes?'

'Truly, I thought you knew. How could you not, after all?'

'It doesn't change anything now I know, does it, Rhun? Your mother is still murdered, my father is who he is...and we are as we are. Married, yet not man and wife.'

There was a long moment of silence but she felt his fingers tremble on her sleeve, as if some battle, silent yet terrible, was raging within him. 'No,' he said, finally. 'It doesn't change anything.'

Eleanor waited for him to say more—if not to absolve her, or even forgive her for being her father's daughter, at least to show he realised that she was not the enemy he believed her to be. But when he spoke again it was as if the matter, now aired and purged, was closed. To be forgotten and never to be mentioned again.

'The storm is getting worse. We should return to the keep.'

His hand fell away and she turned to see him striding down the aisle towards the door. As it was flung open an eerie orange light flooded in from the torches on the wall of the keep. Eleanor blew out the remaining candles on the altar and then walked to the doorway—just as Rhun stepped over the threshold into the rain, pulling his hood up over his head.

'Follow close behind me. It's dark and a fog has come down.'

Before she could reply he moved forward, his boot splashing in the puddle that had formed outside the chapel door. His shoulders hunched, he began to cross quickly towards the keep, leaving her no option but to stay where she was or follow. So, gathering her cloak around her, Eleanor closed the door and, avoiding the puddle, set off in his wake.

The rain was heavy now, driving into her face and turning the ground underfoot into a sodden marshland. She trod cautiously, but even so her foot slipped and she nearly fell as water oozed through her shoes.

Recovering her balance, she called out for Rhun, but his shadowy form was already far ahead of her, almost invisible in the orange fog. Clutching the folds of her gown, she stepped forward again and continued her way slowly across the courtyard. She was halfway across when she slipped again, and this time she couldn't prevent a little cry of alarm, flinging out her hands to steady herself.

Almost before the sound had died on her lips Rhun loomed up in front of her. His hood had blown off and his black hair clung wetly to his forehead. The rain ran down his face and throat, soaking the neck of his cloak and spiking his eyelashes.

'I slipped—nothing more,' she said hastily. God forbid he think her completely incapable of walking in a straight line without falling over. 'Pray, go ahead...but a little slower, if you please.'

'*O'r nefoedd!*' His hand lifted and pushed the hair

out of his eyes. 'Go slower? Eleanor, you are already soaked to the skin. Any slower and you'll drown!'

And would he care one way or the other if she did?

Eleanor didn't ask but, muttering a curse of her own under her breath, gathered up her skirts again.

Before she'd taken another step, Rhun had swept her off her feet and into his arms. Then, pausing only to tuck his cloak around her, he proceeded to carry her across the soggy courtyard, cradled like a child against his chest.

She wriggled and tried to protest, but her head was covered and his arms were like iron about her. Her eyes were blind to everything but the dark wool of his tunic, to which her fingers clung for dear life. The only sounds she could hear were the solid squelch of his footsteps and the steady beat of his heart beneath her ear. And into her nostrils came the musky male scent of him, masculine and so powerful that it quickened her senses and kindled her blood.

Embarrassed, she wriggled harder and tried to push herself away from his chest. 'Put me down. I can manage by myself.'

'It didn't seem that way to me.' From above her head came a blunt reprimand. 'Now, keep still—unless you want us both to end up in the mud!'

His grip tightened and he crushed her against him, making both struggle and speech impossible. Eleanor felt the warmth of him, the strength of his arms, the hard breadth of his chest where her head lay. And oddly, despite what had just been said in the chapel, she felt protected, safe—even if she was hated! How could that be so?

Through cold lips she pressed a whisper of complaint into the rough weave of his tunic, even if she wasn't quite sure what she was complaining of!

'You didn't have to come back for me. I might be clumsy, but I'm not helpless!'

He didn't hear her, however, and soon they'd reached the stone steps of the keep. But instead of setting her down Rhun carried her up them, the muscles bunching in his arms and legs. And there, just inside the doorway, beneath the welcoming glow of the torches, he halted.

Eleanor lifted her head and, relinquishing her grip on his tunic, pushed back the heavy woollen cloak and looked up into his face. He was breathing hard, although carrying her seemed to have placed no great effort on his lean, strong body.

'Y-you can put me down now,' she said, feeling her own breath quicken too under the strange glint of his eyes. At once, he set her down upon her feet, but his hands didn't drop away. Instead, his fingers curled around her arms and he stared down at her as if he was trying to see right inside her. And then he spoke, his voice low and as harsh as the weather they'd just fled through.

'Contrary to what you think, I consider you neither clumsy nor helpless, Eleanor.'

Eleanor began to shiver, but it wasn't with cold— not when her blood still raced through her veins, hot as molten metal. So he'd heard her after all…even though she'd spoken to herself more than to him, never expecting an answer.

'Do you not?'

He shook his head slowly, his eyes never leaving

her face as he unclasped the cloak from around his shoulders and draped it around hers. He fastened it at her throat and then, after a moment's pause, drew her slowly towards him.

'No. In fact, I suspect you are far from being either.' His hand came up and brushed some damp strands of hair away from her cheek. 'And you are mistaken in something else too.'

His forehead came down to rest on hers. Trickles of rainwater flowed from his hair into hers, turning from ice to fire on her skin. Eleanor didn't dare to speak or to prompt him to finish what he'd started to say. She waited, her heart pounding and her body quivering, while the weight of his head on hers rested like a weight on her heart. Then finally he spoke again, his voice as bleak as the rain that still drove relentlessly downwards and yet filled with a passion that drove even deeper down inside her.

'I don't hate you at all. But if I could only be indifferent to you, this marriage of ours might be bearable!'

'I… I thought you *were* indifferent.'

His head lifted and his eyes burned into hers, dark and unblinking. '*Indifferent?* Then you are mistaken in that too. Our marriage may be a mistake, and mayhap we really are not suited, as you said.' His eyes narrowed and his knuckles brushed gently down over her cheek. 'But indifferent…? No, Eleanor, it would be easier for me to stop breathing than to be that.'

And then he was gone from her, turning swiftly on his heel and mounting the stairs that led upward. Left alone, Eleanor sagged back against the wall and pressed a hand to her forehead, where the weight of his still lingered. The scent of him on his cloak was thick in her nostrils...she could still feel his arms clasped around her body. The ring of his footsteps echoed in her ears and his words swarmed like bees in her mind, making her thoughts reel.

Was he really not indifferent to her? And if he didn't hate her, what *did* Rhun feel for her?

Chapter Seven

The following afternoon Rhun sent for Eleanor. She entered his chamber with his cloak neatly folded over her arm. Closing the door behind her, she stopped in the middle of the room as if unsure what to say, before holding the garment out to him.

'Here is your mantle. Alice has cleaned the mud off the bottom and it is quite dry now. She has also mended it where it had begun to fray, at the hem.'

'Thank you.' He took it from her and laid it over the back of a chair, impatient to be done with the subject of his cloak. That wasn't why he'd asked her here today. Moving to the table, he picked up the flagon of warm ale his man had brought earlier and poured himself a cup.

'Will you drink?' he asked, dragging his manners together and half turning to Eleanor. She had taken the chair next to the hearth and was sitting, as she always sat, like a queen, her back straight and her hands folded in her lap. At times she almost made him feel more peasant than nobleman, although last night, as he'd draped his cloak around her and drawn her to him, he'd almost felt like a husband. 'I can send for wine, if you prefer.'

She shook her head. 'No, thank you.'

Rhun leaned back against the table and the speech he'd prepared deserted him, overridden by the events of the previous evening. How he'd held her close as he'd carried her across the courtyard, how soft her cheek had felt beneath his touch, how her scent had infused his senses as he'd rested his forehead on hers. How hard he'd had to fight to stop himself from kissing her.

Taking a deep gulp from his cup, he forced his mind back to today and to the reason he'd called his wife to him. 'It is time you heard what news Father Robert brought, since the revolt is a fact and not mere rumour now.'

'I'm listening.'

She shifted slightly to face him and the silver wedding band on her finger blinked in the firelight. On his finger, his own band seemed suddenly heavier, tighter, as briefly Rhun told her all that he himself knew, though that was enough to make the reassurance at the end of his speech more a warning than anything else.

'So far, the rebellion is concentrated in the north and the south and there has been little conflict in this region as yet.'

'Yet, it is only a matter of time before conflict *does* come here?'

He noted the quickening in the rise and fall of her breasts beneath her tunic, although the calm dignity on her face didn't alter. 'Yes, there has already been fighting in the March, and the King's justiciar in Deheubarth has been killed at Builth by the men of Cynan ap Maredudd.'

Her hand flew to her mouth. 'Geoffrey Clement?'

Rhun nodded. 'His wife and children have fled the attack on Cardigan that followed and are in the castle at Aberystwyth.'

'Oh, poor Margery!'

'You know her?'

'She is distant kin of my mother.' Her gaze dropped, but not before her eyes clouded with sadness. 'They were often guests of my parents.'

'Well, she and her children are safe, at any rate.'

'Safe? But for how long?' Her eyes lifted to his again. 'What has caused this conflict to break the peace now?'

'Peace, yes—but for the conquerors not the conquered.' Rhun felt his blood heat. 'Injustice is rife, Eleanor, and heavy taxes are crippling the Welsh people. We have suffered displacement from our homes in favour of foreign settlers and suffered worse too at the hands of the King's official and Marcher lords. And now the King calls for Welshmen to go and fight his war in Gascony for him!'

'But there is no excuse for violence and murder!'

'I doubt the men who hanged Roger de Puleston at Caernarfon would call it murder, and neither do I. Rather it was due justice for the corruption he has wielded upon the district over the last ten years in the name of royal rule!'

Her face went white and he saw her swallow.

'Then you condone this revolt?' she said. 'You think it just and right?'

Rhun nodded. 'I do.'

At his reply, alarm flared in her eyes and her hands tightened in her lap. But there was no purpose in misleading her or trying to shield her from the turbulence that would soon engulf them all.

'So it is only a matter of time now before the King musters his army. We must be prepared for when that time comes.'

She said nothing for a moment, her gaze moving from his to the fire and then back again. 'And where will you stand when that time comes?'

'Where I have always stood.' He gave Eleanor the same answer he'd given Father Robert the previous day. 'With my people.'

'And against mine?' Rhun drained the goblet of ale in his hand and then refilled it. He stared long into the amber liquid before meeting the cool green eyes that waited for his response. Although she must know already that if he turned rebel and opposed the King in the field it would mean the end of the alliance between their two houses. 'If it comes to that, yes.'

He watched as she got to her feet and moved to the window. There was no sun beyond, but even so her skin glowed as pale as cream. 'So you're asking me to choose sides?'

'There is no *choice* involved, Eleanor. You are my wife.'

'Am I, Rhun?' She turned suddenly, her eyes bright. 'I needn't be if only you'd annul this marriage now, before it's too late!'

Rhun's fingers tightened around his cup. Did she truly want to go from here—from him? Was it only *his* senses that had been stirred in the stable, in the chapel, in the doorway of the keep? Was *she* the one who was indifferent, not he?

'It's already too late. Events have overtaken us—or will do soon.' He put his cup down with an unsteady hand, causing ale to spill over the brim and onto his sleeve. Because it wasn't just the rebellion he was referring to. Other, more private events had overtaken them during the last two days…things that shook the walls of the castle harder than any siege engine ever could. 'But whatever happens we'll hold out. Castell y Lleuad will never yield again before an enemy.'

'Will it not?' Her eyes raked over his face and then she walked across the floor towards him. 'Yet there is more than one sort of enemy, isn't there?'

Rhun drew in a breath as the scent of roses assailed him and the blood began to course through his veins. 'Meaning?'

'Meaning that there are the enemies without and the enemies within,' she said quietly. 'And if you are to do battle with them you need to know the difference.'

Her words were weighted and almost prophetic. 'What would you know of military strategies, my lady?'

'Nothing at all. But I'm not the enemy, Rhun, despite what my father did to you, to your mother. And if you won't let me go, if you insist that we continue to live as man and wife—in name, at least—you must accept the truth of that. Otherwise, this marriage can only end in disaster.'

She stepped closer still, as if she wanted to make sure he both heard and understood.

'Or are you *trying* to make it into a disaster? Didn't you resent me even before I came here? And although

I understand why now, I think that even if you *wanted* to like me you'd not let yourself, would you?'

Rhun's blood began to thunder in his ears. Like? *Arglwydd mawr!* That was far too mild a word to describe the battle he waged with himself every day and every night. *Like* was nothing akin to the passion he fought to conceal and keep in check. And because he couldn't give his desire free rein, could never possess her in that way without betraying himself, his flaws, his weakness, their marriage was already a disaster.

'It's not as simple as that, Eleanor. Things are as they are, and whatever the future holds the past can't be altered or obliterated.'

She looked into his eyes for a long moment and he felt them delving deep into his soul. 'No, the past can't be wiped away, and what happened to your family should never be forgotten. But neither should it be clung to so stubbornly and blindly that it makes any future at all impossible. Can't you see that?'

Rhun made no answer, for there was no answer he could give her—not when the room was shrinking around him and his body was pulling as tight as a bow and his hands itched to reach out for her.

But she'd already turned away, shaking her head. 'No, I don't think you can, or else you won't. So, if you permit, I'll take my leave of you, since there is nothing more to be said.'

Eleanor didn't wait for a response but began to walk towards the door. For there *was* nothing more to say, and trying to say anything only led them both in never-ending circles. And every time she felt the gulf between

them begin to narrow a little, just when she started to
think she might even cross it, Rhun seemed to move
even further away, out of reach once more.

Was there even any purpose in continuing to try or to
hope? Was it not better to accept and make the best of
life? If any of them were left alive, that was, in this war.

Her hand was on the latch of the door when Rhun's
voice came again, stopping her from lifting it.

'Before you go I would ask a favour of you.'

She turned back. 'A favour?'

His face flushed, as if it almost pained him to have
to ask *anything* of her, let alone a favour. 'Cai is ailing.'

'Your hound?'

He nodded and his face creased in worry. 'When I
woke this morning he was not in his usual place at the
foot of my bed. He's not come near the fire, which is
also unusual. So I wondered, given your skill with potions, if you could help?'

Eleanor's gaze followed Rhun's to the corner where
Cai lay, half hidden within the folds of a thick homespun
blanket. She hadn't wondered at it before but this was
the first time she'd ever seen the animal absent from
his master's side. With a nod, she crossed the room and
knelt down beside the hound. He was listless, his eyes
dull and lacking in lustre, the usually sleek coat matted.

'Hello, Cai, what's amiss?' she said, as she began to
examine him, aware that the man still standing at the
table watched her every move.

After a long moment, Rhun spoke again. 'Well?
What do you think? Can you tell what's the matter
with him?'

Cai's tail thumped feebly at the sound of his master's voice, but Eleanor had no answer yet. She carried on feeling her way along the inert grey flanks, slowly and carefully, and then her fingers found the hard lump near the bottom of his ribcage. She took a moment, explored carefully until she was quite sure, and then looked across at Rhun.

'I'm sorry, but there is a canker inside him. I can feel it plainly, low down in the intestine.'

Rhun's face blanched. 'Can it be cut out?'

Eleanor looked away from his stricken expression, biting her lip as she considered. 'It could, but I'm not sure Cai would survive the procedure. He is already very weak and it may not help him anyway. It might even make him worse. Is he very old?'

'Fourteen years.'

She sat back on her heels. 'I don't think he's in any great pain, Rhun, and given his age it might be kinder to let him go.' She looked up at him again and shuddered at the anguish she saw on his face. 'I have a potion of poppies that would ease him. I'll bring it later, if you like?'

Rhun nodded, and then he pushed himself away from the table and came to kneel beside her. As he put his hand out to touch Cai she saw it was shaking.

'Thank you.'

It was the first time he'd ever thanked her for anything! And as she listened to him murmur to Cai in Welsh Eleanor knew his thanks were genuine, for she heard the love behind each word with the keenness of a needle to her heart.

They stayed there on their knees for several moments, Rhun's hand stroking his hound's head, Eleanor's hands clasped in her lap. She didn't know what to say, how to comfort him…whether to leave him alone or whether he wished to talk, share some of his distress.

As if he'd read the question in her mind, Rhun spoke suddenly, half to himself, his voice heavy. 'My mother gave Cai to me on my tenth birthday. Apart from when I went as hostage those two years, we've never been parted. Even when I went to Santiago de Compostela he came with me.'

'You went on pilgrimage?' Eleanor's heart began to beat fast at the unexpected statement. 'When was that?'

'Six years ago.'

They were kneeling so close that their sleeves touched, and she sensed through the whisper of contact not just the present sorrow in Rhun but a deeper anguish too. He would have been eighteen then—younger than she was now.

Carefully, she began to probe, as if testing a festering boil that might suddenly burst. 'Did you go to seek a cure for your leg?'

He shrugged. 'In a way, yes, but I wasn't healed—as you've doubtless noticed.'

She knew that people went on pilgrimage for spiritual as well as physical healing, but if that had been part of his reason for going he didn't say so.

'What is the shrine like?' she prompted, when he fell silent again.

'Like any other.' His shoulders heaved as he drew breath. 'But the route through Castile is treacherous, and pilgrims are prey to thieves and cut-throats. I stayed longer than I'd intended and attached myself to one of the abbeys nearby, to help guard the roadways.'

'To protect the pilgrims?'

'Yes.' His eyes slid to hers and focused, and his pensive, almost confiding mood shifted abruptly. 'But I soon discovered that the tournaments provided a far more diverting and lucrative living, even if they didn't give me what I sought either.'

Swiftly, he rose to his feet and, going to a coffer, took out a blanket. Returning, he laid it snugly over the dog, with slow and gentle care. Then he extended his hand to help Eleanor rise from the floor where she still knelt.

Eleanor wavered, almost afraid to take the offered assistance, given what had happened the last time he'd helped her up in the stable. Finally she placed her palm in his and was drawn to her feet, but this time he relinquished her hand immediately. His face was shuttered now, and all gentleness was gone from his voice, to be replaced by a sort of repressed anger.

'It must be supper time. We'll go down together.' He went to open the door. 'After you.'

In his corner the hound whined and, struggling to its feet, laboured its way pitifully across the floor. Rhun went down on one knee beside him and, burying his hands in the shaggy fur of the animal's neck, laid his cheek on its head. A flood of feeling seemed to pour out of him and, unable to bear it, Eleanor stepped quickly over the threshold and out into the corridor, her eyes blurring before her.

When she looked back Rhun had risen to his feet and the hound was cradled in his arms. 'He can't manage the steps down, and I don't want to leave him alone even if he'd stay.'

The gruff explanation didn't fool either of them and

her heart bled for both man and beast as she started down the stairs before them. For all she didn't know, or understand, there was a bond of pure love between the two—a lifelong bond that would soon be broken by death. But if Rhun was capable of such love for his hound, why could he feel none at all for her, his wife?

All Hallows' Eve saw the first frost. Rhun rode in through the gatehouse from a visit to the Cistercian monastery to garner news. Travellers constantly stopped at the hostel there, for refreshment or overnight lodging, and they brought word of the revolt that was spreading like wildfire, with victory after victory for the Welsh.

The reaction had already begun, and royal forces were mustering. Yet autumn was already giving way to winter—early, as it often did in Wales. Surely even Edward wouldn't march into the midst of the Welsh winter…unless the King intended it to be over by then. The thought made Rhun's blood run colder than any snow.

Settling Eryr in his stable, he glanced in at Eleanor's marc. His wife had been treating the wound daily and it was healing well. She'd also been going to tend to Cai every day, administering her herbal potion, but without such hopeful results as yet. The dog lingered on from day to day, as if he was as unwilling to die as Rhun was to let him go.

'Rhun!' As he left the stable, Huw ap Gruffudd came hurrying towards him, his face grim. 'A messenger has come from Richard de Vraille and awaits your presence in the hall.'

'*Uffarn dân!* What in hell's name does he want?'

'I think I can guess, my lord.'

Rhun nodded and dragged a hand through his hair. 'So can I,' he muttered. 'Well, let's not keep him waiting.'

They entered the hall and found the man sitting in front of the hearth, his sagging shoulders and soiled clothes evidence of his swift and strenuous journey across the March. He was young and vital, however, his body strong and his energy palpable, and the badge of his master was visible on his breast. He got to his feet at once and, bowing low as they approached, held out a parchment.

'My name is Gilbert of Ludlow, my lord, and I am sent from the Baron de Vraille with this message. I must wait for your answer and take it back without delay.'

Rhun took the roll from the man's hand. 'I doubt there'll be any answer, but you are welcome to take some refreshment while I read it.'

As the messenger was escorted to the kitchens Rhun went and seated himself at the top table, Huw taking his place at his elbow. Breaking the seal, he read it quickly, and then passed it to his steward.

'It seems I've been summoned,' he said. 'I am requested to muster as many men as I can and go to help relieve Castell y Bere, which is being besieged by the rebels.'

'Y Bere!' His steward gave a low whistle. 'That's one of the King's most prized castles.'

Rhun gave a wry smile. 'And the last to fall to Edward in the last war. The King must be gnashing his teeth with rage!'

'What will you do?'

'Nothing—at least not yet.'

Huw ap Gruffudd scratched his beard. 'It might be wise to wait a little, until we hear more.'

'I heard enough at the monastery this morning, Huw. Y Bere isn't the only royal castle under threat. Penarlâg, Ruthyn, Cricieth, Harlech and others are all besieged by Madog's forces.' Rhun glanced up at his steward to find the man's eyes burning with the same burn he felt in his own. 'Cardigan has been sacked by the men of Deheubarth, and Cynan ap Maredudd's forces are scoring victory after victory around Builth and Brycheiniog.'

'Then it is only a matter of time before Edward musters his army.'

Rhun nodded. 'He has already mustered, and the King is taking the situation seriously enough to postpone his invasion of Gascony to deal with Wales.'

'It's like the last time.' Huw had fought then, and from the quiver in his voice it was clear he'd fight again. 'When the whole of Wales stood as one man for Prince Llywelyn ap Gruffudd, *Duw a'i gadw.*'

God keep them *all* when this war came!

'But in the end she fell, piece by piece, and Madog isn't Llywelyn.' Rhun felt the shame of that time twist in his gut, remembering his two years as hostage in Hereford Castle, lying helpless as his homeland was conquered. 'Perhaps it will be the same this time, but whether we fall with her is in our hands now.'

And just like that the decision was made. Now that it had been forced upon him it was simple, if not easy. It didn't matter that it made him a traitor, in thought if not as yet in deed, but to fight for the King against his

own people… Against his country… No, that would
be the worst treason of all. But his decision involved
not just himself but his household, his vassals and his
tenants…and his wife.

Rhun glanced towards the doorway, as if he expected
her to appear. Did she know a messenger from her father's house was here? Would she make her choice now?
If she decided to ride back with her father's man, what
could he really do to prevent her? She wasn't his wife
in the full sense and, unconsummated and therefore un-
binding, their marriage could be undone in a moment
if she chose to do so.

Or if *he* chose to.

He was ready and willing to commit treason—in the
King's eyes, at least. For in his heart his decision was
just. But could he really condemn Eleanor to suffer for
his treachery, his disgrace, and his probable downfall?
If they lost this war, if he were imprisoned or killed,
his lands forfeit and his castle in ruins, what would
happen to her?

The question was still rolling around his mind when
the messenger reappeared in the hall and approached
the table with swift strides, clearly anxious to be gone
before nightfall and the danger of ambush in the dark.

Rhun rolled the parchment tightly in his hand and
got to his feet to meet Gilbert of Ludlow's expectant
eyes. 'I have read this message and, as I said before,
there is no answer.'

The man's mouth dropped open. 'But, my lord, the
matter is urgent!'

'Then best you be gone on your way.'

The messenger became wary, his eyes sliding nervously around him, as if he expected a dagger at his throat any moment. But instead of taking to his heels, he put his hand inside his cloak and drew out a second roll. 'There is one thing more, my lord. In the event of no reply to his message, the Baron de Vraille instructed me to give you this.'

Retaking his seat, Rhun broke the seal, his mind racing at this turn of events. As he read the brief but blunt missive, a wry smile played over his lips.

He looked up again at Gilbert of Ludlow. 'Do you know the contents of this?'

The man shook his head. Rhun rolled the parchment tightly again and, placing it down on the table in front of him, curled his fingers over it. They trembled, and even as he forced them to stillness the same quiver rose up through him to echo in his voice. For now the die was truly cast, and without his doing at all. But perhaps that was all to the best.

'Then you may tell my Lord de Vraille that he shall have the answer to his second message in due course.'

Chapter Eight

From her window, Eleanor had seen the rider trot in through the gates and recognised the man as one of her father's retainers. Now, not more than an hour later, the messenger was riding out again over the drawbridge, the gates barred behind him.

She stood a moment and gnawed at her thumbnail. A message from her father following so soon after the outbreak of rebellion couldn't possibly be a coincidence. And since whatever news had come for Rhun must concern her too, she made up her mind.

'Fetch my cloak, Alice,' she said, fixing a coif hastily over her hair. 'We'll go down and find out what's happening.'

When she entered the hall Rhun was standing in the large window alcove opposite the hearth, looking out, his feet planted and his arms folded across his chest. The setting sun glinted off his black hair and his lean, dark figure seemed like a carved silhouette against the light without. Servants were coming and going around him, carrying out their usual duties, but he seemed hardly to know they were there. He looked so solitary, so isolated, that Eleanor felt a pang over her heart. He always *was* alone, she realised, even in the midst of his people. And with Cai curled up in his death corner upstairs, too ill now to be brought down, Rhun seemed not just alone but lonely too.

As if he'd sensed her, he turned his head and his eyes found hers. They were sombre, and a cold feeling seeped into her bones.

She dismissed Alice and went over to him, her legs suddenly weak with dread. 'What news has come from my father?' she asked, without preamble, for it was obvious from his expression that it wasn't good news.

'Nothing for you—at least not directly.' His brow furrowed. 'The King has summoned me to go with your father to raise the siege of Castell y Bere.'

Eleanor swallowed back a little rush of alarm. 'Where is that?' she asked. The name was completely foreign to her, but a forbidding one nonetheless.

'In the mountains to the west, about fifteen leagues from here.'

'And…will you go?'

He shrugged. 'No, and that is why we need to talk.'

Eleanor sank down onto the stone seat to one side of the alcove. 'What do we need to talk about?' she asked, her heart starting to drum in her breast.

He passed her a roll of vellum that she hadn't noticed he was holding until then. 'Read this.' Then he turned his face to the window once more. 'The irony of it is quite amusing.'

Eleanor unrolled the message, and as she read it the paper began to shake in her hand.

My Lord Rhun,
Since you are my son-in-law, I deem it wise to
warn you that if you refuse the King's Summons
hereby sent by my hand you will be declared Trai-
tor to the Realm, and with immediate effect make
necessary the two sanctions herein stated.

First that the Treaty between us will be nulli-
fied and made void, and Second that your mar-
riage to my daughter Eleanor shall be annulled
and she shall be returned at once to my keeping.

I await your response.
Richard de Vraille
Lord of Vennyngton and Fronne

She laid the paper down on the stone beside her, the
elegant Latin script dancing before her eyes. 'Wh-what
answer have you sent?'

'None as yet.' Rhun didn't turn his head and the fading light outside cast an eerie light on the sharp planes
of his profile. 'What response would you have me send,
Eleanor?'

Her heart beat faster and the swirling motes of dust
spinning in the rays of the sunset made her head spin too.
'I… I would rather you didn't turn traitor, obviously…'

'It is the only course I can take.' His shoulders lifted
and then fell again. 'And, since it changes everything,
if you still wish to leave here I will make no objection.'

Eleanor looked down at the paper again as the words
that would finally set her free from this marriage echoed
in her ears. She sensed Rhun turn and look down at her,
waiting for her response. Or perhaps he'd already taken
that response for granted. Perhaps he expected her to

leap up at once, not wait for the morrow, but be out through the gatehouse before nightfall!

She met his eyes. 'Yes, this does change everything.'

He nodded. 'It is only a matter of time before I go and join our army in the field or the enemy comes to besiege this castle.' He looked at her strangely, something dark moving deep within his eyes. 'And your father is right—you should go.'

Should she? And, if so, why wasn't she rushing upstairs and ordering Alice to start packing at once? And what was this sinking foreboding that filled her breast and hollowed the pit of her stomach?

'Only yesterday you were set that I should stay—that there would be no annulment, and that we would remain wed.'

He turned his head, towards the window again. 'Yesterday I wasn't a traitor—today I am. It is as simple as that.'

No, it wasn't so simple. Eleanor looked down and traced a fingernail along a chip in the stone seat to the side of her. Or *was* it so simple to Rhun? Was she nothing to him but a commodity, to be passed from father to husband and then back again as circumstances dictated? And when she became an inconvenience to her father passed on yet again to another husband.

'Do you *want* me to go?' she asked, after a long moment.

'The treaty is broken and I am at war with your father.'

Was that an answer? Eleanor glanced up to see him staring down at her hand, where her fingernail still worried at the fault in the stone, her wedding band glinting in the dying sun.

Self-consciously, she stopped what she was doing and curled her fingers into a ball. 'Then you would prefer that I went?'

'I would prefer you be spared whatever is to come.'

'But you don't know what that may be?'

'No, not for certain, but… Do you know what a siege is like, Eleanor?'

She shook her head and stared away from him at the routine going on in the hall. The boards were being laid out for supper, the fire was being fed, and more torches were lit as the evening crept closer. All was normal and quiet, and a siege seemed as distant as the moon.

'It is long and hard and ugly, and above all futile. It means starving hunger and thirst, lying on the ground riddled with disease and half mad with delirium. A slow, awful and pointless death.'

'Have *you* known a siege?'

'Yes, ten years ago, in the months before my father submitted to yours. It was one of the worst things I've ever witnessed and I don't relish going through it ever again. But I may have to. You don't.'

No, she didn't. Yet how could she run away and leave him to go through it alone? How could she be such a coward?

'The English may not come.'

'They *will* come, Eleanor, sooner or later. And when they do I'll not yield. They'll have to take Castell y Lleuad over my dead body, and if you stay over yours too.'

His words did what she sensed they were meant to

and Eleanor felt a shiver slide down her spine. Yet far more frightening than a siege was the prospect of returning to her father, to be given in time to someone else—someone less kind than Rhun who, for all his curses, and despite the darkness that she sensed in him, had never once frightened her. Wouldn't her present fate and her present husband be preferable, war and all?

'You can't see the future. It might not even come to that.'

'No, I may be killed in the field and the English will just walk straight in through the gates. But the outcome will be the same and it would be better for you if you are not here when it comes.'

'Then you *do* want me to go?'

'*Want?* What either of us *wants* is impossible now!' He turned to her at last, his black eyes blazing and his voice rising. '*Er mwyn Duw*, Eleanor, I don't understand you! Not two days ago you were begging me to send you away. Now you seem determined to stay!'

Everyone in the hall stopped what they were doing and turned to look in amazement towards the window alcove. 'There is no need to shout,' she said under her breath. 'I'm sitting right next to you and can hear you plainly.'

'You can hear, yes, but you are not listening.' He sent a glare down the hall and the watchers turned hastily back to their business. Then he sat down beside her and placed his hand over hers. 'Eleanor, listen to me. If you remain, I may not be able to protect you.'

She looked down at their hands, locked together on the stone between them. Two wedding rings glinted up at her now, not one. The silver rings that bore their names and that bound them together in a union he now meant to break apart. She'd wanted to break it apart too, before, but for very different reasons.

'So what do you intend to do, Rhun?' She raised her eyes to his. 'Lift me onto a horse and tie me to the saddle and bundle me back to my father's house like so much unwanted and inconvenient baggage?'

Rhun's grip tightened on her fingers. 'If I have to, yes.'

And even as he said it Eleanor knew that if he tried she'd dig her heels in to the very last. She couldn't have explained it to him, or to herself either, and perhaps their wants *were* impossible, but she knew, with a strange sort of resolve, what she *didn't* want.

'But who will treat Cai if I'm not here?'

'Cai?' His eyes flared, and then the tense line of his mouth relaxed just a little bit. 'Are you telling me you would stay here, in the midst of a bloody and bitter war, just to look after my hound? No, that is foolish, Eleanor, and you know it.'

Yes, she did know it was foolish to choose to remain with a man who didn't want her, and who had now found the perfect reason to be rid of her. Now the peace treaty was shattered she was no longer necessary to him. But what about the other man she'd glimpsed beyond the invisible armour this one wore? The man she'd heard utter something more below the curses? What about the times when she felt she could almost touch the soul beneath his skin if she reached just that little bit further?

'Tell me truly, Rhun. If there were no rebellion, no summons from the King nor letter from my father, if the peace *weren't* broken, would you wish me to remain here as your wife?'

For a long moment he didn't respond. His grip on her hand tightened a little and his eyes searched deeply into hers. So deeply that Eleanor feared he might see right into *her* soul, and discover the feelings hidden inside her heart that even she had only just begun to discover.

'Yes, if that was your wish too.' The armour slipped for a moment to reveal a naked and undisguised honesty that softened the features of his face. But the next instant it was gone as he got abruptly to his feet and went to the window again, his arms folded once more across his chest. 'However, what we might wish for matters little now.'

Eleanor stared at his rigid back, at the broad shoulders set into an impassable barrier. He stood just as he had that first night, shutting her out. But now, unlike then, she'd seen the other man—the one in the stable in the moonlight, treating Mistletoe's wound. She'd felt his arms around her when he'd carried her from the church and then laid his forehead against hers, watched him bury his face in Cai's fur before picking him up because he couldn't walk down the stairs. All those moments she'd seen Rhun as no one else had, and not just with her eyes but with her heart too.

'Perhaps our wishes *don't* matter.' She stared down at her hand, at the solitary wedding band, and even though she tried to see with her eyes only it was her heart that made the decision for her. The only one it could make. 'But while Cai lives I wish to remain here to treat him. Will you grant me that one wish, at least, Rhun?'

There was a long silence—so long that she looked

up finally at his tall figure, darker now against the dusk that was fallen without. And when he answered his tone wasn't quite as set as before.

'You could leave your potion with me and I could treat him myself.'

'Yes, I know you could. But… I've become fond of Cai. And what difference will a few days make anyway?'

The gleam of torchlight in the hall turned the black of his hair to shining pitch, just as the firelight had done that very first night in his chamber. But when his reply came, an eternity later, it didn't shut her out, as he had then. Instead, the crack in the door opened just that little bit wider.

'Very well, Eleanor, if that's what you want. But once Cai has…gone…you must leave. It is for the best.'

As he turned away and left her Eleanor picked up her father's message and read it again. She *was* fond of Cai, that was true, but she'd also come to care about his master too. When had it happened, exactly? Or had there not been any one moment, but many moments? And were the feelings that pressed so heavily over her heart now the accumulated and combined weight of them?

But one thing was undeniable, and so startling that it made her eyes mist and her father's writing blur into insignificance. If she went from here, and his hound died, Rhun really would be alone. And, whatever her fate would become after that, so would she.

Nine days later Rhun buried Cai in the patch of ground beyond the walls next to where his mother had grown her herbs. The ground was hard, a heavy frost had come the night before, and the early-morning sun was not yet strong enough to warm the ground. But the tearing up of the frozen soil was neither a balm to his heart nor his soul, for he was laying to rest a creature that had been his shadow, his companion and his friend for fourteen years. And now he was gone he'd left a hole in his life far deeper than the one he was digging.

When the grave was deep enough, he picked Cai up, shrouded in his blanket, and clutched him to his breast. After pressing his lips to the cold, lifeless bundle, he knelt and placed it in the earth. Then quickly he took up the spade again and covered it, sweat pouring down his face and his tunic clinging to his back. When it was finished, Rhun knew a part of himself had gone deep into the ground too.

Turning away, he rubbed his sleeve roughly across his face. And then he saw Eleanor, standing just inside the postern gate.

For a moment neither of them spoke. He didn't know what to say to her, or how to thank her for these last days when she'd cared for Cai, easing his final hours with her potions and her kindness, so that the hound had seemed to slip into a peaceful sleep instead of eternal death.

In the event, it was she who broke the silence. 'I sensed that you wanted to be alone and that is why I stayed back here, out of the way...but I wanted to say goodbye to Cai too.'

Rhun nodded, and suddenly he didn't care that she'd seen his grief, even his tears. What did it matter now when she'd soon be gone from here anyway and he'd be saying another goodbye, this time to his wife?

'It is fitting you came, after all the care you've taken of Cai these last weeks.'

She moved forward a little, out of the shadow and into the sunlight. 'Why did you bury him here?'

He looked away to the barren and neglected patch of earth. How many years had it been since he'd last come to this place, full as it was of bittersweet memories? 'My mother grew her herbs here and so…it seemed the only place to lay Cai to rest.'

'You will miss him.'

'Yes… I will miss him.' Rhun heard his voice break and stooped to pick up the spade, driving it viciously into the earth beside the grave. 'But now he's dead and has no need of you, you can leave here. There's no reason for you to remain.'

Except for the one overpowering and undeniable reason that when she went he would miss *her* too—so much that it was torture to even contemplate how much.

Turning away, he began to place the rocks his mason had cut over the grave, so that no scavenging wolf could steal Cai's remains. The stone cut into his hands but he welcomed the sharp pangs of pain, for at least they distracted from the sharper pain that was gripping his heart.

'No, there is no reason for me to remain.'

Her voice behind him was so quiet that he had to strain to hear it.

'My things are packed and I can be ready for tomorrow. Indeed, I can be ready today, if you wish me to leave sooner?'

'No…' The exertion of piling the stones made his breath rasp in his throat—or at least it had to be that, surely, and not the weight that seemed to be falling down upon him with each one he lifted and set into place. The weight of his own folly! 'No,' he said again, 'tomorrow will suffice.'

Silence fell once more, and the only sound was the ring of stone against stone as Rhun piled the rocks one upon the other until the little mound was covered and secure. His back aching, he straightened up and turned around. And as his eyes went straight to Eleanor's the grip on his heart tightened until he could hardly breathe.

'I won't be here tomorrow when you leave. I have business elsewhere.' He didn't, but somehow he'd find some distraction out towards the village, or the monastery, or he'd just ride out on Eryr and not come back until the setting of the sun—if there was any sun tomorrow. 'Huw and a party of men will escort you to the border and beyond to the Abbey of Strata Marcella. There you can relay a message to your father to send escort for you the rest of the way.'

For if he took her himself he might easily bring her back again, and not send her over the border and towards her former home at all.

Her eyes searched his face, seeming to flay the skin from his bones for all the soft greenness of their gaze. Then they dropped to his hands where they hung at his sides. 'You have cut yourself.'

She stepped towards him and took up his right hand, examining the grazes on his palm. Rhun looked down at the long slender fingers as they brushed gently over his skin, and when her eyes lifted to his saw they were moist.

'I have a potion that will help. I will leave it behind for you when I go.'

Her face suddenly crumpled and she spun away and moved swiftly towards the postern gate. But Rhun was swifter still, and as she passed under the arch but not out through the other side he caught up with her and put his hand on her arm. 'Wait.'

She stopped, half turned her head, a flush mounting her cheek. 'Is there something else you wish to say to me, my lord?'

The stone archway blocked out the sun and a shadow seemed to fall down and cover him, making him shiver suddenly. And the voice that echoed back at him from the cold stones didn't sound like his at all. 'This *is* what you want, is it not, Eleanor? To leave here? To end this marriage?'

'We've discussed that already, more than once, and I see no need to go over it all again. Or *is* there a need, Rhun?'

Turning to face him, she raked her eyes over his face, their deep green depths pulling him in until Rhun felt he would drown in them.

'For, if there *is* more to say it must be said today—because tomorrow will be too late.'

He stared at her mutely as the walls of the archway enclosed them. Something squeezed hard at his throat with fingers of steel—pride or fear or something even more paralysing—until Rhun could neither speak nor draw breath. All he could do was move, reach out, draw her into the shadows and into his arms. And as he did so he felt no resistance. Instead she came willingly, lightly—eagerly, even—into his embrace. And then, his heart thundering against his ribs, he bent his head and placed his mouth over hers.

He heard her gasp, but the sound was swallowed up by his kiss. Her hands fisted in his tunic and instead of pushing him away she pulled him closer, and moved backwards until they were against the wall. The stonework was sharp against his knuckles, but he felt only Eleanor's lips on his, her warm body pressing close, her hips cradled between his, making his loins burn. And as her fingers curled into his hair, pulling his mouth down harder on hers, he knew there was no way he could ever let her go.

Why had he never kissed her like this before? How, in God's name, had he resisted for so long? Or at all? For now it was as if he'd been dying of thirst these long months and had refused to see the well of life that was right there in front of him. Now he drank deeply, feeling his whole body swell with the relief of it and harden too, until every sinew trembled as taut as a bowstring.

A shout rent the air, loud and urgent, echoing through the archway in warning. Rhun stiffened and lifted his head to listen, as did Eleanor, their eyes locked together. He was gasping for air, as she was too, their breaths mingling and turning to vapour in the cold air. The call sounded again, louder and even more urgent, shattering the raging of his lust, breaking the moment.

'Wh-what is it?' she asked.

'The watchman over the main gate is sounding the alarm.' He fought for a long moment with the overwhelming urge to pretend he'd never heard it, his body and his mind unwilling to let go of this moment. But finally he took Eleanor's wrists and lowered her hands from around his neck. 'Something is amiss.'

His eyes went to her mouth and it took all the restraint he possessed not to ignore the call, to kiss her again, drink in those sweet lips and forget all else.

Instead he brushed his mouth over her knuckles where they still hovered over his heart. 'Come, we must go and find out what it is.'

Turning, he went in through the postern gate, his hand clasping Eleanor's and a sense of unease prickling at the back of his neck. They rounded the chapel and emerged into the bailey and there, riding in through the gateway at the head of a small retinue of men in blue and gold livery, was Richard de Vraille.

Behind him, Eleanor gasped, and the next moment her hand was pulled abruptly out of his and the sound of her footfall ceased as she stopped dead. Rhun stopped too, in surprise, but only for a moment. For had he really expected the repercussions to take longer? For now *his* time had come and his blood rose to welcome it, fuelled by the hatred for this man that had been his life's compass for many long years. Now, finally, his revenge was in sight, glittering on the horizon, waiting only for him to take up his sword and claim it.

His heart thundering with quite a different beat now, and his soul on fire, Rhun strode forward alone to meet his father-in-law.

Chapter Nine

Eleanor's feet sank into the earth, or so it seemed. Her body had chilled to the bone at the sight of her father. She hung back and watched as her husband halted a few yards from where the English party waited, as if he was drawing an invisible line and daring them to cross it. None did. The riders stayed in their saddles, clouds of steam billowing off their horses' coats, indicating that they'd ridden hard and fast. None of the stable lads came running, no servants offered ale, and nobody went to her father's great chestnut destrier and held the stirrup for him to dismount. The lack of welcome at Castell y Lleuad couldn't have been more obvious if it had been shouted out loud.

And then, after a long and tense moment, Richard de Vraille nudged his horse forward to where Rhun stood, all in black from his hair down to his boots. The sun glinted off the older man's chainmail and picked out the gold that still burned in the greying hair. There was no warmth at all in his greeting, however, as it rang out like breaking ice through the brittle air.

'Lord Rhun.'

The inclination of Rhun's head was so slight it was barely there. 'De Vraille.'

Her limbs coming back to life, Eleanor moved forward and, drawing level with Rhun, dropped a deep curtsy to the man who had sired her. The pale blue eyes looked at her, and all at once she was swept back over the years to her childhood, when he'd always looked at her like that, without any apparent interest but merely acknowledging her presence. And, now as then, a sense of awe filled her and made her feel small once more.

'Welcome, my lord,' she said, aware of that awe in her voice even now, though she was a woman grown. 'I hope you are well, and my mother and sisters too?'

Her father nodded. 'We are all well.' His eyes slid from her to her husband. 'But I am not here on family matters.'

Eleanor turned her head to look at Rhun, standing like a pillar of granite at her side, so still that he didn't even seem to breathe. Only she saw the quiver of his limbs, the perspiration on his brow, the ominous clench of his jaw before he spoke again.

'Then what is it that brings you here, my lord, on such a chilly morning?'

She didn't know whether to be aghast or amused at the irreverence in Rhun's tone. Her father was neither, that much was evident, and his anger began to stream down upon their heads like hailstones from the back of his lofty horse.

'I am come, as you well know, to order you and your men to Castell y Bere.'

There was a murmur around them as if a wind had picked up and, glancing over her shoulder, Eleanor saw that the whole household had gathered in the bailey. Moreover, being the last quarter-year when the tenants' payments were due, there were a dozen villagers and their children within the castle walls. As Richard de Vraille's words hung poised in the air it seemed that everybody held their breath, waiting for their lord's answer.

Eleanor waited with them, as Rhun stood alone before this representative of the King of England. But he wasn't alone, was he? *She* was with him.

Even her father seemed to sense it. 'And to collect my daughter,' he added, like an annoying afterthought— one that sent a thrill of horror to Eleanor's heart. 'As I stated in my second letter which, like the first, has gone unanswered.'

The stamp of hooves and jingle of bits were the only sounds to break the silence until, a long moment later, Rhun's response came, calm and quiet but loud enough so that all could hear. 'As to the first, I thought my lack of response would have been answer enough. But, since you obviously need to be told in plain words, here it is. Neither I nor any of my men will go to Castell y Bere, or anywhere else that the King of England may command.'

The murmur around them rose, growing in volume and intensity, until the castle walls seemed to howl with its echo. Rhun held up a hand and the voices were shut off abruptly, almost on a single breath.

'As to the second—that is up to Eleanor, my lord.'

Eleanor's pulse began to pound in her throat. For Richard de Vraille was at his most deadly when anyone dared gainsay him. His mouth thinned beneath the close-cropped beard and his eyes glittered like steel behind his pale lashes.

'Then you are refusing the King's summons?' her father said after a moment of stalemate, his voice as icy as his eyes. 'Even though that makes you a traitor and all your household with you?'

'That word "traitor" has no meaning here,' her husband said, with such simple dignity that Eleanor's heart swelled with pride. 'And as for taking Castell y Bere, you may try but you will fail, for you'll find the people there as steadfast as those you see here.'

Suddenly her father was out of his saddle and standing almost chest-to-chest with Rhun. Eleanor shrank inside, remembering the violent rages that would come out of nowhere to make her childhood one of constant vigilance. He was tall—as tall as her husband—but his body was thicker set and still strong, despite his fifty years. He could look like an angel one minute and a devil the next, and now, in the blink of an eye, he had become the latter. And she'd never been more afraid of him.

'So you mean to break the peace treaty I made with your sire?'

Rhun stared into the older man's eyes, his gaze unwavering and hostile. 'Yes, I do.'

The Englishmen began to shift uncomfortably in their saddles, the hands of one or two of them moving to their sword hilts. But they were only six, seven with their master, and none of them seemed eager to draw their weapons.

'Then you are a fool as well as a traitor!' Richard de Vraille turned his head slightly and spat on the ground at Rhun's boot. 'I ought to challenge you here and now, you cowardly dog.'

'Then why don't you?'

Eleanor's hand flew to her throat as her husband's response came soft and deadly, the chill behind every word making them all the more dangerous. The armour over her father's chest was quivering, as if his latent fury would split it wide open, and his features were a mask of fury. Rhun, however, was completely still, his face almost serene, his eyes dark and steadfast. But she could see the blood pulsing in his throat, sensed that every sinew of his body was taut, ready to confront violence should it come.

Then Richard de Vraille's mouth stretched into a slow smile. 'One day, perhaps, I'll do just that.' His tone was like poison as his lips curled back from his teeth. 'After I've dealt with your treacherous countrymen.'

The cold blue eyes looked askance over Rhun's shoulder to fix on her. 'Come, Eleanor, away from this pigsty and back to where you belong.'

Eleanor felt a jolt pass through her as if a bolt of lightning had struck her out of the sky. She looked from her father to her husband and back again, and as Rhun's eyes met hers she made her choice—the only one she could.

'No, I'm staying here,' she said, her voice atremble with the thrill of courage that came from she knew not where if not from the man at her side. 'With my husband.'

'What?' Disgust distorted the heavy, handsome face and the pale stare pinned her like the point of a dagger. 'Do I understand you right, daughter? Are you telling me that you'd spurn your own kin to remain *here* with these *peasants*?'

'Yes, you understand me perfectly, my lord!' Eleanor flung her head up and for the first time ever faced her sire without quaking. And all at once she felt strong, and proud, and unafraid, more sure of what was in her heart than she'd ever been before. 'Because these people are my kin now.'

Rhun spoke then, not so much in warning but as a promise, his tone final and utterly dismissive. 'I'd advise you to leave now, my lord, before my *peasants* take it upon themselves to toss you over the walls on the points of their pitchforks. And, believe me, I'd do nothing to stop them. In fact, I might even take up a pitchfork myself.'

The tension suddenly snapped like a bow strung too tight. Her father's clenched fist lifted, quicker than the eye, as if he meant to cut Rhun a blow across the mouth. Instinctively Eleanor ducked, but Rhun didn't even flinch. At the edge of her vision she saw Huw ap Gruffudd step closer, and there was the scrape of metal as one of her father's men drew a weapon.

She'd never stood on the lip of a cliff before, but right then she knew exactly what danger felt like and how easy it was to step towards it or away from it. And while everyone around her braced themselves for the fall, it was Rhun who pulled them all back from the perilous brink to safety. Without any haste, he moved half a pace to stand in front of her like an impassable shield.

'Go on, de Vraille, what are you waiting for?' He spoke so quietly that nobody but they three could have heard it. 'It wouldn't take that much of a challenge, be-

lieve me, to meet you here and now—but in single com-
bat, man to man. After all, you and I have more than
one score to settle, do we not?'

There wasn't a sound to be heard in the courtyard.
Even the horses were silent and still, their ears pricked
and their nostrils flaring, as if they already scented
blood in the air. A child started to cry somewhere, and
Eleanor bit her lip until she tasted blood. For if these
two adversaries came to blows now, even in single com-
bat, there would still be carnage.

The moments crept by so slowly that time began to
feel unreal, and then she saw her father waver. A look
of doubt flickered in his eyes and his shoulders sagged
in a way she'd never witnessed before. It wasn't fear,
but rather surprise…and naked unease before the accusation in Rhun's voice.

'I should have hanged you years ago when I had the
chance—and your father alongside you!'

Rhun's eyes were gleaming black against the ashen
pallor of his face. 'If you're not going to challenge me
then go from here now—before I challenge *you*!'

'I have my orders from the King and, unlike you, I
will carry them out. But I'll be back soon to settle with
you, my lord, once and for all. Unless I have the good
fortune to meet you in battle before then.'

And with that he spun on his heel and vaulted onto
his horse's back, turning the animal so viciously that
its hooves sent clods of earth flying upwards. And then
the blue eyes swept around to lock onto hers once again.

'As for you, daughter, you've made your choice. Stay
here and be damned! But remember that a wife is as

much a traitor as her husband, and I'll do nothing to help you in your widowhood when it comes—as it will.'

Then he led the English party at a gallop out through the gatehouse, the thunder of their hooves over the wooden drawbridge seeming to shake the very walls. They rode westward, towards Castell y Bere.

Eleanor uncurled her hands, her palms stinging where her nails had dug into the skin. Perspiration trickled down to pool between her breasts and made her shift cling to her body, despite the cold of the day. Rhun turned slowly towards her, his eyes dark and his mouth tight. He seemed to struggle with himself for a moment, as if he might leap onto his stallion's back and gallop off in pursuit of the English after all. And then his shoulders relaxed and he smiled at her suddenly, dazzlingly, and it warmed her like a caress.

But as swiftly as it had come the smile faded and a frown settled over his brow, his gaze delving deep into hers. 'Eleanor…are you certain…?'

But he didn't get to finish whatever it was he'd started to say. A crescendo of noise surged around them as everyone suddenly sprang from their stunned inertia into pulsing action. People rushed up from all sides, dogs leaping and barking as they sensed the energy. The whole castle was gripped now with the excitement that gathered about them like a storm.

For a moment Rhun looked as bewildered as she knew herself to look, and then his hand lifted and his fingers touched her cheek. 'It's cold. Go back to your chamber now and get yourself warm again.' His thumb brushed her bottom lip, soft but fleeting, before his hand fell away. 'We'll talk later.'

As he left her, pulled in every direction by duty, Eleanor turned and threaded her way through the crowd making their preparations for the war that had now arrived at the gates. Everyone was behind their lord to a man, no matter what came next, and she'd taken her stand with them too—behind her lord, at the side of her husband.

Rhun stared into the fire. His chamber was empty without Cai, the hearth offering neither warmth nor companionship now that he sat there alone. He lifted his cup to his lips and found the ale that filled his mouth had gone cold. His head still ached from the noise at supper, where everyone had been talking at once, not in whispers but at the top of their voices, about the coming rebellion.

Only he and his wife had sat in silence, as if each of them was pondering on all that had happened that day. Or perhaps wondering what would happen next. And above all of it his overwhelming longing to reach for her had made his body ache too—so much so that in the end he'd muttered an excuse and retired early to his chamber.

But the aching continued, not even the ale he'd drunk easing it, and Rhun knew that only one sort of ease remained to him. Putting his cup down, he got to his feet, his knee stiff after sitting so long.

It was only a step from his threshold to Eleanor's, and at his knock the door opened at once.

Eleanor's eyes widened, yet it wasn't with surprise. 'Come in, Rhun.'

As he passed into her chamber Rhun saw two things immediately.

The first was that she'd made it her own, replacing the faded tapestries with newer ones and hanging fresh linens at the windows. There were more sconces in the walls, making the room bright with candlelight, and the aroma of herbs—lavender and camomile and others he couldn't name—rose up from the floor rushes to greet him. There was a little *prie-dieu* in the corner that hadn't been there before since, unused to praying himself, he'd never thought to provide one. The curtains hanging around the bed were also new, of thick green velvet embroidered with gold, and the fire that blazed high in the hearth made the chamber warm and welcoming.

The second thing he noticed was that Eleanor was alone.

The door closed behind him and she went to stand before the fire, her plaited hair falling to her hips. The flames behind her illuminated the saffron-coloured chamber robe she wore. The garment, although it reached from neck to toes and was thickly woven, didn't hide the curves and lines of her naked body beneath.

Rhun swallowed as she turned to face him and his body began to sing with anticipation. 'Where is your maid?' he asked.

A little smile played on her lips. 'With Huw ap Gruffudd, I don't doubt.'

'My steward?' He felt his brows shoot up. 'Is that fitting?'

'Why not? Alice is the daughter of a knight, and therefore a suitable match for Sir Huw.'

He shook his head, his loins heating as the warmth of

the room reached out and enveloped him. 'No, I meant, is it fitting that she should leave you alone?'

'I gave her permission to go.'

'Why?'

'Because I knew you'd visit me tonight.'

Rhun stared at her. It wasn't what she'd said but the way in which she'd said it—the way she stood there before him with an inner self-assurance that, like her chamber, was new.

'And how could you know something I didn't even know myself until now?'

'You said we would talk later, did you not?'

But all at once Rhun didn't want to talk. He wanted to act, to pick her up and carry her over to that sumptuous bed and possess her, make her his wife at last. For when he'd kissed her that morning he'd felt the response in her body, in her lips, had felt it pulse in the palms that she'd pressed over his heart. It had been a response that surely meant she also wanted to make this marriage of theirs real at last. But first he needed to know...

'Why didn't you go with your father today?'

'Because when he damned me for choosing to stay and not go I found I wasn't afraid.'

'Afraid of what? Of me?'

'No. Of him.' She shrugged, but it wasn't a careless movement, rather a sad one. 'You see, my father hates me almost as much as he does you—perhaps even more.'

Rhun knew the sort of man Richard de Vraille was. After all, he'd had first-hand experience at the time of his father's capitulation, when Richard de Vraille had thrown him into the dungeons of Hereford Castle. 'I gathered today that your relationship with your father isn't a good one, but hate...?'

'It's a harsh word, isn't it, to describe the relationship between a parent and his child?' Her eyes dropped for a moment and then lifted again. 'But he's always despised me for not being a boy. After my birth, which was a difficult one, my mother nearly died. And thereafter she could bear him no more children so he was left without a male heir.'

'That was no fault of yours.'

'Perhaps not, but he blames me for it nevertheless, and can't forgive me for it either. And because I knew he despised and resented me I grew up fearing him.'

But Rhun still didn't understand, and her explanation had raised more questions than it answered. 'Yet you asked me to end this marriage, to send you back to him.'

She smiled, an odd little curve of her lips that drew his gaze and made his heart vault. 'When I first came here marriage to you seemed the lesser of two evils and the easiest one to bear. But when I saw that you resented me too, I began to think that perhaps even my father's wrath—which I know well—was preferable to yours, which I knew not at all.'

Rhun dragged in a deep breath, the aroma of herbs and rose petals filling his lungs, and felt shame close around his heart. He took a step forward to seek her forgiveness, to beg for it if need be. 'Eleanor... I'm sorry—'

But she put up her hand, palm outwards, and stopped him in his tracks. 'No, stay where you are! That isn't all of it. There is another reason and I have to tell you now, tonight, otherwise...otherwise it might never be said.'

* * *

Eleanor felt her heart start to gallop in her breast as Rhun stopped dead, as she'd bade him. Her stomach began to churn in dread, but she forced herself to go on. She'd faced down one fear that day, so surely she could confront and conquer another now?

'Today, when I told my father that I was staying here, with you, it was as if the chains that had bound me suddenly broke and fell at my feet. And now...' The heat from the fire behind her seemed to bathe her in shame but she kept her head high and her gaze steadfast. 'And now, if I am to be the wife I want to be to you, Rhun, the last chain of all has to come off too.'

She found her fingers were shaking as she lifted them to her throat and began to untie the lacing of her robe. The knot came free, and as her wrapping opened and fell to the floor shyness as well as shame swamped her. But she kept her fingers moving, loosening the shift she wore below, letting it slip down over her arms, over her body, revealing her naked flesh. And against the pale skin, showing dark and ugly, was the blemish she'd hidden all her life even from her own eyes, now exposed to her husband's view.

And with all her clothing pooled around her feet, her body bare and defenceless, she waited.

Rhun's eyes were wide and dark, and a streak of red raced along his cheekbones as he looked at her. Goosebumps rose up on her skin and her insides began to quiver. She'd never stood naked before a man, and she knew herself to be more vulnerable than she'd ever been. But somehow she knew she was more powerful than

ever too, in spite of the birthmark that must surely turn
her husband's gaze away in disgust any moment now.

'*Annwyl Iesu...*'

Despite the softness of the words, which were no
more than a ragged breath, Eleanor flinched as if a
knife had ripped at her entrails. But her skin didn't
shrivel away, her flesh didn't crawl out of sight, and
the hurt faded as quickly as it had come. Because her
heart was her shield now, and the new strength she'd
found that day held her steadfast. And stronger than all,
even though it had been born only a few hours since,
was the love that filled her body, heart and soul, en-
abling her to face anything that came now and hereaf-
ter. Her love for this man who looked at her now with
frank and appreciative eyes that didn't turn away at all
at the sight of her.

For a long moment Rhun's gaze explored her body—
her face, her breasts, her belly, and that part of her below
that no man had ever looked at before. Then it lifted
again, lingered long on the horror that covered her right
breast like an evil claw, before returning to hers, where
his eyes lingered longest of all. Eleanor felt her heart
pounding against her ribs but said nothing. She'd said
everything there was to say except the words of love
that couldn't be said, and it was for him to speak now.

At last, he moved forward and reached out his hand
to touch the blemish. Her skin quivered as his fingers
traced the purpled proud flesh down from her collarbone to the tip of her breast.

'I knew you'd be beautiful, Eleanor...but I never
imagined that you'd be even more than that.'

Eleanor swallowed. 'Are you mocking me, my lord?'

His brows drew together but it wasn't a frown. His hand palmed her breast, his fingers closing in a gentle cradle, the warmth of his touch like a flame on her skin. She gasped with shock, and with the response that tugged low down inside her.

'Is this a burn?'

'No, it is a birthmark. I was born with this ugliness.'

'You think this makes you ugly? Eleanor, you are wrong.'

'I don't just think it, I can see it—and so can you.'

He shook his head. 'What I see is that this is a part of you…no more and no less.'

'Then it doesn't…disgust you?'

'No, it doesn't. You *are* beautiful, and your beauty goes deeper than your skin.' His eyes smiled into hers. 'And I saw far worse afflictions at Santiago de Compostela, believe me.'

Eleanor wanted to believe him—she really did. 'My sisters used to tell me it was the mark of the Devil, that I was his spawn. They told me that was why my mother could bear no more children and why my father disliked me.'

'And you *believed* them?'

'As a child, yes, I did. Why would I doubt it? They were older than me and they knew things I didn't.'

His fingers went on caressing her breast, making even her birthmark tingle with pleasure. 'And now?' he asked.

'Now I know they were just the words children say to each other without realising they hurt.'

And she *did* know that, so why couldn't she believe what Rhun was telling her? She'd never known him to lie, and there was no disgust or revulsion on his face. He was even touching her birthmark with gentle fingers, making her feel neither ugly nor repulsive. Making her feel other things too…things that built up inside her like a well filling up not with water but with a sweet sort of honey that left her craving to taste it.

'But that doesn't make my blemish fade or disappear.'

He stared down at her for a long moment, and then his hand left her breast and he laced his fingers through hers. 'Come.'

Eleanor let him lead her over to the bed, but when he drew back the curtains her heart began to throb, and she was suddenly keenly aware of her nakedness. Sitting her down, he stood back, his gaze serious despite the light smile that touched his mouth. And then he began to take off his clothes too, pulling his tunic over his head and letting it drop to the floor. His under-tunic and linen shirt went after it, until finally he stood only his braies.

His body was hard and lean, beautiful and fascinating, and she wanted to reach out and touch it. But as he bent to untie the lacing at his left knee and rolled the linen up to reveal the skin below, her hand flew in horror to her mouth.

From mid-thigh to a handspan below the knee there was a jagged pattern of ruined flesh, with one long, deep scar running down the middle. The knee itself was misshapen, mangled, as if the bone had been broken and set back all wrong. And against the lighter skin tone of his body that part was like a huge bruise that would never heal, blackly purple at the centre, fading to a yellowish-white where it met the undamaged flesh.

Then Rhun spoke softly. 'Do you think this ugly, Eleanor?'

'It is ugly, yes.' The words were out before she could prevent them—but how could she lie? 'And it must have been a terrible injury that caused it. Yet…' She looked up from his knee to his face, stumbling over words as she tried to express herself. 'Yet it doesn't repulse me… only makes me sorry you suffered, and it doesn't spoil the rest of you, which is…beautiful.'

'Then now you know how I see the birthmark on your body.'

Eleanor reached out and with a light finger touched his thigh, feeling the flesh quiver in response. 'What caused this?'

He shook his head. 'I'll tell you someday…but not tonight. That isn't why I'm here or why you knew I'd come, is it?'

'No.'

Her lips trembled over the word—a tremble that spread to her limbs, to her heart, as he pushed his braies down and, stepping out of them, removed his soft chamber shoes. She'd seen animals copulating, knew what they did and why, and yet when she saw his naked loins, his manhood erect and powerful, her eyes shifted away nevertheless and she felt heat suffuse her cheeks.

'Eleanor…' Rhun dropped to his knees in front her and turned the head she'd turned away back towards him. Then, a long moment later, he took the braid that hung down her back, drew it over her shoulder and began to unplait it slowly, pleat by pleat. His eyes bored into hers as he ran his fingers through the loosened locks and smoothed them down over her breasts. Then he took her face between his hands. 'It is time we made this marriage a real one, is it not?'

It was only as he waited in silence, his eyes burning dark, quietly, patiently, but like flames nonetheless, that Eleanor realised it really was a question. That he was asking her, not commanding her, and was waiting for her answer, there in front of her, on his knees.

She felt the quaking of his body in the palms that held her cheeks, the tension in the fingers that threaded into the hair at her temples, sensed the effort that the waiting was costing him. But wasn't it a husband's right to take his wife, whenever he wanted her, without asking if that was what she wanted too?

'Do you understand what I'm asking you, Eleanor?'

She reached out and placed her palm on his taut, smooth chest. His heart was pounding and his rippling stomach rose and fell rapidly with every breath he took.

'Yes, I understand,' she murmured, her breath quickening too as he leaned his body over hers and, kissing her mouth softly, scooped her up in one arm and pressed her backwards onto the bed.

'And do you want what I do, *f'anwylyd*? For us to lie together and make our union binding?'

Eleanor nodded, and then gasped as he straddled her, his knees either side of hers, and planted his palms either side of her head. Shock, apprehension and need all rushed through her at once, like a jumble of rivers in flood, wild and unstoppable.

And yet he stilled himself once more, his body trembling over hers as he stared down at her. 'It may hurt you a little, this first time.'

She heard the words but they didn't seem to matter.

They held no meaning for her because her mind had gone blank. Her body, her physical self, had all the control now, and her heart and soul urged it on to demand what it needed. She placed her hands on his flanks, smoothed them over his back, felt the hardness of his muscles, the sweat on his skin.

'Make me your wife, Rhun,' she breathed.

His mouth took hers, not soft and questioning now, but hard and demanding. His body came down upon her and the heat in his blood fired hers as they lay skin on skin, heart to heart, loins to loins. Eleanor moaned as his lips went to her breast and he took the teat gently between his teeth, his tongue hot and caressing. When his hand slid down over her belly and delved between her legs, his fingers beginning to stroke and play, her back arched and her insides melted.

She'd never dreamed anything could feel like that, soft and tender, yet as powerful as a strike of lightning. She became moist and swollen beneath his hand and buried her fingers in the thick black hair, breathing in the scent of heather and peat. As he entered her body there was a quick, sharp pain, and then only an overwhelming sense of rightness, and of wonder, and of completion and joy. Because as Rhun possessed her, made her his wife and he her husband at last, she felt…beautiful.

Chapter Ten

When Eleanor awoke the next morning she was alone. She lay on her back and stared into the dark as the chill of the room reached through the curtains that enclosed the bed. Her body ached in a way it had never ached before, and as she remembered Rhun's lovemaking her cheeks heated all over again. He'd possessed her. Not just once, but twice, and then thrice...gentle and restrained the first time, then with a passionate ardour that had made her cry with a pleasure she'd never dreamed it was possible to experience.

And yet he'd left her afterwards, slipping out of her arms as she'd slept. Why? Did a man not sleep with his wife once he'd taken her? Was a wife's bed solely for the purpose of coupling and nothing else? In truth, she didn't know. Nobody had ever told her.

The sound of humming came to her ears. Alice! Eleanor threw back the curtains and leapt out of bed. It was only when her maid's mouth dropped open that she remembered she was naked. And not just naked, but dishevelled, with the soft bruises of love on her mouth and on her flesh.

'Pass me my chamber robe, please,' she said, with as much dignity as she was able to draw on.

But it was useless to try and hide anything from Alice. Her maid picked up the garment from the floor where she'd left it the night before, her eyes twinkling.

'Good morning, mistress… Or should it be *madam* now?'

Eleanor blushed, but her heart swelled with a sort of wild pride. 'I could ask the same thing of you! Were you not with Sir Huw last night?'

Annoyingly, Alice never blushed at anything. 'Yes, but not *all* night,' she replied, without a hint of shame. 'It's not as you suppose.'

'Oh?' Eleanor took her robe and pulled it on, trying to keep a straight face at her maid's never-ending cheek, but unable to prevent her eyes twinkling. 'What other way is there, pray?'

'A chaste and honourable way, since Sir Huw wishes to marry me.'

This time it was Eleanor's mouth that dropped open. 'Marry you!'

'His wife is dead and he needs another to take her place, to look after him.' And then Alice did blush, even if it was ever so faintly. 'Besides which, I love him with all my heart.'

It was said so simply that Eleanor had no doubt it was true. During the night, when she and Rhun had lain together, she'd discovered there was nothing complicated in loving. You either loved or you didn't. She loved, and with all her heart as well. She must do— otherwise what was this feeling that made her want to sing and fly, made her feel that she could face and survive anything, even the terrible war that awaited?

'And does Sir Huw love you in return?' she asked.

Her maid shrugged. 'I cannot tell, and anyway that doesn't matter.'

'Doesn't it?' Eleanor sat down on the edge of the bed as Alice knelt to put her shoes on. 'Don't you care if Huw loves you or not?'

'If one loves, then that is enough for both, and I doubt I could compete with the love he has for his son.'

'Huw has a son?'

Alice nodded and sat back on her heels. 'Goronwy Bengoch—which means "crowned with red hair", so Huw told me. And truly I've never beheld such a mop of red hair on a boy! He is eight years old and being raised by his Aunt Gwenllian, the laundress here. Though once we are married I shall take over the care of the boy, of course.'

Eleanor stared down at the girl, who was not much older than herself and yet suddenly sounded like wife, mother and woman of experience all rolled into one skin.

A woman who suddenly tilted her head to one side and looked inquisitively up at her. 'Do *you* love the Lord Rhun, mistress?'

'Of course not!'

The refute came so smoothly to her lips that Eleanor was ashamed. But how could she talk of something she hardly understood yet? And if she told Alice of her love she might tell Huw, who might tell Rhun, and if her husband came to know of her feelings nothing would be simple any more. For, although she might love with all her heart, as Alice did, how could Rhun ever love the daughter of a man who'd abetted the terrible wrong done to him?

'My marriage was arranged, not chosen like yours, so love doesn't enter into it.'

'That is true,' her maid mused. 'And Huw and I have not the same status as you and the Lord Rhun. Huw was born a commoner, but because of his valour in the last war the Prince Llywelyn himself honoured him!' The pride in Alice's voice turned to wonder. 'It is all so different in this place, isn't it? And the people are so strange. But I think I like living here now.'

'You have changed your tune, Alice. Are you wearing blinkers now?' Eleanor laughed, but she heard the wavering timbre below it. 'Or is that the voice of love talking?'

'Mayhap it is love talking—but what's wrong with that?' Her maid's eyes twinkled again as they moved to the bed behind her. 'But now, before I do anything else this fine morning, I'd best change the bed linen and have it washed.'

Still reeling from this transformation in her maid— and in herself too—Eleanor turned and saw spots of blood on the under-blanket. She frowned. 'When did that happen?'

'A woman bleeds the first time, when her maidenhead is broken,' Alice explained, as if to a child. 'It is her husband's proof of her virtue.' And then, in the next instant, their roles seemed to be reversed, her maid now the one lacking experience. 'What was it like, mistress? Did it hurt? They say it does, the first time.'

Eleanor folded her hands in her lap and tried to look

like a woman who knew of such things. But inside, despite the knowledge her physical part had gained, the way her heart had embraced new and wonderful possibilities, she felt oddly vulnerable too—as if there was still part of her as a child within her woman's body.

'For a brief moment at the beginning there was a little pain, but after that, no.'

And, as she spoke her body relived the experience all over again, the exquisite joining that had seemed to go beyond just the flesh. As Rhun had penetrated her, moved so deeply inside her, she'd felt herself disappear into him until their bond was exquisite yet agonising, wrenching at her heart until she'd feared it would burst from her breast.

'And then?' Alice prompted, her eyes wide. 'After the pain was there pleasure?'

'After that it was…pleasant, yes, and the Lord Rhun was considerate,' she finished, her words not betraying anything of the feelings below them, for if they had her maid might ask her to explain them, and she couldn't. 'But now I must dress.'

Alice got to her feet. 'They say it gets better the more it happens, mistress… I mean, *madam*. Some women even come to like it, so perhaps you will too. I hope I will when *my* turn comes.'

Eleanor laughed. She should reprimand Alice for being so forward, but today was too joyful a day for scolding. 'I don't doubt that you will when you and Huw lie together in *that* way! Now, please have my bath filled. I want my hair washed this morning too,' she added, aware that it hung like tangled straw over her shoulders.

As her maid nodded and turned to her duties, Eleanor slipped a hand inside her robe and touched her birthmark. Her fingers traced where Rhun had caressed and kissed the wrinkled dry flesh and tried to see it as he saw it. Not ugly, but simply a different tone of skin. She'd forgotten it was even there as their bodies had become one in the dark. But by day she knew it was still as hideous as it had always been, and nothing, not even love, could change that.

Yet now she'd shown him, and he'd not turned away in disgust, could she learn to accept it as he did? Just as a part of her? After all, when he'd revealed his mangled leg it hadn't made him any less in her eyes, and not ugly at all. In fact as he'd shared the whole of himself with her he'd seemed even more beautiful to her eyes. Could she seem the same to him too?

Alice's voice broke her thoughts apart. 'What gown will you wear today, madam?'

Madam! Eleanor's heart began to skip at the thought of seeing Rhun again at table, her mind searching through the fabrics that lay within her coffer. A smile began in her stomach and rose to her lips. Even if she *was* ugly beneath her clothes, the clothes themselves were beautiful enough to help her forget the fact. And it would soon be night-time again, and Rhun would take them off, and perhaps she'd be so bold this time as to remove *his* clothes too.

'I'll wear my jaune below and the vermilion over,' she replied. The light yellow under-tunic would be warm, and she knew the delicate hue complemented her hair. Vermilion was a bold colour, one denoting status and ceremony, but it seemed appropriate this morning. After all, even if she would never be beautiful, she could at least be bold. And, after last night nothing less would do.

Rhun saw Eleanor at once. How could he miss her? Even if his eyes hadn't gone straight to her, his gut had tightened and his loins had fired as memory of the previous night drove everything else out of his head. When he'd possessed her something had seemed to shift in his consciousness, as if a key had finally found the right lock. Even before that, as she'd stood before the hearth and bravely bared her body and her blemish to him, not just his loins but his heart had fired too. And now, as their eyes met across the heads of the people who stood to greet his entrance, it happened all over again.

He threaded his way through the mass of bodies and the din of noise in the hall, with his guest Cynan ap Maredudd beside him. At the top table, Eleanor looked like a precious gem amid a pile of rocks. Everyone around her was dark of hair and sturdy of form, whereas she was fair and soft, her features so finely drawn they were almost fragile. Everyone else was ruddy of cheek, but she was pale, and nobody had eyes quite the same shade of green as hers. Even her dress set her apart. Everyone wore cloth spun in brown or grey or dun, while she wore…scarlet!

As she rose to greet him, a radiant smile on her face, Rhun's feet halted so abruptly that Huw and Cynan behind him crashed into him. A visor of black slammed down over his eyes, and then slowly black turned to red and began to creep down the hall towards him, like a living, moving puddle of blood.

As Eleanor's smile slipped, he spun away. Pushing past his companions, only dimly aware of the astonishment on their faces, he lurched back out through the doorway. Like a blind man, he groped his way up the stone steps, his hands clinging to the wall, his nails scraping for purchase. At the top, he started to run, but fell headlong, knocking the breath from his body. Sweat streamed down his face into his eyes, but he had to get up! He had to run—run as fast as he could—before it was too late…

But it was already too late. The sound of thunder filled his ears, growing louder and louder, coming nearer and nearer, until the floor beneath him trembled. Rhun ran faster, but his tunic curled like a rope around his legs and the hooves came hammering down upon him. There was the sound of bone splintering, the cruel ring of laughter, and the taste of salt and fear in his mouth.

Choking, his leg crushed and useless, Rhun stumbled to the door of his chamber and flung himself over the threshold. Then, slamming it shut, he slumped to the floor and buried his face in his hands. He sat and shook and wept like a baby, his heart dying of shame all over again, while from some clear corner of his mind he watched himself with disgust and loathing.

Because he hadn't been a baby when he'd watched his mother's gown turned red by the blood that gushed from the place where her throat had been. He'd been a boy of twelve—a man, almost, and old enough. He'd even had a dagger at his belt! And yet he'd lain there in the dirt, dazed and crying and clinging to Cai, and done nothing to save her.

* * *

Eleanor kept the smile on her mouth until her cheeks began to ache with the effort of it. She spoke courteously to the man Huw had introduced as Cynan ap Maredudd, and as lady of the castle she played her part in welcoming their guest in Rhun's inexplicable absence. Inexplicable to all but her, that was. It had only taken one look at the horror on his face when he'd seen her for her to know the reason for his abrupt departure from hall.

He'd lied to her the night before, when he'd touched her blemish, kissed it with his lips, lain with her. And then, his lust spent, he had left her. How foolish she'd been to wonder why as she'd drifted into warm, contented sleep, drugged with feelings of love! Why else but to avoid looking on her again, in the cold light of morning, when there was nothing of passion left to blind him to her ugliness?

But he'd lied so well! Any woman, even one with far more experience than she, would have believed his words, his mouth, his touch. Though a woman of experience would perhaps have seen it all for what it really was. A fleeting moment of pleasure, yet empty for all its passion, and nothing more than a husband's due.

'Is it true, my lady, that you've been learning our language since you wed the Lord Rhun?'

Eleanor didn't like Cynan ap Maredudd. The moment he'd sat down next to her, her flesh had recoiled. He was big, rough, loud, and his manners at table were appalling. He'd also made Margery Clement a widow and her children fatherless, and for that alone she despised him.

'Yes,' she answered, not turning to face him, hoping that he'd go on gnawing at his leg of mutton and not speak to her again. Why was he even here, this leader of the revolt in the Middle March? And not just him but his men too, a score of them sitting at the end of the long table below the hearth, all of them as uncouth and as violent as their leader.

'And is it also true that you've turned rebel too? And said as much to your own sire?' Cynan ripped into the meat, laughing at the same time, spitting food. '*Duw*, I wish I'd come a day earlier to see that!'

'I am not a rebel, sir.' Eleanor shuddered in disgust as a sliver of mutton landed on her sleeve. 'I just happen to be married to a Welshman and not to an Englishman.'

Right at that moment, as if fate had summoned him, Rhun reappeared. His face was ashen, his eyes bloodshot, and his leg dragged horribly behind him. As everyone rose deferentially all eyes stared, but her husband didn't seem to heed them. He sat down at the other side of Cynan ap Maredudd, calling for wine, and the two began to talk in Welsh, too fast for her to follow. Or at least the rebel leader talked. Rhun seemed content to listen, and still he hadn't said a word of greeting or anything else to her.

Eleanor stared down at her plate and the little appetite she'd had vanished. Even the ache that had resonated through her body when she'd woken up that morning had gone, leaving only an ache in her heart. By the time the meal drew to a close a sense of utter loneliness, worse even than she'd felt the day she'd arrived, swamped her, tugging her mouth and her heart downwards in despair. And then, as an excuse to finally leave hall presented itself, Cynan ap Maredudd sat back in his chair, belched loudly, and addressed the whole of the top table in English.

'Your wife tells me she doesn't support our cause, my Lord Rhun.'

Eleanor froze and her scalp started to prickle beneath her veil. Curling her fingers around the arms of her chair, she took a deep breath. For if her husband seemed determined to shun her, Cynan ap Maredudd seemed determined to provoke her. And finally he'd succeeded.

'That isn't what I said at all, sir. Perhaps your ears were blocked by all the snuffling going on to hear me properly?'

Cynan's brow creased. 'Snuffling, my lady?'

'The noise you make when you eat.' She turned to look full into his eyes, so that there would be no mistaking her scorn. 'Truly, you stuff food into your mouth faster than the pigs do, and your manners are even worse.'

The man was on his feet in a flash, but so was Rhun, their chairs crashing back behind them. A stream of Welsh burst out of Cynan's mouth—the mouth she'd just insulted—and rained down upon her like a shower of arrows. And then his voice was cut off, and before she had time to blink Rhun's hand was at Cynan's throat, pinning the rebel back against the wall. He spoke not in Welsh but in English, his voice so deadly that the words would have been understood in any language.

'You will apologise to my wife, both for your insults and your table manners—which, as she has so correctly pointed out, are disgusting. You shame us by sitting at our table, and so too do your men.'

Rhun's face was white, right down to the lips that were drawn back from his teeth in a snarl worthy of any wolf. Anger radiated from him, and yet the self-control he clearly imposed over it was even more frightening than the anger itself. Half the men in the hall were on their feet now, amid mutters of excitement, confusion and speculation.

Eleanor raised herself up too, and with her heart rattling against her ribs stepped forward and laid her hand on Rhun's forearm. It was like iron, the muscles taut and quivering as they held the other man against the wall.

'Rhun,' she said quietly. 'Perhaps if you allow the Lord Cynan room to breathe he will be able to make his apology, as I don't doubt he wishes most fervently to do.'

It seemed that Cynan ap Maredudd agreed, for his voice came again, rather more courteous now. 'Your wife is right, my lord. I apologise for my outburst, as I see now her words were spoken in jest.' The flint-grey eyes flickered to hers. 'Is that not so, my lady?'

Eleanor nodded, though she'd been in earnest when she'd called him a pig and she suspected he knew it too. 'Nobody here intends any insult or enmity. Friendships need to be strengthened now, not torn apart over trifling things said over wine.'

Rhun's head snapped round and his gaze met hers at last, causing a gasp to rise up into her mouth. His eyes were raw and dark with something that made her blood run as cold as ice. For she saw beneath the barely reined-in temper a sort of desolation, as if he'd just emerged exhausted from the bloodiest of battles even though not a single weapon had been drawn.

'You are wise, madam,' he said, removing his hand from Cynan's convulsing throat. 'We have enough enemies to face without making more. But, even so, we need to be certain of who our friends are.' He looked back to the rebel leader. 'My steward will see to quarters for you and your men. We'll talk further later.'

And then he turned and strode down the hall between the spellbound men, walking swiftly despite the limp of his leg. In his wake, an atmosphere of uncertainty and unease ensued, with the men of both parties clearly puzzled by what they'd just witnessed. Eleanor stared after him in confusion too, and in dismay. Even now he couldn't bear to wait and walk out with her, as befitted their rank in front of guests! Shunning her in private was one thing; shunning her in front of his entire household and their visitors was too much.

'May I escort you from hall, Lady Eleanor?'

Huw's arm was already poised and waiting, the man as courteous as always, but Eleanor shook her head. 'No, thank you, Sir Huw, that is not necessary.'

Then, nodding to Cynan, she walked down the hall too, just as quickly as Rhun had done, though he was gone from sight already. She held her head up high and didn't look at anyone as she passed by except Alice, who got up to follow. But Eleanor bade her stay. What she had to do, and what she had to say, needed no witnesses.

Once out of hall she flew up the stairs two at a time and down the passage to Rhun's door. She didn't bother to knock but pushed the door wide and burst over the threshold. Rhun was standing in the centre of the room with his back to her, but as he heard the commotion of her entrance he turned swiftly.

'Beth ddiawl...?'

Breathless after her dash up the stairs, Eleanor let her words come tumbling out of her mouth in a torrent. 'I suppose I should thank you for defending me in front of your *guest* downstairs, but I'd have been more grateful if you'd looked me in the eye!'

Rhun, still motionless in the centre of the room, shook his head. 'What?'

For a moment she might have believed he really was as puzzled as he appeared. But the slow burn of colour into his cheekbones, the way he looked at her askance, his gaze sliding away as if even now the sight of her disgusted him, only confirmed the truth that last night, while she'd freed her heart in his arms, all Rhun had done was take her body.

'And I would have respected you more if you hadn't felt it necessary to lie your way into my bed last night,' she went on, her voice rising along with her temper. 'How could you be so...cruel?'

'Cruel?' Slowly, his eyes returned to hers. 'Lie my way into your bed? What are you talking about?'

'Please don't insult me even more by pretending that you don't know.'

He pushed a lock of hair back from his brow. 'For God's sake, Eleanor, speak plainly!'

'I'm talking about my...my birthmark and well you know it. Why else can't you bear to face me this morning if the sight of me didn't sicken you last night?'

Rhun winced as if a fist had slammed into his midriff. He heard a gasp and realised it was his own. *'Nefoedd...* is that what you believe?'

'What else am I meant to believe?'

Eleanor's gown was redder than ever now against the angry whiteness of her face and, closing his eyes, he shifted through the jumble in his head, trying to go back to before the moment his attack had come upon him. As he recalled, he hadn't even reached the high table. Or had he got that far? Had he said something at table that she'd misread? Insulted her without even realising he'd done so?

'Whatever you think, you are mistaken,' he said, opening his eyes again, but looking down at the floor, not at her. 'Nothing between us last night was a lie.'

That, at least, was clear in his head. When she'd revealed her body to him he'd seen nothing but beauty. So why was she talking of lies now?

'That is hard to believe in the daylight when you turned and left the hall at first sight of me!' Her feet moved, the hem of her gown coming into his line of vision as she took a step forward. 'But if there is another reason for why you are behaving so coldly and strangely today, then tell me and I will listen.'

Tell her? How could he ever reveal the weakness that took away his senses and sucked him helplessly back into the past as if the present didn't exist? She'd seen something of it in the chapel that day, but to talk of it now might drag him back again and then he wouldn't have to explain anything. For she'd see that horror for herself, right before her eyes.

'There is nothing to tell.' Rhun still stared at the floor, willing his eyes to avoid the scarlet that snatched at them like claws. 'But even if there were this is not the time to discuss domestic matters, when we have war on our doorstep and Cynan ap Maredudd awaiting my attention downstairs.'

'Domestic matters!'

After a moment of silence, when he thought she might actually spin on her heel and leave him, she crossed instead to the table against the wall. Rhun forced his gaze upwards to see her lean for a moment on her hands, her shoulders heaving as she drew in a deep breath. And although every sinew in his body screamed out to go to her, he couldn't.

'After yesterday...after last night...' She straightened up but didn't turn around. 'I thought the *other* war, the one between you and me, might be over.'

Rhun shook his head, but it didn't clear his mind at all. What had happened between them last night had been more than the simple consummation of their marriage, yet today everything seemed more confused than ever. And he had no hope of finding clarity while his mind was drowning in a sea of scarlet.

'There isn't any war between us, Eleanor.'

'No, perhaps not war.' She spun around to face him. 'But there has never been peace between us either, has there, Rhun? For peace means trust, and I doubt now that such a thing can ever be truly possible in this marriage.'

'Eleanor—' he began, but she cut him off.

'I know!' Her gaze dropped away, and now it was she who stared at the floor. 'The rebellion is upon us and this is not the time to talk of *domestic matters*.'

'No, it isn't the time.'

Even as he said it, Rhun cursed himself for his cowardice. Why could he not trust her? Admit to her the nightmare that had driven him from her bed? Tell her how he dreaded the contempt he'd surely see on her face had she woken at his cry, discovered the sweat on his body, the fever in his eyes, the clenching of his teeth as his body shook in spasm next to hers?

'In a few days hence I go to raise the men of Caereinion and guard the border for Madog ap Llywelyn.'

Her head snapped up again, her eyes flying to his. 'You're leaving?'

He nodded. 'Huw will remain, to see to things here until I return.'

'I see.'

She folded her arms across her midriff, but that only drew his eyes even more keenly to the scarlet haze that surrounded her and hammered at his skull like a mace.

'And when will that be, may I know?'

'I don't know that myself yet. Before the snow comes, at any rate.' Rhun rubbed a hand over his eyes but the needles behind them only dug deeper. 'And now I beg you leave me. I must speak with Cynan and not keep him waiting any longer. As you've seen for yourself, he is not a moderate man.'

And since he himself was only half a man, his soul tormented by nightmares and not his own at times, how could he be truly a husband to her? She deserved far better than that—better than he. And she knew it too, as she drew herself tall and her eyes glittered. But not in the way they'd done last night before the fire, and later in his arms. Now, for the first time, he saw disgust burning there.

'Of course. I understand you mustn't waste time talking to your *wife* when there are matters of war waiting!'

'Eleanor…'

But she'd already turned on her heel and left, leaving the door wide open behind her.

Rhun went and closed it and then dropped into the chair. As of long habit, he put out a hand to call Cai to him and then dropped it back into his lap. His companion was dead and already rotting in the grave. He sat back and closed his eyes, and gradually the scarlet faded away. But the headache persisted, spreading to his whole face and throbbing along his cheekbones and jaw until he thought the bones would shatter.

So his wife had learned to despise him at last. He almost smiled as he wondered why it had taken her this long. After all, since he despised himself for his weakness, his failure to master himself, why should she do otherwise?

Chapter Eleven

The morning Rhun rode out Eleanor stayed in her chamber and watched from the window as the little band of men assembled in the courtyard below. They weren't many, less than a dozen, for they weren't going to seek battle but to incite support for the rebellion in a land that lay cheek by jowl with England. They wore helmets, however, and chain beneath their cloaks. Because whether or not they sought battle, it could easily meet them anywhere at any time.

She'd never seen Rhun in armour and, despite the distance and coolness that had divided them since the day Cynan ap Maredudd had come, she drew her breath at his magnificence. His tall body bore the armour well, the bright bronze of it contrasting brilliantly with the black of his hair and the darkness of his eyes. Below the short brown riding tunic his calfskin boots reached to his knees, and thick gauntlets covered his forearms from fingers to elbows. There was little colour on his face, however, and his features were stern as he checked over the pack horses that carried supplies and then ordered his men to mount.

Swinging himself up into Eryr's saddle, he sat for a moment as if lost in thought, and then his gaze lifted to her window.

Eleanor flinched inwardly as the piercing eyes locked onto hers. And even from where he sat, as still as a rock astride his stallion, she saw his eyes flame with something that could have been anger or accusation or regret or anything in between. She swallowed and balled her hands into fists. Her feet yearned to run down to him, but she didn't let them.

After a moment Rhun's head dipped and he turned for the gates, leading his men out without once looking back at her window. And as he went Eleanor felt a piece of her go with him.

The nights began to draw in, the sky low and black, the stars so near and so bright that it seemed they would touch the earth. Snow feathered the castle walls as December arrived, though it melted quickly enough when a wintry sun rose weakly in the sky. Conflict was expected daily, and the air was filled with the sound of swords and spears being sharpened, arrows cut and fletched, horses reshod, and shields and mail burnished, all under the efficient eye of Huw ap Gruffudd.

The garrison passed the short daylight hours training in mock battle on the flat area of pasture between the castle and the river. The talk in the hall, now slightly emptier since ten of the men had gone with Rhun, was of nothing but fighting, and rumours flew after every piece of news that arrived.

Eleanor had shut her ears to it all and turned her eyes away from the war that men seemed to live for. Why, when war could mean their deaths? And why, when it could mean Rhun's death too, hadn't she said goodbye to him on the morning he'd left? Now it was too late to regret her stubbornness, but even so her body ached for him as the nights grew longer, and her heart dreaded whatever ill news each new day might bring.

On the morning of the feast of St Nicholas, Eleanor went as usual to the stables to see Mistletoe. The low wooden building was warm with the heat from the horses' bodies and, after a kiss on the mare's nose, she knelt to inspect the wounded fetlock. It was completely healed, with just a slight line of proud flesh visible and the hair already grown back over it. The day it had happened seemed so long ago now, and as the days had turned into weeks, and no word came from her husband, time had ceased to exist. Even the tolling of the bell from the monastery seemed unreal, as if it belonged to a distant world, and she'd stopped counting the hours long since.

Eleanor got to her feet again, and as she did so a frown settled on her brow. For the mare's coat was dirty with stable stains and her mane and tail matted. There was no water pail, and it didn't seem that Mistletoe had been fed yet either. She checked the adjacent stalls to discover that there was no water pail in any of them, and the horses were all standing with their ears pricked, hungry and eager for their food.

Looking about her, she spied one of the stable lads listlessly drawing water from the well, empty buckets around his feet. He jumped as she approached him and the bucket he was bringing up went back down into the well with a splash.

'Do you speak English?' she demanded, but no answer came. 'Why have the horses not had water or food yet? It is well into the morning.'

He shook his head, his eyes sliding from side to side, as if he was terrified to meet hers. Evidently he didn't understand a word of English, so Eleanor filled one of the buckets herself, then took his arm and led him to Mistletoe's stall.

The mare drank thirstily from the pail the instant she put it down. 'I take it she hasn't been fed either?' she asked the boy, but he just gaped at her, so she put her hand to her mouth in an eating gesture, at which point he giggled.

'God's blood!'

For the first time ever, Eleanor cursed out loud at one of Rhun's people. But at that moment something snapped inside her—something that had been building for weeks as the winter closed in and life seemed to stagnate to a maddening dullness.

Dragging the boy back outside, she marched him over to the food store, where she discovered two more lads sitting cross-legged on the ground, playing at counters. When they saw her they leapt to their feet, but she didn't waste time speaking to them as doubtless they had no English either. Instead, she scooped corn into one of the feeding bowls lying empty and neglected, and then dragged the water boy back to Mistletoe's stall. The mare fell hungrily on her food, and in a blaze Eleanor boxed the minion's ear.

'And now you will clean her.' She made a brushing motion on the mare's coat. 'Do you understand me?'

He didn't giggle this time, but nodded his head, rubbing his ear that glowed pink where her hand had struck. Eleanor pushed away the little pang of remorse and, going back outside, took a long look around her. Everywhere was quiet, with not even the men at their training. Huw ap Gruffudd had been ill for the last week, laid up in his bed with the shivering sickness, Alice constantly at his side. And all at once his absence was noticeable, though she hadn't seen it until then.

Briskly, she crossed the courtyard to the clay oven. Bread was baking but there was no sign of the baker. The loaves were turning black and, taking up the long spade, she scooped them out and left them on the ledge adjacent to cool.

Then, climbing the steps to the keep, she turned downwards into the kitchens. The warmth hit her at once, but here, too, an air of idleness hung over everything. A spit boy was turning mutton over the fire, another stirred a pot of *cawl*, while a man chopped winter vegetables. Goronwy Bengoch, Huw's child, sat on a low stool near the fire, whittling wood. They all looked up as she entered, seemingly struck dumb by her presence, but none bowed or showed her any reverence at all.

Eleanor walked past them into the buttery—which was completely empty—and through into the laundry. There she found the baker, with a cup of ale in one hand and the laundress's breast in the other. She knew that they were man and wife, but even so shouldn't they be carrying out their duties? Shouldn't everyone?

The baker straightened up, saying something to her in Welsh, knowing full well she wouldn't understand. The woman—Huw's sister Gwenllian—tugged at his sleeve, but he merely shrugged and murmured something that brought a grin to her lips.

Eleanor's face flamed and fury rose up like a torrent of boiling water inside her. For she didn't have to understand the language to know that what had been said was about her, and also that it was insulting.

With a shaking hand, she pointed behind her. 'Baker, return to your oven and watch the bread at once! If I hadn't come along the loaves would be charcoal and unfit for eating by now!'

Whether the man understood English or not, she didn't know, but it appeared her tone was intelligible enough. He made her a lazy bow—more mocking than deferential—then sauntered past her and out through the doorway. Eleanor opened her mouth to speak to the laundress but she didn't need to, for the woman bent quickly to the soiled cloths on the floor and began to dunk them vigorously into the washing vat.

Going up into the hall, Eleanor looked about her in dismay. Men lounged at the tables, which were no longer being stacked after meals as before, dicing and drinking or just talking. One or two were even asleep, and the evidence of their neglect of duty was even more marked here than in the kitchens. As they saw her some rose reluctantly, even resentfully, to their feet, and then sank back down again. Others merely glanced up at her and then returned to whatever it was they were doing.

Fighting down the urge to retreat back to her room, she searched the tables until she spied the one man she sensed might be of help and beckoned to him. At once Dafydd Genau'r Glyn left off repairing a broken string on his *crwth* and came over to her.

'*Dydd da, arglwyddes,*' the poet greeted her, and then, with a quick bow and a speculative look, went on in English. 'Is there something I can do for you?'

'I require your assistance,' Eleanor said, swallowing down the nervous indignation that filled her throat. 'Since the Lord Rhun's absence, and with Huw ap Gruffudd unwell, the order of things here is not as it should be. The livestock is not being properly tended to, the men are neglecting their duties, and the castle servants are grown lax and insolent.'

'I had noticed, my lady. What do you wish me to do about it?'

'I don't wish *you* to do anything about it.' She heard her voice quiver but pressed on. This was the moment of her testing, and if she failed now she would *never* be lady here. '*I* intend to rectify all that myself, but I need to be able to speak to these people in their own tongue. I have learned some Welsh, but not enough to make my wishes clear, still less command compliance. And so… will you teach me the words I need?'

The man smiled until the corners of his honey-brown eyes crinkled. 'At your service, Lady Eleanor.'

Rhun drummed his fingers on the ground, where he sat before as much of a fire as they'd dared to kindle. Bleddyn ap Gwion, sitting opposite him, related the latest news of the rebellion, having ridden like the wind from the north. His man had embraced the role of spy with open arms, carrying secret messages along the

March and even across it, into lands in England that had once belonged to Wales and where Welsh hearts still beat.

'The battle took place on the eleventh day of November.' Bleddyn spoke in a whisper so as not to wake the men who slept on the floor around them. 'Madog's forces defeated the armies of the Earls of Lancaster and Lincoln, and have captured the towns and castles of Denbigh and Rhuddlan.'

Rhun leaned forward, placing his elbows on his crossed knees, and counted backwards in his head. The eleventh of November was more than a month ago. The night he'd gone to Eleanor's bed had been the day after that. Now it felt as if a lifetime had passed, and yet at the same time it only seemed a moment ago that he'd dragged himself unwillingly from her arms.

'And what of the castle at Conwy?' he asked, forcing himself back to the present.

'Still in the King's hands.' Bleddyn spat into the fire, making the flames hiss. 'Madog hasn't attempted to take it—yet.'

Rhun shivered and drew his cloak closer around him. A freeman of Dolwen, loyal to the cause, had courageously extended to them the shelter of this draughty barn. But tonight it only served to underline the fact that they were renegades, creeping from village to village by day and hiding in the dark by night. Where was the honour and valour in that?

Getting to his feet, he flexed his bad knee, feeling the blood flow down into the calf again.

'Madog's men will never take Conwy,' he said, rubbing his palms together to get the blood flowing into his frozen fingers too. 'That's Edward's route into Gwynedd, and from there to the whole of Wales. He'll not yield it, even if a legion of Welshmen batter at the walls.'

Bleddyn nodded, getting to his feet as well, his eyelids drooping. And no wonder, since none of them had known a warm bed and a full night's sleep for many weeks now. 'Yet the King's forces have failed so far to retake Castell y Bere.'

Rhun thought back to the day Richard de Vraille had ridden in under his gateway to order him to go and help lift the siege. The day that Eleanor had made her choice to stand with him.

He kicked at the fire, causing sparks to fly and smoke to rise up to the rafters, but no more heat issued from it. 'Is it still snowing?'

'Thicker and faster than ever,' Bleddyn confirmed, eyeing his blanket hungrily, his thin face and grizzled beard evidence of the toll this undertaking was having on them.

'God curse this weather.' Rhun stamped his feet to warm them, his aching body longing for his blanket too. 'If the snow worsens, we mustn't get trapped here. It's too close to the border, and the men have endured enough already. Besides, we're endangering our hosts more, the longer we remain.'

As he said it he made up his mind, feeling his heart lifting as a consequence, and even some warmth creeping into his frozen veins. 'We've done all we can here. We'll break camp in the morning and head back to Castell y Lleuad.' He put a hand on his man's shoulder. 'But I have one last favour to ask of you, Bleddyn. Will you ride south to Brycheiniog tomorrow and inform Cynan

ap Maredudd that we're making for home? And bid him
send the same news north to Madog?'

'Gladly, my lord.'

Rhun yawned and, as if it was contagious, caught
Bleddyn in a yawn too. 'And then, as soon as you can,
come home,' he added.

His companion grinned as he turned for his bed.
'That I'll do even more gladly, my Lord Rhun. I've a
sweetheart in the village who misses me sorely. Your
lady is missing you too, no doubt, and you her.'

As he folded himself inside his blanket and watched
the fire die away, wide awake now despite his weari-
ness, Rhun knew the last part of Bleddyn's observation
to be true. As for the first part...he wished he could
be as sure.

Eleanor sat as close as she could to the hearth,
wrapped in thick furs from her chin to her toes. The
malady gripped her belly again and she took another
sip of warm wine, but it didn't help.

'It's an ague, nothing more,' she said, cross with herself for being so weak and so tired all the time. 'It's this
place. It's always cold.'

'It's not the ague, madam,' Alice argued, stubborn
as always. 'You have no fever.'

Eleanor batted away the hand her maid laid on her
brow. 'It must be, for what else *can* it be? Anyway, I
mean to ride down to the village today, as I promised
Geneth a potion for her child. So please be so good as
to bid Huw to arrange for some men to accompany us.'

Since the day Rhun had raged at her for riding
out alone, she'd always taken an escort whenever the

weather had allowed her a ride outside the castle walls.
Although she dismissed the steward's repeated warn-
ings that with the rebellion coming ever nearer it would
be wiser to stay put.

'I suppose you'd like your prospective husband to
come with us too, now he is well again?' She sent her
maid a questioning look. 'When is Huw going to name
the day?'

'He must wait to ask permission of the Lord Rhun
first, madam.'

Inside her layers of fur, Eleanor rubbed a hand over
her belly as the ache bit again. 'Then he'll be waiting
a long time!'

It was only two days to the Christmas feast and
there was still no word from Rhun. Nor had any of his
men come with news, good or bad, and as the weeks
had passed she'd learned the real virtue of patience.
In the meantime, she'd finally succeeded in making
her presence felt among his people here. It hadn't happened overnight, but gradually the garrison of Castell
y Lleuad, and the villagers too, had come to accept her
as their lady. Her words and wishes were obeyed without question now, and she in turn had found that she
enjoyed her new status.

Was it that by possessing her as he had Rhun had
truly made her his wife and lady of his house? Or had
his very absence given her the freedom and the confi-
dence to grow into that role all by herself?

'I wonder, madam…'

Alice's voice broke into her thoughts and Eleanor
looked up to see her maid still frowning down at her.
'What do you wonder?' she asked.

'I wonder, perhaps, if you might be with child.'

'With child?' Eleanor shook her head. 'Don't be foolish!'

'What's foolish about it?' Alice planted her hands on her hips. 'You and the Lord Rhun have lain together, have you not? And would it not be a natural consequence in that case? When were your last courses?'

Eleanor looked down at her stomach, which she knew without seeing it to be flat and firm beneath the furs. Her courses?

'I can't remember...' she began, but even as she spoke, the date loomed large and indisputable. It had been the day after Rhun had carried her back from the chapel in the rain. Her hand flew to her mouth as the sum came out. Almost two months!

'Aha!' Alice beamed, her face smug. 'I knew it!'

'You don't know anything!' Eleanor retorted. 'And neither do I. It may be that this intolerable cold has affected my womb.'

'It hasn't affected mine.'

'No, well, that's as may be...' She stood up and, shrugging off the heavy coverings, ignored the rolling sensation in her belly. 'Now, fetch our riding skirts, if you please.'

'Do you think you should ride, madam? In your condition...'

'By all the saints!' Eleanor gritted her teeth, not because she was angry at her maid's insolence but because she feared Alice might be right. 'We are going to the village today. I promised the medicine. And, anyway, I want to issue an invitation to the Christmas feast.'

'But Huw said they haven't bothered with that here since…'

'Since the Lady Morfudd died,' Eleanor finished for her. 'Yes, I know, but there is a new lady of the castle now, and it's high time the tradition was reinstated.'

Rhun could barely see the outline of Castell y Lleuad through the snow that drove into his eyes. The deep drifts had all but obliterated the road that led homewards, and if Eryr hadn't known the way with that instinct that all animals had they might have strayed from the path and got lost more than once.

He looked behind him yet again, checking that all ten men were accounted for, and his gut twisted at the sight of the cold and bedraggled figures slumped low in their saddles. They'd passed through the village, but the cottages and outbuildings had been swallowed up in a blanket of snow and the hamlet had seemed devoid of life. All around the treetops were white too, and the land was ghostlike and unfamiliar, the sky already dark in the late afternoon.

His fingers were numb inside their gauntlets and he was unable to feel his feet any more. Only the thudding of the horses' hooves disturbed the eerie hush of winter as he ploughed up the hill, the breath of both man and beast steaming like clouds.

A herald had gone ahead to announce their coming, and as they crested the top at last he saw the gates were open and welcoming.

Rhun saw Eleanor at once, standing just inside the gateway, swathed in a thick cloak. Alice and Huw were at her side, also wrapped up against the weather. And

behind them, in the torchlit bailey, men were waiting
to take their horses and packs, and servants held jugs
of warm ale. Despite the cold, a swift warmth filled
his belly when his wife took hold of his stirrup and
walked him in, though she hadn't yet looked up at him
or spoken to him.

Swinging himself stiffly down from the saddle, he
handed Eryr to one of the stable lads and looked around
him. The relief at being home palled a little under an
odd sense of awkwardness, as if his welcome wasn't
all it should be. And yet there was Eleanor, at his side,
holding out a goblet of wine.

'*Croeso yn ôl.*'

The cup he'd accepted nearly slipped through his
gloved fingers. It was the first time she'd ever spoken
to him in Welsh, and Rhun recalled how, when she'd
first come, he'd advised her to learn it, and then done
nothing to see that she was taught. How was it, then,
that she addressed him now, welcoming him home in
his native tongue?

'Dafydd Genau'r Glyn has been teaching me,' she
said, as if she'd read his mind. 'He says I have a gift
for it.'

The snow must have chilled his senses as well as his
limbs. For it wasn't only Eleanor's language that was
changed. She seemed older, even though it had been
only weeks, not years, since he'd last seen her. Had his
absence done that? Had she missed him so little that
instead of aching for him, missing him as he had her,
she'd blossomed instead, like a flower free of the shade
of a fallen tree?

Rhun took a long pull of his wine, feeling it sting

his cold lips and blaze down his throat, and watched as Eleanor gave orders in Welsh, halting but clear, seeing to it that every weary man had wine or ale, that every tired horse was led to the stable to be unharnessed, rubbed down and fed.

Then she looked back to him, her eyes sparkling in the torchlight. 'But, as you see, I have only mastered a few sentences as yet.'

He passed the empty cup to a waiting servant. 'Are there any other surprises to welcome me home?'

His voice seemed to echo back at him from somewhere outside of himself, as if the cold that numbed his body had blocked his ears too.

Her smile was fleeting, gone as soon as it came. 'One or two, yes, but they can wait. Come into the hall. You are frozen to the bone.'

And then, tentatively, she reached for his free hand and led the way to the keep, but Rhun could feel no warmth in her touch through his thick gauntlet. Most of his men had gone before him, and when he entered the hall there was the usual fire roaring in the hearth and the tables were set out where they normally were. But that was all he recognised.

The walls had been repainted a bright white, and tapestries hung at intervals along their length—gaily woven hangings he'd long forgotten or hadn't even known he possessed. There was a new tapestry behind the high table too, depicting the miracle of the Nativity in brilliant and vivid colours. The rushes on the floor were also new, and the aroma of herbs rose to greet him, mingled with the scent of the greenery that hung everywhere, its berries dazzling in their gaiety.

And it wasn't only members of the castle garrison that filled the hall to bursting. All his tenant farmers and freemen were there as well, their families too. No wonder the village had seemed so lifeless! Dafydd, his *bardd*, was strumming his *crwth* to one side of the fireplace, while men diced, women sat and gossiped, and the village children played at Hoodman Blind in the centre of the hall. The aroma of hot, seasoned food spiralled up from the kitchens below, and his mouth watered instinctively as he turned to Eleanor in enquiry.

'Had you forgotten it is the Eve of Christ's Mass?' She spoke before he could ask. 'I know the feast hasn't been celebrated of late, but with the times being so uncertain, and the weather so harsh this year... I thought it fitting to bring back that custom.'

Rhun withdrew his hand from Eleanor's, pulling off his gauntlets and pushing back his hood. 'I begin to wonder if I have come home to the right place.'

'I...we wanted to welcome you home properly.' She pushed her hood back from her head too, and her eyes shone like emeralds in the light of the multitude of candles that lit the hall. 'Does it displease you?'

Rhun stared down at her and saw too, plainer and clearer than all the finery and colour around him, that the barricades he'd built up between them on their parting were not only still in place but towered ever higher. They were there in the way she stood, so near yet so far, and in the expression on her face that was welcoming and warning all together.

'Displease me that you've decided to celebrate the feast even though we're at war?'

'Yet there needs to be no war here—does there?'

The double meaning was unmistakable, and it was as if their last conversation, that day before he left, was to be recommenced exactly where it had ended. And as she stared unflinchingly up at him Rhun saw that she'd altered even more than he'd thought—as if, with the coming of snow, something hard and solid had built itself around her too. And while she spoke and looked like a wife, touched him, smiled at him, welcomed him, it was as if she had perfected the role…learned it by rote, just as she had the Welsh language.

He shook his head and felt his heart, which had begun to thaw with the rest of him, shiver colder than before. 'No, there needs to be no war here, Eleanor.'

'Then when you have bathed and changed come to table.' She turned away and gestured to his body servant. 'You must be famished—which reminds me that I must attend to the kitchens.'

He opened his mouth to respond but she had already left him and was walking towards the steps down to the kitchen. The people came back to life as she passed by, as if she'd sprinkled them with some sort of magic aura. She paused to speak to this one or that, to taste the ale a servitor held out, to laugh at some jest or other. Not once did she look towards where he still stood, like a stranger in his own hall.

Bemused, Rhun turned and nodded to Huw ap Gruffudd, bidding him attend him a little later. Then he made for his chamber, his body servant close behind him. His hunger had deserted him and all he wanted to do now was to get clean and sleep—but not too long.

For even if Eleanor had changed she was still his wife, and he her husband. His absence had not changed *that* at all. And now he was home he meant to prove it to her.

Chapter Twelve

'Perhaps you should give the traditional greeting, my lady, since this is *your* feast, not mine?'

Eleanor felt her face flame. Not because she couldn't give the greeting—after all, Dafydd Genau'r Glyn had taught her well, and she knew it by heart—but because of the challenge in Rhun's suggestion. She looked at him for a moment, trying to see behind the words. But his face was unreadable, so she nodded and got to her feet, banging her cup on the board until the hall fell silent. And then she took a deep breath.

'Bendith Duw ar y tŷ hwn. Bwyd da a bywyd da i bawb!'

Cheering and applause soared to the rafters and everyone fell on the food and drink the servitors had laid before them. For at this special season of the year they were all blessed by God and entitled to good food and good life, just as her greeting decreed, at least for this one day.

Retaking her seat, she took up her goblet and toasted the coming of Christmas.

'Well done.' Again, there was an odd note in Rhun's voice, although it didn't entirely mask the hint of surprise. 'You know far more than the few phrases you claim to have mastered, Eleanor.'

Eleanor couldn't prevent a surge of pride. 'Thank you,' she said, modestly enough. 'But I still have a long way to go.'

She studied Rhun as he picked up his knife and stabbed it into a hunk of meat on the platter. He'd grown thinner, the hollows of his cheeks more pronounced, his shoulders not quite as broad. All the men had come back seeming less than before they'd gone, and she could only imagine how hard a time they'd passed in Caereinion.

But she didn't have to imagine, did she? She could ask, and when it was time she would. There would be no more tiptoeing around now—not when she'd learned to walk with a firm and determined step, to use her own voice and exercise her own will.

So she waited quietly, picking at her trencher, her stomach still feeling too delicate for her to eat very much of the rich food. Alice, as usual, had been right, and sooner or later she would have to tell Rhun that she carried his child within her womb. Would he welcome it at all now that they were at war? And if it were a girl would he welcome it even less?

Many moments later Rhun sat back, wiped his mouth with his napkin and reached for his wine. There was a little more colour in his face now.

Eleanor put down her knife too and folded her hands in her lap. 'You eat like you've not tasted food in months.'

'We had food enough, but not quite as plentiful and certainly not as appetising.'

She followed his gaze as he looked along the table at the fare she'd arranged. Not the simple mutton of ordinary days, but a sumptuous banquet to end the fasting of Advent. There were platters of pork loin, goose in succulent sauce, roast fowl glazed with mustard and honey, mince pasties and plum porridge, spiced pears and apples. And white bread instead of the usual rye, mulled wine as well as mead.

'We lived in barns, like animals, and ate whatever we could get.' Rhun met her eyes again and a ghost of humour hovered in his voice. 'But I hope you won't think my table manners have become as bad as those of Cynan ap Maredudd?'

Eleanor smiled and shook her head, remembering that day when everything that had blended together so naturally and so joyfully the night before had seemed to shatter about them like broken glass. 'No, Cynan's manners would take some beating, I fear.'

'As you most eloquently pointed out to him. And, as I remember, I agreed with you.'

His face wasn't just thinner, she noticed, but older too, the lines around his mouth and eyes more marked. But it was the shadow of disillusionment etched clearly across his fine features that pulled at her heart. 'Did you do all you meant to do in Caereinion, Rhun?'

'No, the men there are either afraid or have become too English after living so long on the border.' He drained his cup and held it out for the servitor waiting at table to refill. 'But tell me how have things been here in my absence?'

Eleanor's hand almost went to her belly, her news leaping to her lips at the same time. But that news would be best saved until they had privacy. Besides, she didn't know how she felt about it yet, let alone how to voice it, or how to receive whatever reaction it met.

She gestured out at the room. 'I've been making some changes while you've been away.'

'Yes, so I see.' His eyes returned to hers. 'And how have *you* fared this last month?'

How could she tell him that she'd scanned the horizon daily for his coming because she'd missed him so much? And that at the same time she'd enjoyed truly being free to do as she pleased for the first time in her life and it was his absence that had made that possible?

'I have fared very well,' she replied, telling him nothing.

His gaze dropped and he stared down at his hands, wrapping them around his cup. It was a long while before he spoke again. 'The hall hasn't looked like this since… since I was a boy.'

'That is a pity.' Eleanor wondered if he'd been going to say since his mother had decorated the hall for the Christmas festival. 'But I hope you think it well that we celebrate the feast properly this year.'

He looked up at her. 'In case we don't see another Christmas?'

She nodded. If he was disillusioned about the success of the rebellion, as he appeared to be, what was the point of her not facing up to the truth too? Not speaking the truth wouldn't keep it at bay or change the outcome at all.

'Yes. If this is really to be our last Christmas, then we must treasure every moment of it.'

There was a beat of silence, and then he put his goblet down and laid his hand over hers. Eleanor almost flinched, so intimate and unexpected was the gesture, but all the same she felt the warmth of his skin begin to seep into hers.

'God willing, that will not be how things turn out.' His thumb began stroking the back of her hand. 'But at least we will have some weeks of peace over the winter, before we have to face whatever comes.'

She searched his face and a stab of fear pierced her. What would happen to their child, to *all* of them, in such a future? When war came would she still stand at Rhun's side, even though it might endanger her babe? But how could she leave him when she loved him more than life itself?

'I see you're wearing the brooch I gave you.'

Eleanor blinked at the sudden change of topic, her free hand going to her throat, where the little silver clasp that had been her wedding gift fastened her cloak. From nowhere came the thought that her gift to him was still in her coffer upstairs—a gift that she'd never had the opportunity to give to him after their wedding day.

'I missed you, Eleanor.'

'Did you?' she asked, trying to keep the tremble of shock from her voice.

'Yes, there were nights...'

His hand tightened on hers briefly, before his fingers relaxed again. Eleanor held her breath as his thumb went on stroking, his eyes lowering away from hers, his voice dropping too as he went on.

'That last day before I left...the things you said to me in my chamber.' His gaze lifted to hers again and locked on fast. 'It wasn't what it seemed, Eleanor. I couldn't explain it then, and I can't really explain it now. But you were wrong in what you thought...that your blemish offended me.' He lifted her hand to his mouth, turned it, kissed the inside of her wrist, his lips burning hot against her skin. 'So let us forget that we ever parted as we did and make amends for that now, as man and wife, while we still can.'

Her heart started to drum in her breast. Apart from their wedding day, Rhun had never kissed her publicly, and the fact that he did so now sent her mind reeling even as her blood quickened in her veins. Did this mean he really was glad to see her? Glad to be back? That he really had missed her? Or had he just missed a woman in his bed this last month and more?

At her lack of response his head drew back and his eyes searched hers. In them she watched the questions, the doubts, and the slow dawning of realisation. 'Perhaps I am assuming too much. Perhaps you didn't miss me at all.'

Eleanor tried to speak but couldn't find the words. She'd missed him more than she could ever tell him— more than she'd expected to miss him. And as she stared into his eyes her heart crumpled. Whether he lied or spoke the truth to her, about anything, he was her husband and she loved him. Nothing would change that now.

'I...' she began, but she'd hesitated too long.

His eyes narrowed and he relinquished her hand,

placing it back in her lap. Then he picked up his cup
and turned away to stare down the hall.

'Of course you have had much else to occupy your
thoughts and your time while I've been gone.'

Suddenly a shout went up from someone near the
doorway and Dafydd Genau'r Glyn leapt from his seat.
'The cock has crowed!' He strummed his *crwth* with a
flourish. *'Dewch i'r plygain!'*

The poet roused the entire hall, waking those who
had fallen asleep at table or were lying alone or with a
companion along the walls. The villagers at the bottom
of the hall stirred, woke their sleeping babies, called to
heel the children still awake in play. The baskets of candles arrived, and as the servitors began lighting them and
handing them out a sense of excited awe filled the hall.

Rhun turned to her, his brows lifting. 'Christmas carols?'

Eleanor nodded, the occasion saving her from having to either confirm or deny his comment about having missed him, from having to betray her heart, her
soul. For she might love him, but did he love her? *Could*
he love her?

'Will you attend?'

His gaze roamed over her face for a long moment
before he answered. 'Yes, of course. Did you think I
would not?'

'Well...you don't go to the chapel very often.' As she
said it Eleanor thought of the three times he had—how
each occasion had revealed a little more of her husband,
yet had also obscured him too. 'And I don't think I've
ever seen you pray.'

His head dipped for a moment. 'I stopped praying

to a God who wasn't listening a long time ago, Eleanor.' His eyes met hers again and then his hand reached for hers once more. 'But it is fitting that both Lord and Lady attend the *plygain*.'

The celebration in the chapel to welcome Christ's Mass Day was beautiful. The carrying of the candles across the snowy courtyard, the carols and prayers led by Dafydd, the hushed sense of expectation as dawn approached. Less than fifty could fit into the tiny chapel, and most stood outside under the stars, wrapped up against the cold, everyone holding a candle, even the children.

Inside, before the altar, Eleanor stood next to Rhun, and prayed and sang—at least those few carols that were in Latin. The ones in Welsh, though beyond her grasp, were equally moving, and, even though the church was cold the occasion infused her soul with warmth. It was all so hopeful, despite the war that would resume come the spring, that her eyes misted and her hand crept inside her cloak to her stomach, to caress the new life growing there.

In the candlelight, the tomb of Rhun's parents looked both eerie and beautiful. And she no longer wondered, as she had when she'd first seen it, why Owain's eyes were not turned upward to heaven but looked aside at Morfudd, his hand over hers above her heart. There was both love and retribution in the essence of it, and she understood now the Lord Owain's desire to lie like that for all eternity, in sorrow and remorse and above all in love for his wife, even within the grave.

She glanced from the tomb to Rhun. His lips weren't moving at all, neither to sing nor to pray, and his face bore no trace of joy or awe. Slowly she inched nearer, until her sleeve brushed his, willing the warmth of her body to pass through her clothes into his. Willing him to find release from his sorrows and troubles too, but in this life, not the next.

Rhun's eyelashes flickered and slowly his head turned towards her. The carol she was singing died on her lips as his hand found hers. He began to sing, in a deep, rich velvet voice that made the strange Welsh language suddenly full of meaning. The shyness that had spoiled their greeting when he'd ridden in through the gates and the awkwardness that had sat between them at table seemed to melt away. And even war and death seemed almost meaningless in this peaceful and joyous celebration of life.

The *plygain* ended and the crowd behind them parted to let the Lord and Lady leave the chapel first. Outside, dawn was beginning to break in a thin edge of blue on the skyline as everyone extinguished their candles and headed off to find a bed for an hour or two.

Rhun and she were about to mount the steps to the keep when he drew her aside, into the shadow of the wall. And, once again, just like that night when he'd carried her across the wet courtyard, he came close and laid his forehead against hers.

'Eleanor… I need to know.'

Eleanor felt the coldness that hung about his clothes clash with the warmth of his breath on her face. 'Know what?'

'Did you miss me as I did you? I was away a long time—too long—but I yearned for you every moment, Eleanor. I needed you…' His head lifted again and his eyes burned down into hers. 'God, you're my wife, and yet when I saw you today I hardly knew you. You've changed so much.'

Eleanor nodded. 'I *am* changed, Rhun, and for the better, I hope. But I… I'm still your wife.'

His arms slid around her waist. 'Are you, Eleanor?'

'Yes,' she said, her blood warming despite the cold that turned her breath to mist. 'And I did miss you… very much.'

In the light of dawn the reflection of the snow against the sky made everything suddenly so clear. And when he dipped his head and took her mouth, even though his lips were cold and the chill of his skin shocking on her face, Eleanor sensed something of the remoteness in him retreat.

He drew her closer still, and his hands delved beneath her cloak as he brought her hips in contact with his, making her gasp. Her heart began to throb as his mouth dipped to her throat, kissed the spot where the blood pulsed fast. Her knees went weak and moist heat pooled between her thighs, and the ache that began to gnaw deep in her belly was almost unbearable.

'Take me to bed, Rhun,' she whispered, with a shake of anticipation in her voice, her need of him making her bold.

He lifted his head and the glaze of desire in his eyes dimmed a little as he shook his head. 'There is something I must explain first…something you need to understand. When I left your bed that night it was because when I sleep my dreams are…troubled and I am…restless.'

The seriousness of his face made the words, which were commonplace enough, serious too. 'But everyone has nightmares, Rhun. I do often.'

'Not like mine.' His mouth pulled tight for an instant, as if he was reliving one of those nightmares right there and then. 'But I'm telling you now so that you know why I will have to leave your bed again tonight, and every night. I do so for reasons of my own and it is nothing in you.' He lifted his hand and his fingers brushed her birthmark. 'This mark of yours does not disgust or sicken me, and it is not the reason I cannot sleep the whole night with you. Do you believe me, Eleanor?'

Eleanor nodded. She *had* to believe him. If she continued to disbelieve, to doubt, to fear ridicule and repulsion, then there would be no change in her after all. She lifted her hands to his face, tracing the bones of cheek and jaw with her fingertips. 'Yes, I do believe you, Rhun.'

His palm moved lower and closed over her breast. 'Then come, *f'anwylyd*, to bed. I have waited too long already.'

'As have I,' she breathed, for it was true.

With the return of the men, winter closed in with a vengeance. The days became short and crisp, and darkness came swiftly and so cold that the water in the well froze. But the nights were long and sweet and full of pleasure, because Rhun lay with Eleanor on each and every one of them. Sometimes, when their bodies joined together so intensely, so inseparably, he wondered how he'd ever managed to exist before without her in his arms. But he always left her before dawn. If he didn't, he knew what would happen, sooner or later.

Not that his dark dreams and tormented sleep were a secret any more. His nights in Caereinion had seen to that. Once, at least, he'd known he'd cried out, for it had not only woken him but his men lying nearby too. Mercifully not one of them had alluded to it. But they must have whispered among themselves, wondered and speculated at what monstrous nightmares assailed their lord at night.

If Eleanor ever had cause to wonder and speculate with them, he wouldn't be able to bear it. And should she ever ask him, what could he answer? No, he would take his pleasure with his wife, give her the same pleasure in return, but he would never sleep in peace at her side, no matter how much he longed to wake up to the new day in her arms.

News of the rebellion ceased altogether as the end of December came and snow enclosed the castle like a thick white blanket. The feast to see out the old year and welcome the new was as lavish as the Christmas feast had been. And, as then, Eleanor invited all the villagers to share it and the hall brimmed over with life, like it had done in the old days.

When the time for gift-giving arrived Rhun bestowed a small amount of money upon everyone in his household, Eleanor likewise upon all the villagers. Huw, looking ten years younger now he was in love, gave Alice a book of hours and rendered the woman speechless for once. Her gift in return was a pair of soft grey-coloured gauntlets that she'd stitched herself, lined with wool and embroidered with intricate cuffs of green silk thread. The last gifts of all to be exchanged, as per the custom, were those between the Lord and the Lady. Rhun gave Eleanor a pair of bosses for Mistletoe's bridle, worked in bronze and pewter, with a pattern on the disc depicting the full moon edged with a circle of stars.

As he pressed his gift into her hand, she gasped. 'Oh, they're beautiful, Rhun!'

'My smith has worked on them day and night for the last week. He'll be gratified that you like them—as am I.'

'Like them?' Her eyes glowed up at him. 'I've never seen anything more skilfully and delicately wrought.' Then her gaze swept the hall until she found the blacksmith among the tables and she smiled her thanks.

Eurig flushed, Rhun noticed, not just with pleasure at producing a good piece of work but with unmistakable affection.

Then Eleanor drew out a bundle from beneath her chair that had obviously been hidden there as a surprise. She held it out to him, her eyes sparkling and a hint of shyness in her voice. 'And here is your gift. It was meant to be given to you on our wedding day, but I hope you will accept it now, my lord.'

Rhun's blood froze and the walls around him seemed to tilt and sway. The noise in the hall filled his head like a landslide. He stared mutely at the crimson folds of cloth and dug his fingernails into his palms, but his skin had turned to ice and sweat broke out between his shoulder blades. He felt his mouth twist in a grimace, but could do nothing to prevent it as his voice came, devoid of any gratitude at all.

'It is very fine, thank you.'

Her face fell, the pleasure fading from her eyes. 'It is a riding cloak, made of Flemish wool…it should keep you warm.'

Rhun's hand shook as he reached out and took the cloak, the scarlet blinding him and the weave, for all its softness, tearing at his fingers. His throat was dry and he couldn't speak, and to his dismay Eleanor took his silence for something it was not.

'Of course, if you don't like it, it doesn't matter.'

His heart heaved at the disappointment in her voice, but he tried to block it from his ears as he called his body servant forward. He'd instruct the man to take the cloak away, place it in his coffer, where it would remain hidden from his sight. And eventually, one day, he'd forget about it—just as Eleanor would.

But he couldn't block out her crestfallen face or the flash of hurt in her eyes. If he dismissed her gift now, he wouldn't just hurt her, he'd shame her too, in front of the entire hall. And he knew, as her lashes lowered and a flush mounted her cheeks, that he could do neither—whatever it cost him. So, his heart pounding in his chest and his breath stalling in his lungs, Rhun put the red cloak down on the table and, taking off the one he wore, handed it to the waiting manservant.

'Please place this upstairs in my coffer.' Then he turned and looked full at Eleanor. 'I will put on my new cloak now and be proud to wear it.'

Aware of not only her eyes, but also those of the whole company, he stood up. His legs felt hollow and his stomach threatened to throw up all that he'd eaten and drunk that night. But he gritted his teeth and, his eyes clinging to Eleanor's as if she might anchor him, fought to conquer himself this one time for her alone.

Shaking out the cloak, he found it was indeed finely woven, soft and thick, and edged with a delicate pattern in silver thread. He'd never owned anything of such quality, let alone worn such a garment, and if he didn't put it on now, he knew he never would. As he swung it around his shoulders his skin shuddered, but he clasped the cloak firmly at his throat. It felt as if it shrouded him in flames, not fine wool, as he retook his seat and placed his hand over Eleanor's.

'Thank you again…very much.' His voice wasn't quite level, and nausea still swirled in his belly, but he forced himself to smile at her. 'How does it look, my lady?'

How did it look? Eleanor shuddered as Rhun's cold, clammy hand enclosed hers and his face stood out wan against the colour of the cloak. Not that he didn't look fine in it—in fact, he looked like a king, with the garment nobly cresting his shoulders, the bold scarlet complementing the black fall of his hair. He looked splendid, and he did the cloak justice as it did him. But there was something in the stiffness of his jaw, the depths of his eyes, that told her all was not well.

She returned his smile, strained though it was, and tried to calm her foreboding. 'It looks very regal.'

But there had been an awful moment when he'd stared down at her gift with horror on his face, and she'd thought he was going to refuse it. Or worse, hurl it from him with displeasure and shame her before everyone. Even as he'd put it on there'd been a strange glimmer in his eyes, almost like that of a warrior going into battle. A look of determination and yet with the fear that always underlaid courage.

'Then I'll wear it with pride and with gratitude.'

He leaned in and kissed her mouth, and everything in the hall resumed as before, or nearly so. Rhun called for more wine, and smiled and applauded at the entertainments. Eleanor also smiled and clapped at the singing. She listened to and was moved by Dafydd's poetry, drank a little more wine than she normally did. But an atmosphere of discomfort had joined them at the table and sat between them now, spoiling the merriment.

At the end of the evening she stood with Rhun and they gave the whole company their blessing for the year to come. They left the hall together, went up to her chamber, and as the old year died made love in her bed. But it was a lovemaking that made her want to weep, and she didn't know why. Rhun possessed her urgently, then tenderly, cherished and fulfilled her, and afterwards, instead of leaving as he normally did, he held her tightly in his arms, as if he'd never let her go.

She lay still, her body tense, waiting for the awful moment when he would place a final kiss on her mouth, then ease himself up and away from her. But it didn't come, and as she finally drifted into sleep, his warm body curved into hers, Eleanor knew that this night he would stay. Even so, she sensed that old distance was back, lodged like a rampart between them. And for the first time since his return, this first time he meant to sleep with her till dawn, she knew he wasn't really there with her at all—not in his soul.

So where was he?

Chapter Thirteen

As the old year slipped into the new Rhun lay awake in Eleanor's arms. The night was so clear and so quiet that he could count the hours as they tolled from the monastery bell in the distance. And with each peal, each passing hour, the crushing weight on his chest grew heavier until his breath laboured. His whole body was bathed in sweat and a rising panic gripped his throat and filled his nose and mouth with fear.

Eleanor must have sensed his unease, or perhaps felt the searing heat of his naked skin next to hers, because she slept but fitfully, half waking from time to time, her hand feeling for him, touching his chest, his face, as if to reassure herself that he was still there.

The curtains of the bed weren't drawn and the room encroached upon him all around. There were no candles burning, and the boards over the windows shut out the moonlight. From the hearth came a dim glow, but Rhun didn't need any light to see the scarlet cloak. It was lying on the floor where he'd dropped it, along with the rest of his clothes, and Eleanor's too. The garment, for all it was invisible in the blackness, seemed to glare out its colour and its challenge as clear as daylight. Taunting him, blinding him, daring him to face it.

And as he sensed Eleanor drift back once more into sleep Rhun knew that face it he had to. Because that night, when Eleanor had held out the red cloak, his eyes had been opened. He'd seen the truth of his fear and now he had to confront and conquer it. And he had to do it tonight. If he didn't, what future was there for either of them? Wars could be fought, causes won or lost, but the inner battles would still be there—the enemy inside, always waiting to strike. Even Eleanor had said that to him, so long ago now it seemed like another lifetime and he another man altogether.

Perhaps she had no love for him beyond the passion they shared in bed. Perhaps she never would, never could love somebody like him. But that didn't matter. What did matter was that he had to become a husband she could trust, rely on to keep her safe and well. And how could he do that if he wasn't whole?

Quietly, Rhun slipped out from under the furs and, steeling himself, picked up the scarlet cloak. His flesh shuddered, and a mist of red fell over his eyes, but he pulled the garment tightly around him. And with the soft material scraping like chainmail against his naked skin he left the chamber, closing the door softly behind him.

Eleanor awoke, startled by a noise that had broken into her dream, and felt the emptiness of the space beside her. She put out a hand, found nothing, and knew that Rhun had left her again—though not long ago, for the place where he'd lain was still warm. She turned into the imprint of his body, breathing in the scent of him that lingered, but into her mind drifted a strange sense of unease. This wasn't like all the other times he'd left her, after claiming her body and capturing her heart at the same time. This absence was different somehow, as if he had left something behind. Something that hadn't gone with him. Something that hinted he might return—and yet might not.

She sat up and peered into the darkness, a chill touching her bare flesh, causing goosebumps to break out on her arms. There was nothing to be heard now, but her scalp prickled in the eerie silence. Getting out of bed, she picked her way over to the hearth and, from the dying embers, lit a taper, and with it some of the candles on the walls. Her clothes were where she had left them the previous night, in a pile on the floor next to the bed. As she stooped to gather them up she saw Rhun's clothes were still there too, entangled with hers. All except the scarlet cloak she'd given him.

Her heart pulsing in her throat, Eleanor pulled on her shift and under-tunic and, taking a candle, turned for the door. The torches still burned in the passageway but there was no sound from down below, or from Huw's room where Alice now slept, the gallant steward having decamped to the men's quarters over the gatehouse until they were wed. A draught touched her face and she saw the door to the turret was wide open. Her first thought was to close it, but even as her hand reached out Eleanor paused.

Something was wrong. She could feel it in the air

that came down the stone steps to greet her, as if it was calling her upwards.

A step at a time, she climbed up and went out through the door at the top, which was open too—although it shouldn't be. The battlements had been cleared of snow, but the landscape around was startlingly white and it was freezing. The moon was huge and low in the sky and the stars glittered like jewels carved out of ice. And beneath it Rhun stood like a spectre, looking out over the rampart wall.

Eleanor blinked, for he was hardly clothed. His feet were bare, and he had only the scarlet cloak wrapped around him like a shroud. Putting the candle carefully down on the stones, she moved towards him. As she did so she saw that he was trembling and that his face was ashen. Fear closed around her heart.

'Rhun...what are you doing up here?'

He half turned his head and, illuminated by the moon, his profile seemed to be chiselled from stone, his lips colourless, his eyes dark and yet vivid. Despite the cold, his brow glistened with sweat, as if he was burning up with a fever.

'What do you want, Eleanor?'

He spoke curtly, but she resisted the impulse to turn and go back the way she'd come. 'I woke and you were gone, so I came to find you.'

He looked out again over the rampart wall, pulling the cloak more tightly around him. 'I woke you... I'm sorry.'

'You didn't wake me...though something did.' She glanced about her for clues, for some sign of disturbance or danger, but there was none. 'What is wrong, Rhun?'

He didn't answer for a moment, and when he finally did his tone was empty and the words made no sense at all. 'I know now what it is.'

'I don't understand…'

'Neither did I…until tonight. Although I should have realised that other time.'

'Rhun, you are not making any sense. What should you have realised?'

'That it wasn't just the cloak…'

'The cloak?' In the moonlight, the garment seemed to spill like black blood over Rhun's shoulders. 'What about it? Is there something wrong with it?'

'*Uffern*, if it were only that simple…' A harsh sound came from his lips and he shook his head, turning away to look out into the distance again. 'Go away, Eleanor.'

Eleanor took a step closer. 'No, not until you tell me what it is that brings you out here to stand naked in the freezing cold.'

The night was so crisp and so clear that the footsteps of the watch over the gatehouse, and the sudden gruff cough the man gave, could be heard plainly. The noise seemed to startle Rhun into speech.

'Do you remember the day Cynan came, when you wore scarlet?'

Frantically, Eleanor cast her mind back to the day after she and Rhun had first lain together. What had she worn? 'I wore my vermilion tunic,' she said. 'But I still don't understand.'

'That colour…' His voice shook so much her ears struggled to catch the words. 'It took me back there, to that day.'

'Back where?'

In the sharp air, she heard him drag in a breath, saw it come out again like white mist, to dissipate into nothingness. 'To the day my mother was killed.'

Eleanor hardly dared draw her own breath. She wrapped her arms around her as her limbs began to shiver, not only with cold but with premonition too. 'Why does scarlet take you back to that day, Rhun?'

'It's not the colour alone, Eleanor...' He sighed heavily, as if weary. 'I've seen blood countless times—in tournaments, in fighting. I've seen men slain and not flinched. But when I saw *you* wear scarlet, saw *you* touch it...you, my wife... I watched my mother die all over again...'

He stopped, and Eleanor had to bite her tongue so as not to urge him to go on. If Rhun was to tell her the whole story of that terrible day it had to be in his own time, and by his own volition. And then, God willing, she'd understand everything, and might even be able to comfort him.

After a long moment, he began to speak again. 'We were returning to the castle when they came. We ran back to the village, tried to stop them, but they didn't listen. They were bent on slaughter.'

Eleanor realised her legs were trembling, and heard the same tremble in her voice. 'M-my father's men?'

He nodded. 'Their leader—the knight I told you about—rode me down with his horse, breaking my leg. My mother ran towards me...screaming at him...and then...'

There was a choke in his voice and his head bowed for a moment before it lifted again.

'And then he rode on and took her throat out with his sword.'

Eleanor's hands flew to her mouth, and the tears that

sprang to her eyes were shockingly hot in the cold air. 'Oh, dear God!'

'I just lay there and watched the blood run down the front of her dress…so much blood, Eleanor… And her gown turned red as she fell…'

'Oh, Rhun!' His name came out on a sob. 'Oh, I'm so sorry… I don't know what to say…how to comfort you…'

He turned so swiftly that she gasped. 'Comfort me? Didn't you hear me right? I said that I just lay there, crying like a boy, cringing like a coward, and did nothing.'

'But what *could* you have done?' She stepped forward, reached out a hand and let it drop again as he jerked away. 'Rhun, you were a *child*,' she said softly, but with weight on her last word. 'You were hurt…there *was* nothing you could do. Don't you see that?'

'But I didn't even try…' His knuckles were white where they clutched the edges of the scarlet cloak, and as his voice broke so did her heart. 'I couldn't get up. I… I couldn't move…'

'Your leg was broken, and you must have been dazed too. Even if you *had* been able to rise, go to her, you would have been too late to save her. Rhun, you were lucky not to have been killed as well.'

'Lucky!' In the moonlight, the grief on his face changed to fury. 'What does *luck* have to do with it? I should have stopped her running back to the village. I should have made her flee to safety—dragged her if necessary. It should have been *me* who died, not her!'

Eleanor's heart wept at the brutal self-punishment she was witnessing. How could she make him see how it really was? That he was blameless, innocent of his mother's death, and as much a casualty of that day as she'd been, even though he'd survived. For Morfudd must have died quickly, if horribly, whereas Rhun had clearly lived every day and every hour since in hell, tormented by his self-inflicted wounds.

'She wouldn't have wished that. Any parent would give their life to save their child. I would. *You* would.'

His eyes blazed furiously into hers. 'That doesn't change what happened.'

'No, it doesn't.' Carefully, Eleanor reached out again, touched his arm, felt the icy chill of his skin beneath the cloak. 'But you can't go on punishing yourself. Your mother would be heartbroken to see you suffer like this, to know you've carried this burden for so long. Rhun, you must forgive yourself.' He started to shake his head, but she moved her hand from his arm to his cheek. 'You *must*—otherwise your mother will have died in vain.'

'What do you mean?'

'She went back to try and save the villagers, and she tried to save you too. Don't you think she would want to spare you from a life of grief and remorse? A living death is still a death, Rhun.'

He shook his head. 'Even if I could forgive myself, how can a man be a husband to his wife when he can't bear to look at her if she wears red? When he goes to pieces right in front of her eyes, shaming himself and her before his whole household? When he can't guarantee that he won't crumble when she's in danger, when she needs him most? Eleanor... I couldn't bear to lose you too...'

His voice cracked again. 'You won't lose me!' Eleanor gripped his arms fiercely. 'And I won't wear red, and neither will you. We'll put those garments away until the time comes to take them out again.' He broke away from her but she followed, made him look at her, tried to make him listen and believe. 'There is no shame in that. It doesn't mean you are a coward. It makes you even braver that you try to face your fears and conquer them.'

'You would not say so if you knew how I long to fling this cloak away from me, Eleanor, and never look at it again—even for your sake.'

'You are putting yourself through this for *me*?'

There was no answer, and she didn't need one, for she understood everything now—not just his pain but his pride, his honour, his courage.

'Rhun, please…don't torture yourself any more. Have compassion for yourself as you would for anyone who suffered. Come down with me. Take off the red cloak. For you don't have to prove anything to me, my love.'

Under the moon, Eleanor saw the battle in his eyes— the denial, the rage, the grief and the guilt. Things she'd never seen clearly before, although there had been glimpses right from the beginning. Slowly, carefully, hardly daring to hope, she opened her arms, offering him the only thing she could. Her love and her forgiveness.

Rhun stared for a long while, and then, with an inarticulate sound, he stepped into them. His cheek was like ice against hers, and he was shivering so much that it made her shiver too. But there was warmth in her heart nonetheless. Because he hadn't just stepped into her arms, he'd allowed her to step into his soul. A bridge had been crossed, up here in the quiet moonlit night, and surely now they could only go forward, not back?

She closed her eyes, breathed in the frosty air and felt it invigorate her, filling her with a new strength that would help sustain them both, whatever came. For a long time—hours, it seemed—they stood like that, not speaking, hardly breathing. And then Eleanor opened her eyes again and smiled.

'Rhun!' she whispered, awe filling her sight with tears. 'Look!'

His head lifted and his gaze followed hers to where the walls were turning to silver. At first the moon bathed the frost that lay like tiny jewels along the top of the ramparts, making them glisten. And then slowly the whole of the stonework changed from black to grey to white to shining silver. At her side, Rhun gave a breath of awe too, and Eleanor felt some of the tension leave his body. And she knew that not just a bridge but a chasm had been crossed as they watched as some celestial hand painted the walls with moonlight.

It was only a matter of moments before the strange occurrence vanished. But it had happened, and they'd seen it together. When Rhun looked back at her his gaze was still dark, but not quite as desolate as it had been. And his voice, though achingly empty, carried no pain in it now, just the thin echo of anguish.

'It's just a trick of the heavens, Eleanor...'

'Is it, Rhun?' Her heart beat faster. 'How does the *englyn* go again?'

'"*Yn y nos daeth y lleuad...un hudol...*"' The words faded away into the night and he shook his head. 'This is foolish, Eleanor.'

But Eleanor took the words up, reciting the poem in the Welsh Dafydd Genau'r Glyn had taught her. '*"Blodeuad, ein gobaith heb amheuad"*—"a flowering of our hope without doubt—a beginning…"' She placed her palm over his heart. 'Rhun, perhaps tonight is our hope, our new beginning. This wondrous thing we've seen must *mean* something—a blessing, or perhaps even a miracle. Miracles can happen. They *do* happen sometimes, if we can see them and interpret them correctly.'

'A miracle?'

Rhun's hair glistened with frost and the bones of his face were stark in the moonlight. And then, at last, he smiled at her—a bleak smile, but a smile nonetheless. He drew the scarlet cloak around them both and held her close to his naked body, though he still trembled and his skin was clammy with sweat.

'If miracles really do happen, then one happened the day you rode in through my gates. *You're* my miracle, Eleanor.'

Eleanor swallowed down the sob of joy that rose into her throat. She lifted her eyes to the moon again, so low that she could almost reach out and touch it, and sent her thanks soaring upwards. What they'd just seen might have been simply a trick of the heavens, as he'd said it was. Or it might be so much more than that, if they only believed in hope, in each other, and in the future.

When Eleanor opened her eyes the following morning Rhun was still beside her, his arm lying warm and heavy across her breast, fast asleep. She gazed at his face, so beautiful beneath the black tousled hair. It was impossible to recall now the habitual scowl that had once marred his brow, or the sullen set of his mouth. For as he slept his face seemed younger and his lips, slightly curved, almost smiled as he breathed peacefully, his whole body relaxed and content.

And then, as his mouth stretched wide into a real smile, she realised that he wasn't asleep at all! His lashes flickered open and the daylight brightened his dark gaze, making her heart swell with love.

'*Dydd da.*'

'*Dydd da,*' she repeated, smiling back at him.

There was a little pause as his eyes roamed over her face keenly, as if he'd never seen it before or was seeing it differently now. 'Did we really watch the walls turn silver last night, Eleanor—or did I dream it?'

When they'd left the battlements last night, and returned to her bed, Rhun had fallen asleep as soon as he'd drawn the covers up over them and folded her in his arms. They hadn't spoken further of what had happened up there, beneath the moon.

'No, not a dream,' she replied, 'but a miracle, Rhun.'

He stared deeply into her eyes and then lifted her hand and kissed her palm. 'Thank you.'

'For what?'

'For what you said…what you did last night…for being my wife and my miracle.'

As he reached for her, drew her close, Eleanor felt herself wrapped not just in his arms but in the sense of hope that seemed to embrace them both. A hope that, as they lay quietly and long moments passed, spurred her to speak at last of something else.

'Well, this morning there may be no moon, but there is another miracle that I need to tell you about.' Taking his hand, she placed his palm over her stomach. 'The one growing inside me.'

His head lifted off the pillow and he leaned up onto his elbow, his eyes growing wide and incredulous. 'You're with child?'

She nodded. 'Our child.'

'Our child…' A frown darkened his brow, darkened the bright morning. '*Arglwydd*…and I left you alone. I should have been here.'

'The babe won't come for many months yet,' Eleanor reassured him. 'And whether I'd told you a month ago, or today, it wouldn't have hastened its arrival.'

But still he stared down at her, his expression shocked and concerned, and her joy faltered a little. Had she chosen the wrong moment to tell him after all? Should she have waited until the throes of those tortured hours on the battlements had faded completely?

'Then I'm to be a father…' His voice was sombre, distant, as if her news hadn't quite touched him yet. 'When will it be born?'

'In summertime, I think.'

As she said the words, now that he knew, it suddenly became real. Now they were truly man and wife at last, and their child was proof of that. All men wanted a child—a son, an heir—and their child would bring them closer still… But what if their child wasn't a boy, but a girl? Would Rhun be disappointed? Resent it as her father resented her?

Like a black cloud obscuring the sun, dread settled over Eleanor's heart, obscuring her joy.

'Rhun…' She had to ask—now, not later—and confront the fear that had been brewing since the moment she'd accepted that she was with child. 'I know all men hope for a son…but if this child is a daughter, you won't be…disappointed?'

His brow cleared and a smile reappeared at the corner of his mouth. 'And when did you come to know so much about what men want, *fy'nghariad i*?'

Eleanor felt herself blush right down to her toes at the memory of those blissful hours when Rhun had taught her much about what men wanted from their wives. She gave his arm a little thump to cover her shyness, even as her blood quickened in her veins. 'That's not what I meant! All men require a son and heir, and I fully intend to give you one, but should this first child be a girl, will you welcome her?'

Rhun's smile was the first to fade, his eyes growing sober. 'I will welcome all the children you give me, Eleanor, whether they be boys or girls.' His hand smoothed tenderly over her still flat stomach, his gaze intent on hers. 'I am not your father.'

Eleanor placed her hand over his. Her husband had never displayed any of the cruelty, in thought or deed, that she knew her father to be capable of. And she knew now, with a certainty that went beyond mere knowing, that he never could. 'I know. I just needed to hear you say it.'

'I seem to be saying a lot of things lately.' A shadow of regret flickered across his face. 'Perhaps I should have said them much earlier.'

'The important thing is that they are said. It is only then that healing can come, Rhun.'

His hand left her belly and cupped her face, his thumb brushing her mouth. 'But there are times, too, when words are not necessary for healing to happen.'

Her lips parted as his touch moved to other places, to her throat, her breast, her belly again, and then between her legs. And when he moved over her and possessed her Eleanor prayed that they would *both* heal together over the years.

The morning of Huw and Alice's wedding dawned and Eleanor awoke to find herself alone. At once, her heart turned over in dread, for there were still nights when the horrors took Rhun from her. Sometimes she would wake too, and he'd kiss her, hold her briefly, then go swiftly, without a word. Other times she didn't miss him until morning, when only the cold and empty space beside her told her of his anguish. But the pain was always as sharp, either way.

Then she heard the shutters being opened at the windows. The next moment the curtains around the bed were swept back, and Rhun's dark eyes were laughing down at her.

'Get up, *ngwraig i*! No time to lie abed today.'

He turned and poured two goblets of wine. He wore a dark blue chamber robe belted loosely around his lean body, and her blood quickened. Her husband was so comely, his face noble in every line and hollow, the black hair in disarray from their lovemaking the night before.

Eleanor lifted herself onto one elbow as an ache of need opened up inside her. She yearned for him so ardently that sometimes it shocked her. Did all wives become so wanton? Did all wives spend so much time in bed with their husbands? Or was it only those who loved their husbands more than life itself?

'Come back to bed, Rhun,' she murmured. 'Surely it is not as late as all that?'

Leaving the wine where it was, he came over and dropped down beside her. As he always did, after his first kiss good morning, he moved his hand to her belly, caressing both her and the life within. 'It is already the hour of Terce, *fy'nghariad.*'

Eleanor smiled. He did that often now, murmured soft words of affection, the sort of words that she hadn't learned from Dafydd Genau'r Glyn. These sweet and intense words were murmured in the ecstasy of their lovemaking, uttered by day too, when they were alone. He'd never told her that he loved her, but nevertheless, as each of those precious endearments fell like honey into her ears, she felt herself becoming a part of him.

Her heart lurched. She *was* part of him, whether he was with her or away from her, in her bed or about his business, whether he loved her or not. *She* loved, and Alice had been right—if one loved, that was enough.

'And we must soon do our matrimonial duties—I know!' she said, her voice quivering with the knowledge that she would be a part of him even when he rode away to face battle. 'But not just yet...'

Wrapping her arms about his neck, she drew him down, pushing the bedcovers back, offering him her naked body and her naked heart too. Their lovemaking was slow and tender and, despite his insistence that there was no time to linger in bed this morning, he drew her to him afterwards and they lay quietly, her head on his chest, his fingers playing with her hair.

Eleanor smoothed her palm down over his body, tracing the magnificent pattern of bone and muscle. And then, with a boldness that no longer shocked her as it had at first, moved lower down still, to caress his loins, the manhood in the hollow between his hips, the taut thighs. One knee was bent, his foot supporting the raised leg, but the other leg, the damaged one, lay stretched out, stiff and awkward.

She passed her fingers gently over the scarred flesh. This also no longer shocked her, but it did and always would move her to pity. 'If I ask you something, Rhun, will you consider it?'

'I must hear it first, *f'anwylyd.*'

'I understand now that when you leave my bed it is to spare me your nightmares…' Eleanor felt his body tense beneath her but she took a breath and carried on. 'Perhaps if you talked with Father Robert you might find the peace you need to conquer and banish them?'

There was a little silence, and when he spoke again his voice was distant. 'Why spoil so happy a day with such things?'

Had her suggestion been too much, too soon? Lifting herself up so that she could see his face, she dropped a kiss onto his mouth, feeling his response come swift and ardent. But even as she yearned to answer the demand of his lips she drew back. 'Did you not seek healing before, when you took your pilgrimage to Santiago de Compostela?'

'And found none.' His eyes became shuttered below the gleam of desire she'd kindled. 'My leg was not mended then and it will not mend now, but it serves me well enough.'

As if to prove it, Rhun hooked his damaged leg over her hip and Eleanor felt his heart begin to drum where her hands rested on his chest. Her own heart had quickened too, with the knowledge of this new power she had to arouse him, and he her. But even as she got to know his body intimately, and as he got to know hers, there was still a part of her husband that he kept hidden from her.

'Yet you didn't go only for a cure for your leg. Weren't you also seeking a cure for your soul?'

The fingers that had begun to curl once more into her hair stilled. 'Are you asking me if I went to rid myself of the remorse I felt over my mother's death?'

She held his gaze. 'Did you?'

He nodded. 'Yes, and I found nothing of that either—until now, with you.' His knuckles brushed softly down her cheek. 'But, since you are so insistent to know, very well… The other thing I sought in Castile was the man who killed her.'

Eleanor's heart skipped a beat. 'Who is he?'

'He is called Rainulf Dallarde.'

'Did you find him?'

'No, although I came close once.' His hand dropped down onto the covers and his eyes slid past her to somewhere far away. 'I heard he was competing in a tournament at Burgos so I entered as well, but he never came.'

A vision of Rhun clad in armour, with a lance braced at his shoulder, galloping towards his mother's killer, rose up in a terrifying scene before her eyes. 'I'm glad he didn't come, for it might have been he who killed you.'

His eyes returned to hers and the resolve in them was like steel, despite the strange softness of his words. 'No, he wouldn't have killed me, Eleanor. He had his chance once and he'll not have another. I had justice on my side and will again, should we meet in battle, or otherwise.'

'He may be dead now, after all these years.'

'And he may be alive still. And if he is one day I will find him and I will kill him. But not today.' Abruptly, the mood shifted, and as he rolled her beneath him again the topic was closed, like the lid of a coffer being shut and locked. 'Today is for more pleasant matters.'

For once Eleanor held him at bay. She hoped that Rainulf Dallarde was indeed already dead, and brought to justice by a hand higher than man's. For if he still lived he would always be there, like a terrifying black cloud on the horizon of this new life she and Rhun had found after that moonlit night up on the battlements. A cloud dark enough to obscure even the fullest and brightest of moons.

'Rhun,' she said, carefully. 'If I make up a potion to help you sleep, will you take it?'

He frowned. 'A potion?'

She nodded, grasping the moment quickly. 'Valerian, perhaps. It won't impair your abilities during the day, but it may keep your nightmares away.'

His head started to shake and Eleanor threaded her fingers into his hair. 'Please, Rhun, try it at least. And if it doesn't help, then no harm is done.'

He dragged in a slow breath, though whether that was to control his desires or his patience she hardly dared wonder. 'Very well. If it pleases you.'

But she wasn't finished yet. 'And…will you talk with Father Robert? Tell him the truth about your mother's death?'

This time the pause was longer. His beautiful eyes bore down into hers, and in them she saw the struggle between shame and pride, resistance and fear, and her heart bled for him.

'I have never spoken of that with anyone but you, Eleanor.'

'And I hope you always do, for I will always listen. But you need spiritual guidance too, and that I cannot give you.'

'Spiritual guidance?' His body seemed to shrink from her, though he hadn't moved a muscle. 'I stopped looking for that long since.'

Eleanor took his face between her hands. 'Then you must look again, Rhun. You cannot live your whole life with this burden. Please, promise me you will think on it, at least?'

The ardour faded from his gaze and she knew there would be no more lovemaking that morning. But after a long silence, while she watched the battle inside him wage to and fro, feeling her heart fighting for and with him, he kissed her mouth softly. And then, as he pulled her up from bed and into the day, the response she'd longed for came almost lightly, though she knew it was anything but.

'Very well. Since you ask it of me, Eleanor, I will think on it.'

Chapter Fourteen

The weather was kinder to Alice and Huw than it had been to her and Rhun four months earlier. The sun shone brightly over the day, though it was still only two weeks into the new year. Rhun was Huw's best man, and Eleanor herself the matron of honour, though the gesture was more one of genuine affection than of custom or largesse. The feast that followed was merry, and there were no doubts in the hearts of the bride and groom, like those that had lurked in hers and Rhun's hearts that faraway September day.

But those doubts were long gone now, as if yet another miracle had been granted to them that night the walls had turned silver. And, whether or not those miracles were real, or just imagined, or merely coincidence, Eleanor embraced each and every one and believed in them wholeheartedly. For who was to say there wasn't to be a fourth miracle? That the war, seemingly as far away now as it ever had been, wouldn't come to Castell y Lleuad after all? That it might even end soon and leave them to live in peace?

When the time came for the married couple to go upstairs, the bride didn't escape with her garter in place this time. Eleanor herself captured it, tussling with Alice as if they were sisters, not lady and maid, until both of them fell laughing down onto the rushes. Her prize at last in her hand, she waved it aloft in triumph and then hugged her maid to her. When their respective husbands hauled them to their feet again, she saw Rhun was laughing just as helplessly. And, as the newlyweds escaped at last, and he led her to their bed, Eleanor prayed with all her heart for that one last miracle of peace instead of war.

But there wasn't to be another miracle. Winter began to wane and spring started to show its tentative colours in the slow greening of the landscape, the reappearance of buds on the trees, the new warmth in the sun that crested the mountains to the east. And finally, in the middle of the month of February, the call to war came and Eleanor felt the world shift beneath her feet.

It was on a bright morning that Rhun sought her out. She was in the herb patch, just outside the postern gate, where Rhun had buried Cai. Over the winter the ground had lain dormant, but now she discovered traces of long neglected yet still thriving herbs—Bishop's Weed, Tansy, Lady Thistle and Gentian, and others that she didn't recognise. Could this little garden bloom again, even though its produce might never be gathered?

As she bent to pull up some weeds around an emerging sprig of Heart's Ease a shadow fell over her. She looked up, shading her eyes against the mid-morning sun, at Rhun's lean figure, dark against the blue sky behind. And her heart turned over at the realisation of how much she loved him.

'What are you doing out here, Eleanor?' He squatted down on his haunches next to her and brushed his knuckles down over her cheek. His other hand reached out and caressed the earth pensively. 'Herbs haven't flourished here for many years.'

Their eyes met, and she saw in his a shadow of memory—one that she understood now, because he'd shared it with her. And although he'd never spoken of Rainulf Dallarde again, and she'd never asked, she knew that the resolve in Rhun's heart was unshakable. As long as that man lived he would always seek him, and if he never found him, he would never truly find peace. Yet he'd agreed to take her potion, and it was soothing his sleep a little. Didn't that mean he must yearn for peace as much as she longed to help him find it?

'Perhaps they haven't, but they've been here all the time nonetheless,' she said, forcing her thoughts back to the moment. For she'd resolved something too, and that was to live and embrace every moment as it came, like a gift to be cherished, not laid aside in worry. 'I think your mother would be glad if they flourished again, don't you?'

He nodded. 'Yes, I think she would. And I too, since I know their benefit now.' His gaze softened. 'Thank you, *fy'nghariad*, for your potion. If not for you...' He stopped and she saw his fingers clench in the soil and relax again. Then, taking her hand, he drew her to her feet. 'Let's walk.'

As they went down the slope that led to the river,

pausing a little while by Cai's grave, Eleanor wondered if being by the herb patch had brought back too many painful memories for Rhun. Yet he spoke much about his mother now, allowing Eleanor to see her through his own eyes until she felt she knew the Lady Morfudd intimately. But something told her it was of other matters he meant to talk about today. Something ominous that had hung over them for the last weeks and that she knew, with every beat of her heart, was about to fall and shatter everything.

They reached the river, lower now that the rains had stopped, its surface dappled with the sun, and a bright young growth of green on the bank beneath their feet. And it was there, as they walked hand in hand in the new grass, that Rhun told her.

'A message has come from Madog ap Llywelyn.'

The simple statement turned the beauty of the day ugly, drove the joy and hope of springtime scuttling backwards to the dark depths of winter. Her free hand went instinctively to her belly, not quite as flat now, but rounded into a small smooth bump as yet invisible beneath her clothes.

'And what does Madog the Rebel want of us?' she asked, aware of the bitterness in her voice but too miserable even to attempt to hide it. 'Or should I say Madog, Prince of Wales, as I hear he calls himself now?'

Rhun felt the flinch of Eleanor's hand in his, the quick jerk of shock that ran through her body. He laced his fingers tighter through hers and led them on, going nowhere in particular. Was it because she carried his child that she seemed more beautiful, more precious to him with every day that passed? Or was it simply that she had become a part of him now, as vital to him as the breath he drew to keep him living?

He couldn't imagine life without her. His nightmares were diminishing since he'd been taking her potion, and if he did wake, with his skin sweating and terror gripping his throat, she was always there with him. He had found his faith in God Almighty again, and lately had even reconsidered her advice about seeking out Father Robert, although he hadn't done so—yet.

'Prince or not, in the end I think it will count for little,' he said. 'We are all rebels in the eyes of the King, whether we be lowly or high-born.'

She looked away from him towards the river they walked beside, and he thought the rippling sunlit water an unsuitable accompaniment to the disaster he was about to lay before her.

'Tell me the worst, Rhun. I need to know.'

Yes, better to speak of that which was urgent—not of his need of her, of his fear of losing this woman who'd become an inseparable part of him.

'The King has retaken all the castles in the northeast and will soon penetrate into the west,' he said. 'Elsewhere, too, we are being driven back, our early victories lost. So Madog intends to deflect Edward's attention here, to the Middle March, while the other regions try to regroup.'

She stopped walking, bringing them to a halt beside a bare oak tree. 'And what will that mean for us?'

'It means that when he comes I will go and fight at his side.' Rhun took both her hands in his. This wasn't news to her. He'd told her long ago where he would stand, and nothing that had happened between them since changed that. 'For Castell y Lleuad it will mean a stand to the bitter end, whatever that proves to be.'

She laid her forehead against his chest. 'I hate this rebellion, Rhun. And I hate Madog and Cynan and all the others who began it. Why must there always be war?'

Encircling her in his arms, Rhun held her close, breathed in the hint of rose petals that scented her hair. A part of him hated this rebellion too, now, and yet not three months ago he had been ready to fight, to kill and to die. But then he'd had nothing to lose, and death hadn't mattered. Now he had everything to lose. Now he wanted to live—for his wife, for his child, and for the first time in a long time for himself.

'Perhaps one day there won't be wars.' He drew back and brushed his knuckles softly down her cheek. 'But, whatever happens, I promise I will keep you and our child safe.'

She looked up into his face, her gaze moist but unafraid. 'I know you will.'

His gut twisted and his heart swelled until he felt it would burst through the wall of his chest. For how could he make promises that he might not be able to keep? And how could she trust him so implicitly when she knew the truth of that? The old feelings of guilt washed to the surface again, but he fought them down. Remorse had eaten at his soul like maggots for long enough already. It was futile, destructive, and it had no place in his life, in his marriage. And he had no time for it now.

'So when I leave here to join Madog I want you to go to the nunnery at Llanllugan.'

Her eyes flew wide, so green and so dismayed that it hurt him to look at them. 'A nunnery? No!'

Rhun took her face between his hands. 'Eleanor, if I am killed, and the castle lost, at least in sanctuary you and the babe will be safe.'

'You won't be killed!' Her face was white between his hands, her lips trembling. 'And Castell y Lleuad will never fall—you said so yourself.'

He shook his head. 'I said I will never yield it. That isn't the same thing, Eleanor. There'll be no bargains this time, and I wouldn't make one even if I were offered the choice—which I doubt I would be. This will be a fight to the end now—whatever that end may be.'

She opened her mouth to say something and then closed it again. Tearing herself away, she turned her back on him, her arms wrapped around her midriff. 'So you are still determined to send me away, my lord, even now!'

Rhun moved up behind her, wrapping his arms around her again, around the child that lay sleeping inside her, blissfully ignorant of war and of parting, and rested his chin on the top of her head. 'Do you remember the day your father came?'

Her head moved in a little nod, her silken hair tickling his jaw. 'Yes, of course I do.'

'Do you remember what he said? That you'd made your choice and now you had to live with it?' He brought his cheek lower to rest against hers. 'You have another choice now, *f'anwylyd*. My course is set, but yours can still be determined. And if you live, if our child lives, then I can go into battle with an easy heart.'

* * *

Eleanor blinked as his words fell down upon her like rain. Time had run out for them, and the life that she'd begun to look forward to with hope, in spite of the rebellion that had hovered like a storm on the horizon, had ended before it had even begun.

She turned in his arms and placed her palms on his chest, feeling his heartbeat strong and steady, not like hers. Hers thudded unevenly with fear and with dread, and to her shame she tried to bargain with him.

'My heart would be easier if you stayed and became a father to our child—not leave and throw your life away for nothing in a war that is already lost!'

'Eleanor, don't make this any more difficult than it already is. Instead, do as I ask. Then, if the worst happens and I don't come back, I shall at least know you are safe.'

'What good is a wife without a husband, or a child without a father? Rhun, if you die...' Eleanor's voice failed her and she clenched her hands until her nails dug into her palms. 'What will be left for me?'

'Our child.'

'A child that will have no father and no home.' She raised her fist and brought it down hard on his chest, hating him then almost as much as she loved him. 'And that is supposed to be my consolation?'

The irony of that word was like a bitter reflux of poison. Alice hadn't foreseen any of this when she'd advised her on her wedding day what the lot of a wife was, and how her children would be her consolation, would make her happy if her husband had no love for her. Yet here she was, with everything—husband and child and love and happiness—and all of them in peril.

'Eleanor, I'm not dead yet, and pray God I'll live and return to you.' He caught her hands, enclosing them in his, holding them both over his heart. 'But I cannot ride away unless I know you are safe. Please, promise me you'll go to Llanllugan when the time comes. For if anything should happen to you…to our child…how could I ever forgive myself?'

All at once the scene of his mother's death rose up before Eleanor's eyes. And all at once she knew Morfudd's fear when she'd seen her son fall beneath Dallarde's horse and had run screaming to save her child. Wouldn't she do the same? And shouldn't she do the same now and flee to safety for her child, even if she herself wanted to stand and fight and die with Rhun? For if anything *did* happen to them and he blamed himself, took up that terrible burden of remorse all over again… No! That was something she couldn't allow.

'All right,' she said, turning her cheek into his shoulder so that he shouldn't see the sheen of tears in her eyes, although he must have heard in her voice the breaking of her heart. 'I'll go to Llanllugan when the time comes.'

But as they rode out, on the first day of March, it was Rhun who doubted the wisdom of what he was about to do. He was taking only a dozen men, battle-hardened volunteers all, leaving the rest behind to hold the castle under Huw's command. For surely it was madness to march into battle when this war was already lost? And was it really wise to send Eleanor to Llanllugan? Would she be safer at Castell y Lleuad?

There was no answer to any of those questions, and no other course than that he'd already decided upon. Yet the doubts hammered away at his mind until his head felt it would split. He wouldn't have to send Eleanor away if he remained to protect her. If he turned back, even now, he might yet keep his castle, his lands, his name and—unlike his father, but most important of all—the wife who had become as necessary to him as life itself.

The fork in the road loomed up ahead. Madog would go on to Caereinion with his army and Rhun would turn south and escort Eleanor and Alice, and young Goronwy ap Huw, to Llanllugan. The nunnery lay not more than four leagues in distance.

There was still time. All Rhun had to do was bring Eryr to a halt, tell Madog he'd changed his mind—even if he was judged a coward and a traitor. He could close his ears and his heart…turn and lead his men back the way they'd come. It was so simple that it didn't even require much thought. He might even have done it had Bleddyn ap Gwion not ridden up alongside him and spoken quietly in his ear.

'It looks black, my lord. There are rumours that many of the border men we recruited before Christmas have deserted, or taken the King's money and joined the enemy ranks.'

'I expected as much,' Rhun replied, his heart heavy at the news. It was just like the last war. He'd been too young to fight, but that battle had also been lost because the Welsh had failed to stand together behind their Prince. Would it ever be any other way?

'There is more. The Earl of Warwick has three thousand men at Montgomery, ready to march against us, and among them are mercenaries from Hainaut, commanded by Rainulf Dallarde.'

Rhun's fingers tightened on the reins and his blood turned to fire and to ice all at the same time. Twelve years fell away as if not an hour had passed since the moment he'd lain in the dirt and watched that man murder his mother.

'Then the news isn't all bad, Bleddyn.'

'My lord...?'

But Rhun didn't answer as he looked back over his shoulder to where Eleanor rode, Alice at her side, with Goronwy Bengoch sitting behind her. Both of the women were white-faced and unsmiling and even the boy, who'd chattered with excitement as they'd ridden out of Castell y Lleuad, had fallen silent at last, his face blank and uncomprehending.

There had been no arguments in the end, and the last-minute protests he'd expected from his wife hadn't come. But a moment ago, if she'd called to him and urged him to turn back, he might well have done so. Now, as they left the main group and turned southward, his ears were deaf to all but the name Dallarde, and his eyes saw nothing but the road that would lead him to his mother's killer.

As they arrived at the gates of Llanllugan Eleanor schooled her features to quiet resolve, willing herself to betray nothing of what was in her mind, only what was in her heart. Rhun dismounted and rang the bell of the door in the high wall, before lifting her down from the saddle.

Enfolding her in his arms, he held her close without words, so that in the silence everything around took on a keen and agonising significance. The ground beneath their feet, the smell of horse sweat, the birdsong in the trees, the bubbling of a stream nearby, the plainsong that came from beyond the wall. And, above all, Rhun's slow and heavy heartbeat beneath her head. Eleanor fixed it all in her mind, because these might be the memories that would have to sustain her for the rest of her life.

'I will be back for you soon.'

Rhun's promise rumbled in her ear, piercing through the quiet moment, echoing in her soul like a distant dream. She lifted her head and stared up into his face. It had been so short a time that she'd known this man, and in so many ways she still didn't know him at all. And yet she seemed to know him on a level that went beyond familiarity or even the sharing of their bodies. And as she looked into those eyes she saw that while he meant to keep the promise he'd just made, a part of him was already riding away from her.

'God keep you safe, Rhun,' she whispered, curling her hands into the folds of his cloak. The new cloak of ivy green she'd given him, a colour that would blend into the trees, shield him from the archer's arrow, keep him alive and bring him home to her.

As if he read her thoughts, or simply saw them in her eyes, he moved his hand up to her cheek. 'God keep you too, Eleanor, until I return. And I *will* return—I vow it.'

A sob rose up into her mouth but he was already

kissing her, swift, savage and fleeting. It was a kiss goodbye. Turning away, he helped Alice and Goronwy down from their horse, ruffling the child's hair and saying something in Welsh that she couldn't catch. Then he swung himself up into Eryr's saddle and, with a last long burning look into her eyes, spurred the stallion into a gallop.

Eleanor watched until Rhun was out of sight, and only then did she turn away and enter into the calm simplicity of the little nunnery. Its austere buildings offered little comfort, and neither did she seek any. For her heart and her soul, if not her body, had gone with Rhun.

Their cell was clean and white, barely furnished and tiny. There was no window at all. The nuns here, like all of the Cistercian order, lived a frugal and self-sufficient life, as well as a devout one.

'You are very welcome at our table, Lady Eleanor, and at our prayers too, if you wish. I am Sister Agnes, the Mother Superior here, and we will try and make your stay as comfortable as we can.'

Eleanor turned to the nun who'd escorted them. The woman was older than she'd first thought, and from her speech and bearing clearly a noblewoman. A widow, perhaps, or someone who'd escaped marriage and chosen to become a bride of Christ instead of a man.

'Thank you,' she replied. 'However, we will be staying only this night.'

'Oh?' Sister Agnes's forehead wrinkled beneath her wimple. 'But we understood that your stay would be indefinite?'

'No, we will be leaving in the morning. So please have our horses ready as early as it is possible.'

The nun hesitated for a moment, and then inclined her head and left them. Eleanor sank down on the narrow trestle that served as both a bench and a bed. Alice sat down on the single chair that stood beside it, and Goronwy dropped down onto the floor, crossing his thin legs.

'So you really mean to disobey the Lord Rhun, madam?' asked Alice.

She nodded. 'Yes, tomorrow we go back. It's our home, and our place is there, not here.'

'How will we find our way?' Alice asked. 'What if we take the wrong path?'

Goronwy leapt up, his eyes fierce. 'I will guide you!'

Her maid drew her stepson to her and dropped a kiss onto the boy's head. 'Of course you will, *machgen i*.'

With his mass of red curls and bright blue eyes, the child was a mirror image of his father. And it was clear that Alice loved them both deeply. Eleanor's hand went to her belly and her eyes misted. Would her babe look like Rhun or like her? Or a bit of both?

'Indeed you shall, Goronwy Bengoch.' she said. She stood and took off her cloak and veil, but found there was nowhere to hang them. 'But I will ask Sister Agnes to spare one of the laymen to escort us as well…just in case.'

Alice got to her feet too. 'Here, madam, give me those things. I'll find somewhere to put them.'

Eleanor looked at her maid and, suddenly she saw only two women, two wives, two mothers—and two desolate hearts stranded far from home. What did their station matter now, as they were faced with such shared anguish? Impulsively, she kissed Alice's cheek, smiling

for the first time that day at the look of astonishment
the gesture invoked.

'My name is Eleanor.'

The pleasure on Alice's face almost brightened the
otherwise dark afternoon.

'And from now on we shall be sisters, not maid and
mistress. You never were very reverent anyway!'

Tears brimmed in the other woman's eyes, though her
smile was wide and as impish as ever. 'I did my best...
Eleanor. Oh, I'll never get used to calling you that!'

'Yes, you will.' Eleanor folded her cloak and veil and
laid them on the floor. 'Now we must rest, for we've
an early start tomorrow. And we'll not take the wrong
path, Alice. I noted our route carefully. There are only
two roads to take, and if we keep the sun at our backs
we'll know we're heading in the right direction.'

There were two roads to everywhere and everything,
it seemed: hope or despair, love or hate, war or peace,
life or death. But only one road led home.

It was folly, but there was nothing that could be done
now except stand and fight. Rhun waited alongside
Madog ap Llywelyn for the inevitable and felt his nerves
tingling. The Prince knew as well as he did that they'd
been betrayed—and by spies of Welsh blood. Warwick's forces had crept up on them as they'd camped
by night and had them surrounded by daybreak. And
now, whether they fought or ran, the result would be
the same.

With less than a thousand men they were vastly out-
numbered, but tactically Madog had done all he could.
He'd formed his force into a defensive square in the

middle of the plain, with the spearmen on the outside, their shafts dug into the ground and their deadly points skyward, glinting in the sun. The foot soldiers and the few mounted men were formed in neat yet pitifully thin lines behind him, and there they waited for Warwick's army to descend.

The ground shook as the cavalry charged. There were not more than a hundred of them, and at least half came to their doom on the Welsh spearheads. But as Eryr plunged and snorted beneath him, Rhun knew this was only the beginning. For as the second charge came he saw through the slit in his visor that there were archers and crossbowmen now, within the ranks of approaching horses, and infantry behind wielding weapons far superior to those of his countrymen.

The Welshmen around him began to fall like corn beneath the enemy arrows and the defensive square broke. As chaos ensued, Rhun gripped his sword and spurred Eryr into the attack. It wasn't the first time he'd engaged in pitched battle, or witnessed such awful carnage, but as the hours of fighting wore on he prayed it would be his last.

Half the time he struck blindly, recognising only the colours and nothing more of the English knights he engaged. Two he unhorsed, one he wounded, and an English foot soldier had certainly perished at his hand. And all the time his eyes scanned the heaving, sweating, screaming throng of men for Rainulf Dallarde.

But he was nowhere to be seen, and Rhun began to doubt the presence of the mercenaries at all. Then the sound of fighting came from their rear, where Madog's supply train waited under cover in a clearing in the

forest. Calling to those of his men he could see to follow him, Rhun turned and galloped to meet the new
attack. But their baggage was guarded by boys and old
men, not warriors, and when he got there it was already
nearly over. Those Welsh left alive were fleeing deeper
into the forest or heading for the Banwy river, hoping
to cross it to safety, or they were just running desperately, whichever way they could.

And it was here, amid the brutal killing of the defenceless, that Rhun spied the Dallarde colours at last.
They gleamed black and gold in the dappled shade of
the trees and the mercenary's sword-edge ran thick with
blood. The man was urging his destrier in pursuit of a
boy who was running, gasping for his life, his clothes
already torn and bloodied. And as he fell and died helplessly beneath the flashing hooves white-hot rage rose
up into Rhun's throat.

He roared out a challenge that had Dallarde twist-
ing in his saddle. For a moment the man hesitated, then
drove his mount forward. The bloody sword swung
again, its red-gilded blade a dazzling arc, but it was too
late. Rhun's weapon swung faster, higher and truer, slic-
ing into the crown of the mercenary's helmet, splitting it
in two, its cutting edge shearing down into bone below.

The man slid from his saddle without a sound and
landed almost softly on the ground, his sightless eyes
staring upwards in disbelief. Rhun stared too, in horror and in revulsion, as all those years, all that hate,
all his pain and guilt, seemed to seep away into the
bloody ground.

Pulling off his helmet and gauntlets, he sheathed his
weapon and rubbed the sweat and the blood from his

face. *Er mwyn Duw!* Why wasn't he weeping or laughing or yelling his victory out loud? Why wasn't his heart singing instead of lying unmoved in his breast? Why, at this moment of long-awaited vengeance, did he feel so empty? No, not empty, but filled with shame. Because killing—even in justice—was still killing, and he'd seen too much already that day.

The sound of hooves breaking through the undergrowth came to his ears and swiftly he drew his sword again. A moment later Rhodri ab Ifor emerged from the trees to greet him. His constable seemed unharmed, apart from a nasty gash that split his cheek from ear to jaw.

'The day is lost, my lord. Madog ap Llywelyn's men—what's left of them—are in retreat, and Warwick's forces are after them like staghounds.'

'And Madog?'

'Alive. Though he only barely escaped death, as I hear.'

'What of our men?'

'Two dead that I know of, my lord, the rest scattered.'

Rhun's heart twisted and he bowed his head for a long moment. Only two, thank God, but still two too many. 'Then find them, Rhodri,' he ordered. 'Get them all home.'

As his constable rode away again, Rhun guided Eryr over to where the dead boy lay. His eyes were staring sightlessly upwards too—not astonished, as Dallarde's had been, but glazed with fear. And as he looked down at the twisted body and terrified face Rhun saw the boy he'd once been, and also the boy his unborn son might become.

Something broke inside him, shattering into a thousand tiny pieces, tearing his whole soul asunder. The past had ended here, this day, and it was only tomorrow that mattered now. And in the midst of all the death around him he swore a vow. Not his son, nor his daughter, nor his wife, would ever stare up at him with such eyes. Never, not as long as he drew breath or could hold a sword in his hand, would he fail to protect them.

Yet in trying to keep Eleanor safe he might very well have placed her in the most danger. For with Dallarde's death his band of bloodthirsty mercenaries wouldn't stop at killing old men and defenceless boys. Every village they came across would suffer at their hands. Even the religious houses would not be spared—especially if they offered sanctuary to a fleeing rebel...or the wife of one!

Turning Eryr southwards, his heart raging in his chest, Rhun dug his heels into the stallion's flanks and galloped like the wind for Llanllugan.

Chapter Fifteen

Eleanor waited outside the gates of Castell y Lleuad. All the villagers and their livestock were safe inside the castle walls, the lookouts on the hillsides having warned them of the approach of the English. It hadn't been until they'd come into sight, however, that she'd recognised her father's colours. Then she'd ordered the gates barred behind her and gone out alone to meet him.

It had only been four months since he'd ridden away to Castell y Bere, but as she watched her sire ride up the hill, leaving his men assembled below, shock ran through her. He looked ill…his trim figure wasted, his face older, the gold in his hair gone to grey. His left arm was bound in a sling, though he guided his horse expertly enough with one hand and with his heels.

Halting, he stared down at her in silence for a moment, and when he finally spoke the contempt in his voice was one thing that hadn't changed since last they'd met.

'Has your husband sent you out to beg for the terms of his surrender, daughter?'

'My husband isn't here.' Eleanor stared steadily back into the icy blue eyes, still as hard as ever. 'But, since I am the Lady of Castell y Lleuad, you may state whatever it is you have to say to me.'

'Have you forgotten that I am your father, girl?'

She shook her head. 'No. But I am not a child any more. I am a woman grown and a wife.'

'So...'

Richard de Vraille leaned forward in his saddle. Once upon a time, that piercing stare would have bowed her head and bent her spirit but now Eleanor stood firm before it. 'You will find nothing to pillage or destroy in the village,' she said. 'All are safely within, and neither you nor any of your men will gain entry through these gates.'

He got down from his horse, his movements hampered by his injured arm. 'You mean to hold this castle against me? *You?*'

'To the last stone.' Eleanor tilted her chin higher, for her father was still much taller than she, despite the stoop of his shoulders. 'But I doubt it will come to that. You are ill, my lord, and I imagine your men below fare little better after a winter siege at Castell y Bere. We have heard of your failure to break it.'

'Ho-ho-ho!' Her father gave a soft yet menacing chuckle. '*We*, is it? Have you gone over to the Welsh, then, body and soul? Is this cause of theirs your cause too, even though it is a hopeless one?'

'It may be a hopeless cause, but at least it is a noble one.' She stepped towards him. 'And as for going over to the Welsh—this is my home, and I will defend it as any of them would.'

His face changed in an instant. 'God's blood, Eleanor, listen to yourself! You have lost your wits! Or has your husband twisted your mind until you can't recognise what is right and what is not?'

'My wits have never been clearer. And it was yourself who sent me here as Rhun's wife—which is one thing, at least, for which I thank you.'

His hand clenched where it rested on the saddle. 'When this rebellion is crushed, and your husband hanged for the traitor he is, I doubt you'll thank me then.'

Eleanor swallowed back a rush of fear, for her father might well be right—though not in any way he'd understand. 'Then you'll have to hang me with him.'

Richard de Vraille laughed, but there was no mirth in it. 'You must be demented, child.'

'Don't call me child!' She felt herself begin to shake, though not with fear. 'I've *never* been your child.'

His face flushed. 'Of course, you are my child!'

'Then why were you so unkind? Why despise me for being born female and not male? Tell me, my lord, for I would really like to understand.'

'There is only one thing you need to understand, Eleanor. I am come to take this castle in the name of the King. Surrender it now and there need be no bloodshed.' There was a pause before he went on. 'And as for this *kindness* you speak of...that doesn't provide a man with heirs!'

Eleanor drew herself up taller. 'Yet you are not unkind to my sisters. And I know you capable of a sort of love for my mother.' Her father spun away to remount his horse, but she put her hand on his arm. 'Is it because of my birthmark that you hate me? If it is, I can understand, even though it would be nonetheless cruel of you.'

'For God's sake, Eleanor!' His eyes flashed. 'What would you have me tell you?'

'The truth, my lord. After all, since I am now your enemy, and not your daughter, why not speak it? You can't hurt me any more than you have already.'

'Very well, then. If you must know. When you were born, there *was* no mark on you.'

Eleanor gasped and withdrew her hand as if stung. 'N-no mark? What…what do you mean?'

'I put that mark there—that's what I mean. It's not a birthmark. It's a burn.'

'A burn?'

He nodded, but his gaze slid away to rest on the walls behind her. 'I was in my cups, cursing the fates that had given me yet another daughter. You were only a few days old, your mother still in her confinement bed. Everyone thought she would die with the loss of blood she suffered birthing you…'

Eleanor felt horror begin to crawl over her skin. 'Go on…'

'I stood over your crib, looking down at you, hating you. I didn't intend to harm you, but…'

'For pity's sake—what happened?'

'The torch fell out of my hand and set your blanket alight. My reactions were slow, and by the time I doused the flames you'd been burned on your shoulder, your skin scarred by the hot pitch.'

'But…but why have you never told me this before? Why let me think it was a birthmark?'

'Because of my shame! Why else?'

His voice rose and his eyes returned to hers, glittering in a way she'd never seen them before.

'Or do you think me so cruel as to be incapable of feeling shame, Eleanor?'

Eleanor shook her head, struggling to take in what he'd told her—what she'd asked to be told. But it didn't seem possible. 'But my mother knew, surely, and my sisters? You couldn't hide what you'd done.'

'Your mother knew, naturally, but what had happened couldn't be undone. Your sisters were too young to know anything. Your wet nurse kept our secret because she was ordered to. Nobody ever discovered the truth, not even you, for you didn't remember anything.'

'So you've hated me all these years because you feel *guilty*?' Eleanor stared at him and a fury such as she'd never known possessed her. 'You! A man who doesn't even know the meaning of the word!' She took a step towards him. 'But this admission has enabled me to understand you at last.'

'How so?'

'I know now how you were able to condone the killing of Rhun's mother. If you can treat your own child so callously…well, that was nothing to you, was it?'

He shrugged, but his shoulders didn't seem as broad or as arrogant now, and the motion was that of an old man. 'Things happen in war that are not pleasant.'

'Not pleasant? You allowed a murderer to go free and unpunished.'

'The woman was an enemy, a casualty of war, and a loyal knight cannot be punished for doing his duty.'

Eleanor gasped. 'Is it your duty to kill women and children, helpless villagers, just in the name of war?'

Her father pulled off his gauntlet and ran his hand over his face. He was sweating, as if in fever. She realised he really was ill, and that only his will and his constitution kept him on his feet.

'Yes, if it is necessary.'

Even though she'd always known her father to have little compassion, the statement shook her to her core and a chill lifted the hair on her scalp. 'That night when I burned in my crib…was it really an accident, Father? Or was it *necessary* that you dropped that torch onto my blanket?'

There was no answer and Eleanor's blood ran cold. Her hand went to her belly and fear gripped her heart—not for herself, but for the innocent life inside her. 'My God! I'm ashamed to call you my father, and when my child is born he or she will never call you grandsire either.'

The blue eyes flared. 'You are carrying the Welshman's child?'

'Yes. And if you lay siege to this castle you will have to kill not just me but my babe too. But then, it may be born a girl, and mayhap you will consider it wise to kill it in the womb to save it from the disgrace of being female!'

Richard de Vraille looked down at her as if he'd never seen her before. His stare wasn't icy any more, but bewildered, uncomprehending, as if she spoke in a language he couldn't understand. And then, deep within the pale blue depths, something moved. Something she'd never seen there before. And when he spoke again, after many moments, in his voice was the grudging respect a man had for his enemy.

'Very well, Eleanor, keep your castle. I won't be the one to take it from you. And keep your rebel husband and his child too. But I won't help you when this place falls—as it will.'

'We don't want your help.'

'Brave words. I'll give you that.' His mouth twisted with the cruelty of old. 'If you *had* been born a son I would have been almost proud of you at this moment.'

Once Eleanor would have been crushed by those words, by the confirmation that she meant nothing to the man who'd sired her. Now she knew them for what they were: the words of a man who, despite all his outward power, was empty inside, bitter in his disappointment, and perhaps even sad.

'I don't think you have the heart for pride or anything else that is good. I feel sorry for you, my lord.'

But he wasn't listening any more, and as he climbed back into his saddle Eleanor realised that she'd never be afraid of him after today. And perhaps he sensed that he could never touch her now. For as he turned his horse away, looking older than ever, the echo of defeat in his farewell rang loud and hollow against the castle walls.

'Goodbye, Eleanor.'

Without a backward glance, he rode down the hill, and as the English disappeared in a dispirited line of weary men and horses Eleanor knew that the thread of kinship that had connected them was severed for ever.

With a sense of sadness, of anger, but most of all of regret, she raised her hand to knock on the gate. And then a searing pain, like the sharp point of a dagger, pierced her belly and she cried out and fell against the doors.

Rhun fought against the impulse to gallop through the night, although it took every shred of restraint he possessed. But Eryr was tired, his coat stiff with dried sweat, his footing unsure. To gallop in the dark, to fall and break their necks, would serve for nothing. Nevertheless, wherever the ground was open and level he coaxed his horse into a trot, and Eryr didn't let him down. But still the journey back to Castell y Lleuad, short though it was in distance, seemed to take for ever.

From the moment the nun at Llanllugan had told him his wife was gone a fear such as he'd never known had gripped his bowels. For if Eleanor died, and their child too, and he wasn't there to save them, there would be nothing of life left for him.

The new moon, just a sliver in the clear sky, was barely bright enough to light his way, and at every moment he expected the thud of an arrow in his back. The aftermath of the battle, the hunting down of the defeated Welshmen, had been as brutal as the actual fighting. More than once he'd pulled into the cover of the trees and listened, his heart raging helplessly as the sound of the pursuit carried clearly through the night. But there had been nothing he could do back there—he had to keep going forward to hope, to life, not backwards to futile death.

He arrived at the village just as dawn broke and his blood turned cold. It was empty, the doors and windows of all the houses shuttered, no glow of firelight from within. Nothing moved or breathed, not man nor beast, and not even the morning birdsong broke the silence. The only sound was the river flowing nearby, as it always did.

But he didn't stop. Spurring Eryr into a gallop at last, Rhun sped for the castle, high on the hill, its walls glowing as the light from the east touched them. The gates were barred and the voice of the watch on the wall above challenged him as he rode up.

'It is Rhun ab Owain, your lord, open up!'

The bailey was full of people and animals, and, as he dismounted it took him a moment to realise the villagers were encamped within the castle. But when Huw ap Gruffudd came hurrying towards him, his face grim, his question as to why died on his lips.

'Rhun…' His steward took Eryr's reins. 'The Lady Eleanor is ill…'

'Where is she?'

'In her chamber. Alice and the physician are with her.'

Rhun turned and ran up the steps of the keep, and went on running right to the top, to where Eleanor's chamber lay. Bursting through the door, he found it dark, the shutters closed, the air stale.

Alice rose from a low stool at the side of the bed. Even in the dim light her eyes betrayed the traces of weeping. 'Lord Rhun, thank God you've come!'

'Tell me.'

The woman's head turned towards the bed and the choke in her voice filled the room. 'We feared a miscarriage, my lord…yesterday eve…but the babe lives.'

His heart heaved in his chest and terror filled his throat. 'And…my wife?'

'She is sleeping, Lord Rhun.' The physician moved forward from the other side of the bed. 'There is no cause for alarm. Both your lady and the child are well.'

Rhun pushed past them and dropped to his knees at the side of the bed. Eleanor lay like an alabaster statue beneath the coverings, her hair loose and spread out over the pillow and her face pale down to her lips. Was she truly only sleeping? He placed his hand over hers, feeling bones so fragile that he thought they would break if he pressed too hard. Had she always been this fragile? Had he been so blind, so stupid, too driven by his misplaced quest for vengeance to see it? Gently he touched her cheek, finding it warm and alive, and the heart that had shuddered to a halt inside him began to beat again.

'Eleanor...'

The closed eyelids flickered and her lips parted slightly. Behind him, Alice spoke again. 'She was fretting and calling for you, my lord, so I gave her some poppy juice to help her rest. Now she won't wake!'

The woman's panic ripped at the edge of his nerves, even though he knew it stemmed from love. 'It is all right, Alice, but please leave us now—both of you.' He nodded his gratitude to the physician. 'Thank you, Idwal.'

As the door closed softly behind them, Rhun leaned over and kissed Eleanor's brow, his lips tasting the salt of cold perspiration. '*F'anwylyd*...my love... I'm here... I've come home.'

There was a whisper of a sigh, and then silence. It was as if the walls began to crumble around him—the walls of this chamber, the castle too—as the foundations of his entire existence shook. What if his physician was wrong? What if Alice *had* administered too much poppy? What if Eleanor never woke again? If only he hadn't sent her away…if only he hadn't gone to war… if only he'd been here…if only…

Laying his head on the pillow next to Eleanor's, Rhun placed his hand lightly on her breast. The heart beneath seemed to flutter like a bird, its beat scarcely there.

'*Fy mai i*…my fault…'

But as soon as the words echoed back at him Rhun denied them. He knew now that blame and remorse were futile, a waste of time and of strength, when other words, more vital words, were needed. Eleanor had shown him that.

'Forgive me, my love. Curse me for leaving you, hate me if you will, but please open your eyes and look at me.'

And as dawn became day without Rhun fought against the overwhelming surge of guilt that rose to swallow him and prayed—softly, desperately, and with all his heart.

'*Tad nefol…trugarha wrthym…*'

A voice seemed to call her from a long way away and Eleanor opened her eyes, though it took an eternity for her lashes to part. Everything was dark at first, the torches in the room only slowly coming into focus. And then, by their light, Rhun's form took shape beside her. His head was close to hers, his eyes shut as if he slept, though his lips moved and a quiet murmur like a prayer reached her ears. His hand rested on her breast, just over the birthmark that she now knew wasn't a birthmark.

But something else she knew too…something that had happened after her father had ridden away…something that eluded her for a moment, lingering like an awful fog at the edges of her mind.

What was it?

And then it came back to her—that awful sharp pain in her womb, the overwhelming feeling of terror that she was going to lose their child. Quickly, her hand went to her belly, and when she felt the bump, still round, still whole, tears of relief welled up inside her. Stretching out her other hand, she touched her husband's hair, the thick black unruly hair she loved, now matted with the sweat of battle.

'Rhun?'

His head snapped up, his eyes opening and latching onto hers. 'Eleanor?'

'You've come home…'

He leaned over her, his gaze bright and bloodshot, his face creased with worry. 'Don't try to speak, my love, lie quiet. You've been ill, and from now on you must rest.'

'Our babe…it is well, isn't it?'

He nodded. 'Yes, *f'anwylyd.*' His hand stroked the hair back from her brow. 'Our babe is well.'

Eleanor closed her eyes again. The staleness of the room filled her senses and made everything seem to happen all over again. Those agonising moments that had seemed like hours as terror had gripped her worse than the pain. Moments when she'd almost believed she would lose both her child and her husband, if Rhun didn't come back. But he *was* back. He was here, he was alive, and her child lived and grew within her.

'Open the shutters, Rhun. Let the daylight come in.'

He took down the boards over the windows and the warmth of sunlight seeped into the room, falling over the bed, warming her limbs.

'I thought I was going to lose...' She turned her head on the pillow to look at Rhun as he came to kneel at her side again. 'I was so afraid...'

'No!' His fingers curled fiercely around hers. 'Our child will be born whole and healthy, Eleanor. I won't lose either of you—ever.'

Eleanor's eyes adjusted to the gradually brightening room. 'Rhun, I *had* to leave the nunnery and come home. If you hadn't returned I wouldn't have wanted my babe to be born there. I want it to be born here, at Castell y Lleuad...our home.'

Tears came then, in a silly but helpless weeping that stemmed from exhaustion, relief and happiness. She should be joyful—she *was* joyful—and tomorrow she would smile and laugh. But for now she needed to weep.

Rhun seemed to sense it, because he caught her up in his arms and held her close against him, strong and steady as he supported her...supported them both.

'You did right by coming home, my love. It might not have been safe at Llanllugan after all.'

'Rhun, there's something else.' She laid her cheek on his breast, feeling his solid strength beneath. 'I told my father that our child would never call him grandsire, but I never meant to tempt the fates.'

His hand went on stroking her hair, but she felt his body stiffen. 'Your father has been here?' he asked, his voice gentle.

Eleanor watched the sunbeams play over the rushes

on the floor and curled her fingers tightly into Rhun's tunic, clutching on to his strength to give herself strength too.

'He came yesterday afternoon with soldiers to take Castell y Lleuad. That's why I was so upset…why the griping started in my womb…'

'*Iesu…*' She felt the jerk of his heart beneath her head. 'Did he harm you?'

'No—at least only with words. But he'll never hurt me ever again. And now I know everything you said about him is true, because he told me of another crime he'd committed…a crime against me.'

Rhun put a hand under her chin, and when he tilted her face up to his again his gaze was tender and fierce at the same time. 'Tell me.'

Eleanor braced herself for the pain as her father's confession came back to her, but strangely there wasn't any. There was only a sad sort of acceptance. 'My birth-mark isn't a birthmark at all. He burned me with a torch when I was but a few days old. And, God forgive me, I think he did it deliberately.'

'*Y cythraul.* I'll make him pay for that, Eleanor. I swear it.'

She shook her head. 'He's become an old man, Rhun, and he is ill. I almost pity him. I could even forgive him for what he did if he'd told me sooner and not let me believe all these years that I was abominable. That no one would want or love me because I was ugly, cursed, unworthy. That was the cruellest thing of all.'

'He doesn't deserve your pity, Eleanor, less still your forgiveness.' His eyes clouded. 'I should have been with you when he came…shielded you.'

In his eyes Eleanor saw shadows rise up, ebb and flow as he struggled with remorse, and she watched as the dark threatened to conquer him yet again. And then, after a long moment, the dark receded and his eyes were light once more.

'I'll not leave you ever again, Eleanor, no matter what comes. And you will be well soon. You won't do anything from now on—no tasks or duties. Only rest for you, *nhrysor*, until our child is born.'

She lifted her fingers to his mouth, tracing the cracked lips, the bruise at the corner of his jaw, the gash high on his brow, not deep, but black with dried blood. There was no blood on his clothes, however, and his body was whole and sound.

'We heard the news of the battle. But most of your men are back safe. Only one is still missing, and he may yet make his way home, God willing.'

'God will be merciful. I know it.' Rhun pressed his lips to her forehead. 'But now lie down, sleep and regain your strength.'

'No, I have slept enough. Tell me what happened. Why didn't you come back with the rest?'

Rhun's face shadowed again, though it was different now. 'Because yesterday I slew the man who killed my mother.'

Eleanor gasped. 'Rainulf Dallarde? He was fighting for the King?'

'Yes—but for money rather than any higher motive. When we were riding towards Llanllugan, Eleanor, I almost turned back…brought us all home. Then I heard that Dallarde was with Warwick's forces and nothing else mattered. Not me, not even you. Only my revenge.'

'And you took it?'

He nodded, his face grim. 'He was leading the attack on the supply train in our rear. I spurred Eryr forward and the next moment he was dead by my sword. It was done so quickly that it hardly seemed real—but it was.'

Eleanor's hands tightened on the folds of his tunic and a wave of relief washed through her. 'I'm glad it was you and no other who engaged him, Rhun. You might never have found peace otherwise, and you would always have sought him.' And although all killing was a sin, she *was* glad. For now that man was dead Rhun might begin to really live. 'It was justice,' she said.

'Perhaps. And yet... I felt nothing, Eleanor. No satisfaction, no vindication, not even hate. Nothing. All I could think of—all I thought of the whole time I was fighting—was you.'

'Me?'

He nodded. 'I saw Dallarde kill a young boy. He rode him down, as he did me all those years ago. I got there too late to prevent it, and I saw it all happen again—just like it had then. I knew in that moment that there was nothing I could have done to save the boy or to save my mother, just as you said.'

His eyes left hers and looked towards the window.

'At that moment I vowed to myself that I would do anything, whatever was necessary, to protect you and our family...our home. And I will. Even if it means submitting to the King.'

'Then we will *all* go down on our knees with you.' Eleanor laid her palm on his chest, felt the strong solid thud of his heart. 'This war is lost, isn't it, Rhun?'

He nodded, his gaze returning to hers. 'Yes.'

She searched his face, reading in his mind the words he didn't say. Submitting was one thing, but there would be a price to pay. She swallowed, tried to speak and failed. But just as she'd read his thoughts, her husband read hers too.

'Whatever happens now in this war it is out of our hands. I've lost too much time in hate and remorse and regret and I'll waste not a moment more. When I feared you dead…' He shook his head. 'But we will talk no more of death—only of life, of hope, of our child.'

But her father's shadow still hovered, dragging her doubts back in its wake like the debris left after a storm. 'Rhun…if it should be born a girl…' She sought reassurance again.

'I will love her as much as I love her mother.'

Eleanor smiled then, joy breaking through her foreboding like the dawn after darkness. 'You've never said that to me before…that you love me.'

'No—and I don't know why I didn't. For I think I loved you on that first night, when you came to my chamber, soaked to the skin, your hair like rats' tails.' He smiled and his fingers touched her cheek. 'You were so beautiful, Eleanor, and you are even more beautiful to me now.'

'I love you too, Rhun, so very much. But…' Dread rose up into her breast again, vying with her love. 'I fear what the King will do when the end comes.'

'We will survive. My part in this was small compared to others… God have mercy on them.'

Rhun's voice echoed with sadness for those men who would suffer, but also with resolve for his own, whom she was certain he would save.

'I promise you, *f'anwylyd*, we'll have many years yet to cherish each other and our children.'

As Eleanor laid her head against his chest once more she heard the strong, steadfast beating of his heart. And his words of love—a love that she knew was true— chased the fear away.

'Do you know what I said to my father yesterday? I told him I was glad that he'd sent me here to be your wife...that it was the only thing I had to thank him for. And it's true, come what may.'

'*Daw eto haul ar fryn*, Eleanor.'

'Yes,' she echoed. 'The sun *will* shine again.'

And as he bent his head and kissed her Eleanor knew that everything would be as Rhun promised. Even if that meant a miracle. Because she believed wholeheartedly in miracles now.

Epilogue

Eleanor and Rhun stood on the battlements and watched the English party approach. Not soldiers come to lay siege, but her mother and her sisters, their respective spouses and their entourage. It had been her husband who'd suggested her family be invited to the Christmas feast now that the war was over and there was peace again—albeit a harsh one. The toll taken in hostages, confiscated lands and fines was heavy, and the rebel leaders had all suffered death or imprisonment.

But as she'd bowed her head and prayed for them— even for Cynan ap Maredudd, for how could she not?— she'd thanked God that Rhun and Castell y Lleuad had been spared. And that it had been her father in the end who'd intervened and stood as surety for them with the King. There was a huge fine of money to be paid into the royal coffers, but their lands and their people would be left unmolested and at liberty.

Eleanor leaned her head into the hollow of Rhun's

shoulder. His arm tightened around her and her heart swelled with love and pride, as it always did, when he spoke the words that needed to be said by one of them on this day.

'I would never have forgiven your father, Eleanor, for what he did to you. Even what he did on our behalf in this war could never atone for that. But I would have welcomed him today for your sake.'

She shook her head. 'He would never have come, and truly I don't know if *I* could have forgiven or welcomed him. Perhaps what he did for us was his way of atoning for his wrongs, but he's at peace now—at least I hope he is. My mother said the illness he contracted at Castell y Bere took him quickly in the end.'

Rhun's lips brushed her hair. 'Then perhaps he will find mercy and forgiveness from a higher power than ours.'

'Mayhap he will. And we've been shown mercy too. We have much to be thankful for, Rhun.'

'Yet we lost, Eleanor.' His voice grew solemn. 'Even though I knew in my soul that we could never win, there was always a part of my heart that hoped.'

'I know, but we have won in so many other ways. We have our freedom, our home, our family.'

As she spoke Morfudd Fechan, their seventeen-month-old daughter, was knocked over by Cadno, Rhun's new hound, who was bounding about with excitement as usual. Still a puppy, russet-brown with paws too big, he threatened to be even larger than Cai!

As Morfudd landed lightly on her bottom he licked her face, as if to say sorry, and her eyes—Rhun's eyes—grew round with shock. Tears welled like pools, and

Eleanor turned swiftly to comfort her. But Rhun was quicker. As her father swept her up into his arms and kissed her dark curls Morfudd's tears vanished like magic and she giggled with mischief and delight.

The scamp had her father wrapped around her little finger, and the two were inseparable, but Eleanor felt no resentment or envy at that. From the moment their daughter had been born Rhun had proved his love for her every moment of every day. Now it was hard to believe that she'd once feared he could be anything like her father.

But that was the past, and this was today, and it was going to be filled with joy. She tucked Rhun's green cloak more snugly around Morfudd, for the air was sharp. The red cloak was still in its coffer—but not for too much longer…she was certain of that. Her husband's talks with Father Robert, and lately with Ieuan Ddu, the new priest at the castle, were bringing him a gradual yet steady healing. Now he hardly used her valerian and there was only the occasional night when he left her bed.

One day soon he would leave her no more but be truly at peace, with himself and with God, his nightmares only memories.

'Talking of family…' Eleanor squeezed her husband's arm to bring his doting gaze from Morfudd's to hers. 'My sisters are as wilful as I am, so please don't glower at them as you did me when I first rode in through your gates!'

He smiled down at her, contentment shining in his dark eyes, making them even more beautiful. 'I will love them at first sight, as I did you, except I was too dull to see it.'

Eleanor lifted her mouth to his, feeling her body start to sing as he kissed her and the snow began to fall around them in large white flakes. She laughed as one landed on her nose and Rhun kissed it away. 'Do you think the walls will turn silver this year?' she asked, wrapping her arms tightly around her precious happy family.

He nodded. 'I know they will.' Snowflakes glistened on his black hair and Morfudd stared, astonished, old enough now to wonder at snow. 'You called it a miracle, Eleanor, so I can't see any reason why there shouldn't be more miracles in the years ahead. Can you?'

Eleanor shook her head, for so many miracles had already happened. One was their beautiful daughter, born in war but growing up in peace and love. Another was the seed of life that had been planted in her womb not long since. In due course they would have a son or another daughter, and Morfudd Fechan a brother or sister, although she wouldn't tell Rhun until she was sure. And she would tell him here, high up on the battlements, on the eve of the new year, when her mother and sisters had gone and they were alone once more to watch the moon turn the walls of Castell y Lleuad to silver.

'No,' she said, smiling up at him as they turned to go down and greet their guests. 'I can't see any reason at all.'

Historical Note

The rebellion of Madog ap Llywelyn, 1294-1295, sparked by injustice, discrimination, the abuse of Welsh laws, heavy taxation and local and personal grievances, was an organised and determined effort to throw off the King's rule in Wales. Ultimately the revolt failed, but it cost Edward I enormous resources in men, machinery and money to subdue it.

The battle of Maes Moydog and the attack on the supply train are as described, although Rainulf Dallarde is fictional. Madog ap Llywelyn surrendered in July 1295 and spent the rest of his life a prisoner in the Tower of London. Cynan ap Maredudd was captured and hanged at Hereford in September 1295. The two men who hanged Roger de Puleston at Caernarfon were themselves hanged.

Hundreds of hostages were taken, heavy fines imposed, and the lands of dead rebels confiscated by English lords or the Crown. The common people faced devastation and pillaging at the hands of soldiers of the King and his earls. Discrimination and injustice were even worse than before the revolt, and the ripples were felt for decades afterwards.

Castell y Bere was never reoccupied by the English, but destroyed by the rebels and thereafter abandoned. Ystumanner in the Dysynni Valley, where it still stands in ruins, was the last to capitulate in the autumn of 1295, as it had been the final bastion of Welsh resistance to surrender to Edward in 1283.

Rhun and Eleanor and Castell y Lleuad and its occupants are fictional. Nevertheless, they embody the political, social, marital and emotional dilemmas that individuals, families and communities face when two neighbouring lands go to war. Their happy ending, however, reflects the diplomatic solutions that over time established peace between Wales and England.

I am indebted to Craig Owen Jones's book, *The Revolt of Madog ap Llywelyn*, and to Dr David Moore for sharing with me his expertise on the medieval period.

* * * * *

If you enjoyed this story, be sure to look out for more great books from Lissa Morgan, coming soon!